Wolf Moon

Wolf Moon

Book 3 of The Wolves of Vimar

V. M. Sang

Published 2018 by Creativia

Cover art by Cover Mint

Other books by VM Sang

Fiction

The Wolves of Vimar Series
  Book 1: The Wolf Pack
  Book 2: The Never-Dying Man

Elemental Worlds
  Book 1: The Stones of Earth and Air
  Book 2: The Stones of Fire and Water

Non-fiction
  Viv's Family Recipes

To my mother, Marjorie Broad,
in thanks for all the love you
gave me.
I miss you.

Contents

What Has Gone Before

In Book 1, The Wolf Pack, the friends found Sauvern's Sword, a magical sword that chose its wielder and protected itself from others by a variety of methods, such as getting either too hot or too cold to hold, becoming too heavy to lift, causing an electric shock, feeling as if it were covered in prickles, and other means. It chose Randa, heir to the duchy of Hambara as its wielder.

A prophesy that Carthinal found in an ancient book suggested they would need this sword to save the land of Grosmer from an unspecified threat. They deduced this threat could possibly come from someone called 'The Immortal Mortal' in the prophecy. On returning from this adventure, the members of Wolf settled down to normal life.

Carthinal, a half-elf mage now married to the elf, Yssalithisandra, was about to become a father. The couple worked on finding spells lost during the Forbidding, when the king banned use of magic in Grosmer, on pain of death.

Thadora tried hard to settle in to her new life as the daughter of Duke Rollo of Hambara. Until he had adopted her, she had been a thief in the Warren, the poor quarter of Hambara. She found this change in lifestyle difficult to adapt to.

The Horselords, Kimi and Davrael, worked with the Duke's horses. They ran away from their homeland after their parents tried to stop them from marrying. They joined with the others in Hambara and went in search of Sauvern's Sword with them. *(See The Wolf Pack)*

Randa, elder daughter of Duke Rollo of Hambara, at last decided to accept a proposal of marriage from Prince Almoro, the second son of King Gerim. This, in spite of her love for the ranger, Fero. She knew he could never settle down in the city and become the consort of the Duchess, but she had to produce an heir to the duchy.

Asphodel, who had become a fully fledged cleric of the goddess, Sylissa, contented herself with healing any who came to her. The Great Father of Hambara banned her from entering the temple after she disobeyed an order from the Most High of the Church of Sylissa, himself.

Basalt, the dwarf, returned to his previous employer and had become a partner in the business and Fero, with his dog, Bramble, had settled in a hut he built himself in the forest outside the city.

One day Fero had a visit from Grnff, a yeti who saved the members of Wolf from death in the Mountains of Doom. He also helped them to find the valley where Sauvern's tomb lay.

The huge Yeti asked for help to rescue his cub from kidnappers. The members of Wolf all agreed that they owed their friend a debt of life.

Meanwhile, Carthinal happened to meet Grimmaldo, a young man who took the apprentice tests with him. Grimmaldo asked to go with them on their adventure and they all agreed.

On their journey to the place where Grnff last saw signs of his cub, they met another of Carthinal's past friends. This time a cat burglar from Bluehaven, known only as The Cat. The Bluehaven guard had discovered evidence incriminating him in a series of burglaries and had come a little too close to arresting him.

With Grnff, the company first went to the caves where the Yeti had their cubs and met Zplon and her other cub, Crthnl, called after Carthinal, then they set off after the kidnappers.

They tracked the signs to a troll camp where they saw negotiations for the hand over of Tadra, the cub named for Thadora.

The other group in the negotiations were human soldiers. The ten Wolves and one Yeti attacked and rescued the cub, but not without destroying all the patrol of soldiers and the trolls.

On their way back to Grosmer (they now found themselves in Erian), they met a patrol searching for their missing companions. The patrol questioned them as to their motives in travelling through Erian, and if they had seen any signs of the missing patrol.

In order to provide an excuse for being in Erian, they posed as a troop of wandering entertainers and the soldiers took them back to the battalion of the Erian army. Here the captain became suspicious of their cover, and decided to draft them into the Erian army where they learned of plans to invade Grosmer.

Now read on

When Kalhera descends from the mountains
And orcs once more roam the land.
When impossible beasts occur
And t he Never-Dying Man is once more at hand,
Then the Sword that was lost must once more be found.
Only it can destroy the threat
And kill the immortal mortal
To balance out his debt.

The Continent of Khalram

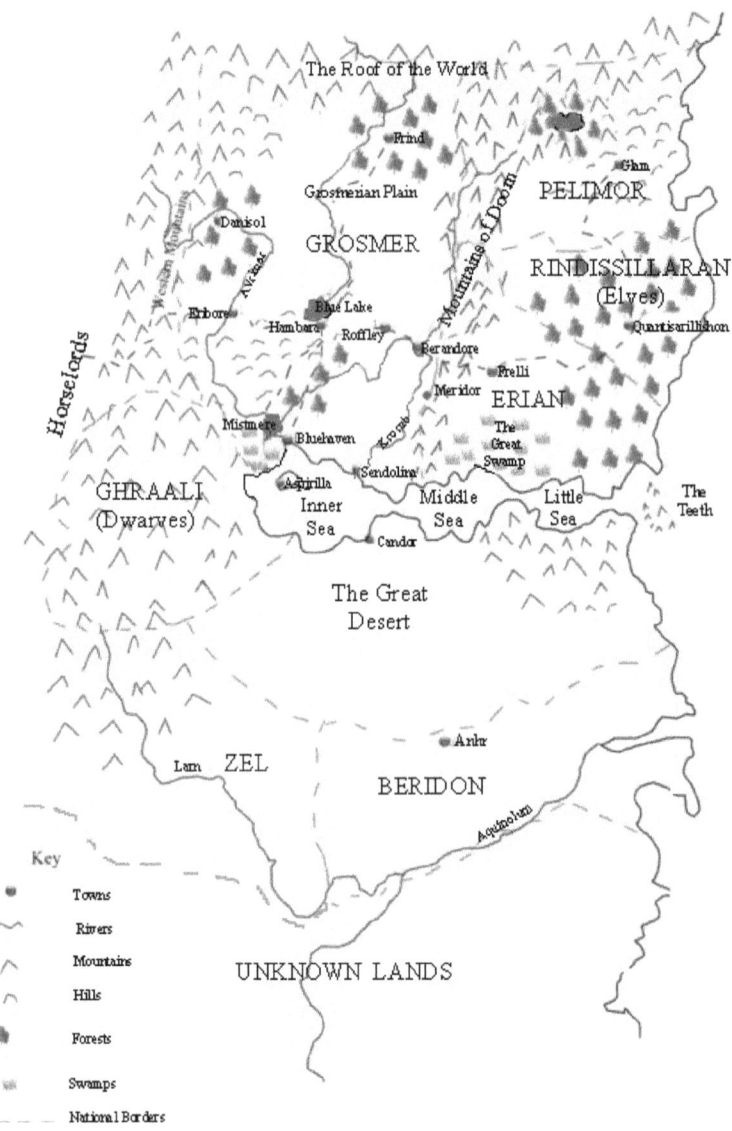

The Roof of the World

Prind

Ghm

Grosmerian Plain

PELIMOR

Danisol

GROSMER

RINDISSILLARAN
(Elves)

Erbore

Blue Lake

Quantisarillishon

Hambara

Roffley

Berandore

Mistmere

Frelli

Meridor

ERIAN

Bluehaven

The
Great
Swamp

Aspirilla

Sendolina

GHRAALI
(Dwarves)

Inner
Sea

Middle
Sea

Little
Sea

The
Teeth

Candor

The Great
Desert

Anhr

Lam

ZEL

BERIDON

Aquispolian

Key

- ● Towns
- ～ Rivers
- ∧ Mountains
- ⌢ Hills
- ♠ Forests
- ⁘ Swamps
- – – – National Borders

UNKNOWN LANDS

Horselords

Western Mountains

Awiras

Mountains of Droth

Krypor

Prologue

Yssalithisandra sat in her study in the house she and Carthinal owned in Hambara. In a cradle at her side slept their daughter, Starralishinara, known as Starr. She rocked the cradle absently as she waited for the arrival of her two new apprentices.

She shifted, stood and walked over to the window. Starr moved in her sleep and Yssa turned to look at her daughter, but the baby did not wake. Yssa brushed her long golden hair from off her face and went back to her chair.

Carthinal sold Mabryl's house in Bluehaven. As Mabryl's heir, he inherited everything Mabryl owned. The older mage had never married and had no children of his own, and so he had adopted Carthinal, an orphaned street child with a talent for magic. Mabryl sadly died in the flood on the Bramara the previous year when he and Carthinal travelled from Bluehaven to Hambara for Carthinal to take the tests that would end his apprenticeship. Yssa said that they could not live in the apartments in the mage tower and bring up their daughter and so they had bought a house in the town.

Now she waited for Tomac and Emmienne to come down for their first lesson with her. They had been Mabryl's apprentices and she agreed to take them on. She and Mabryl had once been close friends, and she mourned his death, even though they had seen little of each other since Mabryl moved to Bluehaven. She turned from the window to return to her seat at the table, brushing a tear from her eyes and banishing thoughts of Mabryl.

Suddenly the door flung open and fifteen-year-old Tomac rushed in. He stopped just inside the threshold, brushed his unruly dark hair out of his eyes and stammered out an apology.

'Sorry for bursting in like that. I thought I was late.'

Yssa smiled. She liked this young man and his exuberant spirit.

'No, you're not late, Tomac. Emmienne isn't here yet.'

Just a she said this, the door opened again and a rather plain girl with wavy brown hair entered.

'I'm not late am I?' she said, sitting down at the table.

Yssa took her place alongside the others.

'I thought we'd start with a bit of astronomy to-day,' she told her charges eliciting a groan from Tomac.

'I don't know what you've already learned about this topic, of course, but from Tomac's reaction, I gather that you've done something.'

'Phases of the moons.' Tomac cast his eyes up-wards 'I still can't work them out properly.'

'You didn't try,' Emmienne told him. 'It comes eventually if you concentrate.'

Yssa smiled at the young man.

'Some people find it easier than others and some never really manage. I always had trouble and now if I need to know I look it up in an almanac. I don't really understand why it's given such prominence when people cleverer than I am can do it and put it in a book for the rest of us to look up.'

Tomac looked impressed that Yssa should admit to finding something hard, but then his face fell as he realised that their teacher still intended to press on with the lesson on astronomy.

'But today we're not going to consider phases of the moon, but something that neither you nor I are ever going to need to calculate.'

Tomac breathed a sigh of relief and Emmienne looked at him in disgust.

Just then, Starr began to stir. Yssa went over to the cradle and rocked it, hoping to get the baby back to sleep. After about five minutes, she decided her daughter had settled again and she returned to the table.

'Today I'm going to tell you of a phenomenon that's due to happen later this summer. It's a very rare occurrence and the complicated calculations to establish when it will occur are not for the likes of us to perform.

'Have any of you heard of a Wolf Moon?'

The pair shook their heads.

'A Wolf Moon, as I said, is a very rare occurrence. It's a bit like an eclipse, but happens when both moons are full and so it doesn't look like a dark shadow passing in front of one of the moons or the sun.

'As you know, Lyndor is smaller than Ullin and is nearer to Vimar. Sometimes it passes in front of its bigger sibling. If this happens when both moons are full, we get a beautiful phenomenon. Lyndor, the golden moon, appears to be surrounded by a halo of silver.'

Yssa went on to explain the phenomenon by using a lamp and an orrery, showing how the sun shone fully on the moons and so they showed their full discs as one passed before the other.

'How often does this occur?' asked Emmienne, fascinated by this.

'Not even once in a human's lifetime,' replied the teacher. 'Even in my long life, I've never seen it. I'm just hoping the night's fine and that clouds don't get in the way.'

'Why is it called a Wolf Moon?' asked Tomac, interested in spite of his dislike of astronomy.

'Superstition has it that, on that night. the hunting wolves are watched over by a celestial wolf whose eye the moons are. This 'wolf' will protect its corporate protégés against any harm. For this reason, people have come to believe that on that night the wolves lose their natural fear of people and will attack anyone whom they think is interfering with their hunting.'

'So people don't go out on that night?'

'Not in the countryside. The towns and cities are different, of course. There aren't many wolves here. Having said that, there are still people who believe that wolves will come into the cities on a Wolf Moon night and stay firmly in their houses.'

'What do you believe, Yssa?' asked Emmienne.

'I am an elf and was born in Quantisarrillishon. The elven homeland is kept as natural as it can be and so wolves roam around. I was brought up to stay indoors on the night of a Wolf Moon, although I've never lived through one.'

Yssa smiled at her two charges and then continued. 'However, I'm a mage and have learned much since my childhood. No, I don't believe the superstitions.'

Just then, Starr began to cry.

'I'll have to leave you for a bit,' Yssa told her charges. 'Starr is due for her feed. I'll be back as soon as we've finished. There are some books on the shelves about the Wolf Moon if you want to read some more while I'm gone.'

She picked up her baby and left the two apprentices to their own devices.

'A Wolf Moon. And happening in our lifetime. Fantastic,' said Tomac as Emmienne got up to look at one of the books. 'I wonder where Carthinal is and if he'll see it?'

Part 1
Escape

Chapter 1
On the Run

One morning, as chance would have it, Captain Ellint decided to split each patrol of the Battalion, in which the members of Wolf found themselves, into two. The soldiers had started to become restless and bored in spite of the entertainment supplied by Wolf Patrol, as they had now become known. The battalion waited for the arrival of another one in order to continue the manoeuvres, and time weight heavy on them.

Captain Ellint spoke to the whole battalion. He stood on a rostrum erected for this purpose.

'Sometimes,' he began, 'in a battle, when people have been captured or killed, it will become necessary to amalgamate two separate patrols. You must learn to work with others whom you don't know, so today's exercises will be with mixed patrols.

Wolf Patrol split and joined with the Griffin Patrol. Carthinal, Randa, The Cat, Davrael and Kimi stayed in the camp, along with half of the Griffins, while the others went off to take up their positions as though in an ambush. Shortly after, those who remained behind set off to act as a battalion passing by. They would not know exactly where the others had set up the ambush, so there would be some element of surprise.

Just after the group, with Fero as acting sergeant, left to join up with the half of Griffin Patrol, the expected second Frelli Regiment arrived. A large, fierce-looking hobgoblin appeared to be in charge and he carried a swagger stick that he looked as though he would use on any who did not obey him quickly enough.

This did not cause any comment, since all of the first Candor regiment, of which the Wolves now formed a part, expected non-humans in the second Frelli. Captain Ellint warned them of this before hand, and told them anyone who caused trouble with the non-humans would suffer for it.

The fact that this hobgoblin captain had a wooden leg caused some comment and stares. No one who had received such injuries in the past had continued serving in the army The hobgoblin captain marched over towards the tent of Captain Ellint, barking orders to his lieutenants to halt the march and to set up camp. He passed close to Carthinal and his company as they prepared to march out on their manoeuvre.

The others having left the camp had got a little distance away, but the arrival of the new regiment caused all to pause. No one had seen an active soldier with a wooden leg before, and not a few people whispered questions as to why he had not been retired.

Fero saw the hobgoblin march past the others, and then he saw him turn and look back at them. The hobgoblin hobbled towards them and appeared to speak to Carthinal and then Randa, eyeing her Sword suspiciously. He turned to his men and barked an order.

Several hobgoblins came running over, along with some humans. The captain gave another order that Fero could not hear, and then he saw the hobgoblins and men seize the others. They searched them and removed their weapons, He felt Asphodel come up beside him.

'It's Khland!' she exclaimed. 'The Sword must have damaged his leg more than we thought, and he had to have it removed.'

With her superior elven eyesight she had been able to recognise the cruel hobgoblin leader who had captured their little group after they found the Sword last summer.

Fero scowled, then an anxious look filled his eyes. In spite of the argument he had with Randa, he still loved her and made to rush down to her rescue. Grimmaldo came to his side and put a restraining hand on his arm.

'Getting yourself killed in a rescue attempt will serve no purpose, Fero,' said the young mage. 'Our best bet is to get away from here and try to rescue them later. They'll surely know that you, Bas, Thadora and Asphodel won't be far away. They'll come looking soon, mark my words.'

'How can we sneak away with all these people to see us?' asked Thadora.

Grimmaldo thought for a moment and then said, 'I've a scroll that may come in handy for that,' He scrabbled amongst his things. 'Invisibility that will act on everything in a ten foot radius. It bends light rays, much the same as a normal invisibility spell, but bends them more, so more is invisible. Ah, here it is. The only problem is sound. It doesn't stop people from hearing things. Anyone around here will hear us moving away and probably put two and two together.'

Asphodel looked at him. 'I think I can help there,' she said. 'I can cause sound to be silenced in the same area.'

'Excellent,' replied Grimmaldo. 'Now get close and hold on to someone else as we'll not be able to see or hear each other. Let me cast first, Asphodel. It'll be no use if I'm silenced.'

They crept close together and each one held the belt of the next person. Fero grabbed Bramble by the scruff of the big, black and tan dog's neck. He yelped as Fero dragged him close. A man from Griffin patrol looked round at the sound, then looked back at the "arrest" being made in the camp, which he found much more interesting. He turned back to ask Fero to confirm what he thought he saw, that the new arrivals had dragged the rest of Wolf patrol none too gently away, but to his surprise, the five had disappeared.

'Where in the name of Kassilla's tits 'ave they gone?' he asked the air.

'What the heck are you gabbing about now, Grondo?' asked his friend.

'Fero and the others. They was 'ere a second ago, now they've gone.'

'Seen their friends bein' arrested I s'pose,' replied the other. 'Run away. Allus knowed they must be spies. 'Alf of 'em was Grosmerian. Cowards all Grosmerians are. They'll find 'em an' 'ang 'em. I 'ope they does it in camp so's we can watch. I likes a good 'angin' I does.'

* * *

Bramble felt Fero grab him by the scruff of his neck. He yelped in surprise rather than pain. After all, his mother had carried him like that as a pup, but he knew Fero did not intend to carry him, and he thought the man rather rough. The dog looked at his master with an expression of accusation and anxiety mixed. He heard Fero's apology, and although he did not understand the words, he understood the meaning behind them.

Fero had looked and smelt anxious ever since he saw what had happened back at the camp. Bramble had looked too and saw the hobgoblin approaching the rest of his pack. He knew it meant danger for them and he itched to go to their aid, particularly the pale female. The dog thought of Randa as Fero's mate, and Fero was pack leader as far as he was concerned, so she was the alpha female. He did not know those terms, but he knew what every dog or wolf knew about pack hierarchy. He whined his anxiety as he looked at Fero for the command to go to their aid. A command that never came.

Then, suddenly, he could no longer see Fero and the others. He could smell them, hear them and feel Fero's hand on his neck. He could see everyone around, but not his companions. He let out a small whine as his tail crept between his legs. He felt his limbs begin to tremble.

'Quiet, Bramble,' whispered Fero.

He heard chanting coming from the dark haired female they called Asphodel, then suddenly it seemed as though he had gone deaf. He shook his head, but still he heard nothing. The dog had no understanding of deafness though, and he whined again. He felt the vibrations in his throat that came when he whined, so he knew he had done so, but no sound came.

Fero's still had his hand on his neck. He knew his pack still surrounded him because he could smell them, but all sound and sight of them had gone. He tried barking, with the same result as when he whined. His tail went further between his legs. This was beyond his understanding and he did not like it at all. Then he felt a tug on his neck and he followed Fero's scent, staying close to the ranger's heels as the group slunk away from the rest of the army. He looked back towards the camp. They walked in the opposite direction from the rest of the pack who

seemed to have been taken prisoner by the hobgoblin.

Once they left the vicinity of the camp, they
speeded up, as the silence and invisibility wore off.
Bramble shook his head once more as hearing and
sight returned. One moment, he could see nothing
of his companions, nor hear anything, then they all
reappeared again, and the sounds of the mountains
seemed to hit him. He whined again, and licked
Fero's hand for reassurance.

The ranger bent down and stroked his ears saying, 'Sorry about that, boy. We had to get away. I
wish I could explain to you, but you wouldn't understand if I did.'

Fero turned to the others and said, 'We must
move away from here quickly. As soon as they get
Carthinal and the rest of them somewhere safe,
they'll be coming after us as Grimmaldo said. However, we must take a few minutes for me to ensure
that following us will not be easy. I'll try to cover
our tracks a little way back, and then we must move
quickly. From here, I'll obliterate as much as I can,
but if they get the dogs out, anything I can do will
be in vain.'

Fero walked back the way they had come with
Bramble pressing close to him for reassurance. Ev-

ery so often, Fero paused to stroke the dog and speak gently to him until he had calmed down. The dog slowly lifted his tail as things returned to normal and he watched as Fero continued in his task of straightening a bent branch or rubbing out a footprint.

Bramble and Fero arrived back within fifteen minutes and Bramble went round them all to check that no one had disappeared in his absence. He looked at Fero as if to say, *'Let's go then.'* He now felt much better, and although he did not like the idea of leaving half the pack behind, the pack leader said to carry on and he would follow him anywhere, even into the underworld itself.

The small group walked up towards the mountains that surrounded the valley in which the Erian troops had their camp. The dog followed his pack leader but kept pressing close He had still not got over the confusion of the deprivation of sound and sight and felt relieved to feel Fero's hand caress his ears every so often. The dark man understood his fears and gave him the comfort he needed. However, he still did not like leaving the rest of the pack, and kept stopping and looking back.

Whenever he did so, he whined and looked at Fero, but the man said, 'Don't worry, boy. We'll rescue them.'

Of course, he did not understand the words, but he interpreted the body language and tone enough to have a hazy idea of the meaning the ranger wished to convey. He knew the captors of the others were not human, and he knew that all the members of their pack were not human too, although he did not know those words. They smelt different somehow. He liked Asphodel. She smelt of woods and soil, of growing things and the wilderness. He liked that and had done so from the start.

The small, hairy one they called Bas, or sometimes Basalt, smelled of metal and deep places. He did not know how he knew such things, but he felt sure that the places lay deep under the ground. It made him a little uneasy, but he the dwarf was part of the pack to protect and he respected the dwarf even if he did not feel the love for him as he did for Fero.

The others had unmistakable smells, too, which, although he did not realise it, was human. Each had their own individual scent, but the underlying scent smelled the same, with the exception of Carthinal who seemed to have a scent between that of the humans and Asphodel.

The dog looked back once more and then trotted off after Fero. He kept looking behind, and sometimes ran ahead to scout the land, but he saw nothing amiss and so the pack continued onwards and upwards towards the higher reaches of the mountains.

Chapter 2
Caves

They walked until it the sun disappeared and dusk began to fall and then Fero called a halt.

'I think we're probably safe enough for now,' he told them. 'We've seen no sign of pursuit for several hours so we'll take a rest. We'll probably be able to stay here until dawn, then we'll see if we can backtrack and find out what's happened to Carthinal, Randa and the others. No fire though,' he warned them. 'Anyone searching would see the smoke. We have little food anyway, just what we took with us for the exercise, so we've nothing to cook. We must try to conserve our water supplies, too, until we can find some more. I only took a couple of water skins, what about the rest of you?'

They each placed what they had in a pile. They had seven water skins between them. Fero noticed Bramble's tongue hanging out and he poured some water into a helmet for the dog. Bramble looked up with an expression of pleading as he saw the small amount of water the man poured out for him.

'Sorry, lad, but you'll have to make do like the rest of us, and hope we find a spring before we run out,' Fero told the animal, and he rubbed his ears. Bramble, realising he would get no more water, drank the little Fero allowed him, then flopped down onto the ground and put his head onto his paws. He sighed and closed his eyes.

'We'll need to conserve this,' the ranger told the rest of them. 'We don't know these mountains, so we've no idea how long it will be before we find some clean water.'

Fero set a watch and they all took turns, but nothing approached them except a small fox and that ran away as soon as it saw the size of Bramble. He did not even have to growl, just raise his head.

Dawn came all too soon, and the weary folk sat up and rubbed their eyes. Their tiredness came as much from worry and tension as from their exertions the previous day. They did not eat as they had hardly and food left. Even Thadora did not complain about her hunger as she knew there was no point.

'I'll go out later and see if I can catch something,' Fero told them. 'Maybe we'll risk a fire tonight and then we can eat. Water will be a problem though if we don't find some soon.'

The friends set off once more, hoping to be able to circle back and look down over the army encampment to find out what had happened to their friends. The sun beat down on them, but towards noon, large cumulus clouds began to gather in the previously clear sky. Bramble felt an ominous prickling sensation in his fur and he whined. Basalt looked up anxiously at the darkening sky.

'Looks like thunder,' he said.

He had hardly got the words out of his mouth when they heard the first rumble. They all looked up anxiously. Storms in the mountains could be dangerous.

'Maybe it'll bypass us,' said Thadora. She always looked on the bright side.

Bramble pressed nearer to her. She was the closest to him. He hated the loud noises of the thunder, and the sensations the build up of the static electricity gave him, the prickling sensation in his fur as though hundreds of tiny insects ran races up and down his skin. His tail went down. Thadora reached down and patted him. It reassured him a little. This pack of his seemed, to him, to be afraid of nothing, and he licked her hand to show her he was not afraid either, although his every instinct told him to hide away.

A flash lit up the sky and for a moment they saw the mountains clearly. A loud clap of thunder followed the flash almost immediately. Bramble shivered, Thadora jumped and Basalt swore. Then the rain started. Not gradually, but a sudden downpour as though someone had just opened a sluice in the sky. Within seconds their clothes had become drenched and they shivered in the cold wind that had suddenly risen.

'We must find some shelter,' Asphodel said.

'Why?' asked Grimmaldo. 'We can't get any wetter. Even my bones are wet!'

'So we can get dry, of course,' replied the elf archly. 'We can't afford anyone getting sick through being soaked. Fero nearly died last year from pneumonia, which developed from 'flu he caught from being exposed to the elements. This happened after we'd been captured by Khland and his men. The first time he captured us. He took us over the moors and cold and damp weather then he made us sleep outside and Fero got sick.'

They hurried to the side of a cliff they could see, in the hope it would afford some shelter from the storm. The thunder and lightning continued to rage around them and the swirling wind meant even the slight overhang they found gave them little shelter from the pouring rain. All of them began to shiver with cold, even though the day had previously been hot.

Bramble wandered off along the cliff base. After a few minutes, he spotted a dark place. Wandering towards it out of curiosity, he found a cave. Venturing in and sniffing carefully for any danger he noticed a scent of bear, but it was faint and obviously the bear that had occupied the cave had long gone. He sniffed further and could detect no danger. Small animals had lived here at some time, but now it appeared to be empty. He barked once to alert the pack. He heard the leader call him.

'What is it, Bramble?' said the ranger as he approached. Then he saw the cave. 'Good dog!'

He praised the animal and patted him, and Bramble wagged his tail in pleasure. Fero called the rest of the pack to the cave. When they arrived, they all praised him, and he had never felt more pleased. His tail felt as though it would wear out, he wagged it so hard. Even the small hairy one called Basalt patted and praised him.

He and Basalt, hardly ever took any notice of each other and Basalt always seemed a little nervous around the dog, but now even he stroked and patted him. When they had all finished, Bramble padded over to a corner of the cave and lay down as the others poured into the cave and sat down to rest.

'I think we can manage a fire here without it being seen,' Asphodel commented. 'If you look carefully, you can see a crack in the ceiling. I think the smoke would go up there.'

'Finding dry wood will be a problem in this,' pointed out Basalt, indicating the weather outside.

'We need some way of getting dry and warm,' Grimmaldo said. 'If we can find some wood that's not too wet, I can probably light it.'

Shivering and wet, they sat looking out at the deluge falling from the sky, but rain so hard could not possibly last long, and soon it began to ease. They began to search near the cave for wood and soon had a small pile. Although the damp had seeped into it, Grimmaldo decided he could manage to light it with a little magic, and shortly after, a small fire burned near the cave entrance. Their shivering gradually stopped and they held hands out to the warmth of the fire, pleased to have some warmth. Bramble shook himself hard to divest his fur of the loose water droplets running over his skin, then he crept as close to the blaze as he dared.

'Hey!' a voice protested. 'Stop that. I'm wet enough as it is!'

It came from Thadora and she hastily retreated as far from Bramble as she could. The others also scattered and protested, then Grimmaldo began to laugh.

'What's so funny!' grumbled Basalt as the mage continued his laughter.

'Well, here we are, as wet as we can be, clothing soaked and us wet through to the skin, and we're running away because a dog shakes a few drops more onto us.'

Once the fire got going and gave off a decent amount of heat, each removed their armour and as much of their clothing as they deemed decent, then put it to dry near the fire. Bramble lay down with a sigh of contentment and closed his eyes. Basalt then noticed Thadora had disappeared.

'Curse that girl,' he muttered getting to his feet and wandering towards the back of the cave. 'Where's she got to now, I wonder?'

Just then, her voice came from the back of the cave.

'There's a crack here. I think I can get in and see where it goes.'

Basalt groaned and called back to her.

'Come back to the fire, lass, and get warm. Many caves have cracks in the back and sides too. Most are just that; cracks that are dead ends.' With that he returned to the fire and sat down.

They still had no food, but Fero put an upturned helmet outside the door to collect some rainwater, so at least they had something to drink. When the rain had filled it, he carefully poured it into some of the water skins. They all, including Bramble, drank some and then he put the helmet outside again.

'When the rain eases up, I'll go and see if I can find some game,' Fero told them. 'I can't go out in this as my bow string will get wet and useless.'

'My sling won't though,' pointed out Asphodel. She had become good with her sling since their quest to find the Sword, and she had also been practising with the mace and had now become quite proficient with that as well in a combat situation.

'I'll go and find us something to eat.'

She stood and moved towards the cave mouth.

'You planning on going out like that?' asked Grimmaldo, grinning. The elf had completely forgotten her state of undress, now wearing only undergarments. A year ago, she would have been most embarrassed to be seen by the male members of their little group in her underwear, but now she grinned back at the young mage and sat down again.

'Perhaps I'd better wait until the rest of my things are dry,' she said.

Grimmaldo looked at her appreciatively.

'I don't know. You look pretty good like that, I'd say,' he teased.

This time, Asphodel blushed prettily and turned her eyes to the fire.

'Stop teasing her, Grimmaldo,' Thadora scolded. 'You're embarrassing her.'

Grimmaldo looked Thadora up and down then.

'You don't look so bad yourself, either, Lady Thadora,' he grinned.

Thadora's blushed now, and Fero grinned even as he spoke.

'Stop teasing the girls, Grimmaldo,' he admonished the mage. 'It's not fair to take advantage of them in our adverse situation.'

Bramble lay with his head on his paws throughout all this. His eyes moved from one to the other as they spoke, and, although he could not understand the words spoken, he became aware of Grimmaldo and Fero's amusement and the embarrassment of the two girls. What strange creatures. If they wanted to mate, why not just get on with it? All this talking and teasing confused him.

Of course, if Grimmaldo wanted Asphodel, he would probably have to fight Carthinal for her. The dog sensed that Carthinal and Asphodel had strong feelings for each other, even if no one else realised it. Even Carthinal and Asphodel did not seem to be aware of it. He closed his eyes. Strange creatures indeed.

The rain and thunder began to ease at last. Their clothing had almost dried by the fire and they felt much warmer, although ravenously hungry. Asphodel rose and put on her clothing and armour, picked up her sling and moved towards the cave entrance. Grimmaldo's eyes followed her and he gave a grimace of disappointment as she dressed.

Basalt noticed, and hoped that either he would forget her when she had dressed, or that she would forget Carthinal and turn to Grimmaldo instead. They did not need any jealous confrontations between a pair of mages. Basalt had a feeling life would soon get interesting enough without added complications.

Fero said he would go with Asphodel and Bramble followed. Sitting by the fire had dried the dog's fur, and now he had rested, he felt in need of some exercise. They had been in the cave for half a day while the storm raged around them.

Fero and Asphodel wandered towards a small stand of trees not far away, where they thought there might be some pigeons at least. Bramble's stomach rumbled as they walked back along the way they had come.

The sun had come out again, and the air smelled fresh. Occasional drips of rain fell from the scrubby trees onto the three as they walked between them. This place looked well off the beaten tracks and they did not find any pathways to follow they had to scramble over boulders and stones not to mention the roots of trees and stands of nettles and brambles to make their own routes.

Suddenly, Bramble paused in his inspection of what he thought might be the run of some small animal. He thought he heard something not too far away. He sniffed the air and got a definite whiff of dog and human, as well as the foul stench of those others that they called hobgoblin. He growled deep in his throat. Fero looked round.

'What is it?' he asked the dog. Bramble's hackles stood up and he growled in earnest.

Fero, realising what had alerted the dog called to Asphodel that they should go back to the cave and warn the others to be ready to move again.

'I think Bramble has smelt pursuers,' he said, as they began the trudge back up the mountain. Then they spotted the searchers.

Half a dozen men and more than that of hobgoblins climbed the hillside towards them. They had six dogs with them, all casting about for a scent. The rain had done them a favour in preventing the dogs from picking up the scent as readily as before, and that slowed them. However, it had slowed the companions too as they needed to shelter in the cave. It would be touch and go as to who reached the cave first, Fero, Asphodel and Bramble, or the followers.

Asphodel almost fell into the cave, followed closely by Fero.

'Searchers... behind us,' she panted. 'Quick. Must go.'

The others quickly gathered up their things and put out the fire.

Just before they exited the cave, Fero called, 'Too late. They're nearly here. Go to the deeper parts. Perhaps they won't go deep in. Try that crack of Thadora's and pray to the gods that it goes somewhere and is not a dead end.'

'What are you going to do, Fero?' asked the young thief.

'I'll stay here and buy you a bit of time,' the ranger told her.

'Oh no you don't, Fero,' said Bas. 'At least, not alone. I'll stay too.'

The others all agreed that Fero would not stand a chance, even with the aid of Basalt, and refused to go unless he accompanied them. They had no time to argue as they rushed for the deeper parts of the cave and the crack Thadora had found.

Basalt went first for two reasons. First, being a dwarf, he had grown up in such places and he could see much better than the rest of them in the dim light. They had no lights with them, not having anticipated going caving, or even being out after dark. Thadora came next, followed by Asphodel. Grimmaldo and Fero brought up the rear with Bramble reluctantly trailing behind.

They found it a tight squeeze, especially for the larger men. Fero banged his head on the roof several times in places where it dropped low. Bramble whined as he followed, little puppy noises in his throat.

The crack was dark and narrow. At first, some light filtered in from the cave behind them, but soon that faded away and Bramble could not see, He hated that, but he could smell and this time he could hear. He heard the drip, drip of water from the roof, and smelled the scents of his companions ahead. He kept as close as he could to Fero and his nose bumped his pack leader's knee from time to time.

Neither he nor Fero worried about that; it gave both of them some reassurance. Even Fero felt a bit disorientated in the dark of the cave. The darkness had now become complete. The dog could not even make out the outline of anyone else. If the ground suddenly fell away, they would be over the edge before knowing it. He had no idea whether he traversed a narrow passage or an open cave except where in the places where it became so narrow it scraped his sides. Fero, he knew, had to turn sideways occasionally to get past.

The crack twisted right and left, and steadily went downwards with the occasional short climb. When they came to a fork, they followed Basalt blindly, trusting he had some idea as to where the passage led them.

They passed places where the tunnel widened, and places where it narrowed. Occasionally they passed through caves, and always water dripped down onto them. They kept on going as they could hear noises of the pursuit still behind, but getting fainter.

Then the roof came lower and the walls pressed in. Bramble became aware of Fero getting down onto his knees to continue onwards, then eventually Fero ended up wriggling along on his stomach and Bramble had to crouch down and wriggle too.

Whimpers came from ahead. They came from Thadora.

'I can't do this. I can't go on. The bloody mountain's going to crush us. The blasted roof is going to cave in. The damned sides will squash us. It's getting narrower and lower. I can't breathe. We're running out of air.'

Panic sounded in her voice. Bramble could smell her fear and it added to his own. He howled in sympathy.

'Not you too!' grumbled Fero. Then he called to Asphodel. 'Try to calm her. We can't afford to have her panic in here. There's no way she can get past us to get out so we'll have to go on. Bas, what do you think of the chances of this crack opening up?'

'If it's not ended now, it may go to another cave at least. If our luck holds, we may be able to find another way out.'

They came to a standstill while Asphodel talked to Thadora. In the pitch darkness she did not find it easy. Asphodel reached out to the girl and took her hand. Thadora's gripped her hand so hard that the elf thought the other girl would break all the bones in her hand.

After what seemed like an age, with Thadora still crying, but calmer, Fero called for them to move again. Time crawled as slowly as they did as they made their way through the crack, but eventually the crawl-way roof rose and gave more freedom to move. Soon it rose even more and became a passage similar to the one they had entered. Fero could not stand completely upright at this point, due to his height but the group moved along a little quicker, especially as they managed to light a torch. Fero said only one torch at a time, though. They had no idea how long they would be in these caves and he did not want to try to travel in the dark.

'What's that?' Thadora stopped and peered through the gloom. I thought I saw a light flickering ahead. Could it be the damned way out?'

'Perhaps we should go and see,' Asphodel suggested.

Just then, a shadow flitted ahead of them, disappearing along a tunnel to the left. The friends stopped, confused.

'Perhaps it was a ghost,; suggested Grimmaldo. 'If it's truly a ghost, we shouldn't follow it.'

Then another shadow from the left, ran along the tunnel ahead of them.

Asphodel turned to Grimmaldo.

'They aren't ghosts,' she told him. 'They're living things. they're giving off heat. You can see it too, Can't you, Basalt?'

The dwarf agreed, and gave his opinion they should not follow them. They had no idea what those shadows were, and perhaps they deliberately led them to their deaths in the form of a nasty creature from the depths.

Thadora shuddered and nearly screamed at that thought, but she managed to suppress it and the little group continued in the direction they had been travelling.

Then, suddenly, the passageway opened and they found themselves free from confinement and in a large open cave.

Chapter 3
Walchin

On entering this large cavern, they noticed they could see, if only faintly. Looking around, dim lights glowed high on the walls of the cave.

'They could be phosphorescent fungi,' mused Basalt, who had experience of living deep underground, 'or they could be some kind of creature that gives off light, like glow-worms or fireflies.'

'Look,' Asphodel said, pointing. 'Those formations over there look like buildings.'

'Perhaps they're natural stone formations,' Grimmaldo mused.

Basalt shook his head. 'No, those are not natural. They've been built in here.' He approached one standing closer than most of the others. 'It looks a bit like dwarven work, but there are aspects of the building work that aren't dwarven. At least, not modern dwarven workmanship. For a start, they're round. Dwarves used to build round buildings centuries ago but not any more.'

'Perhaps they've been here for that long. Abandoned by the dwarves who built them,' Grimmaldo suggested.

As they walked through the buildings, though, Thadora noticed something odd. She pointed at the door of one of the houses.

'That wood looks fresh. It's certainly not hundreds of bleedin' years old, Basalt.'

The dwarf frowned.

'You're right, there, Thadda,' he said. 'This wood is no more than ten years old.'

'Then someone lives here,' said Asphodel. 'Perhaps they'll show us the way out.'

Basalt frowned. 'Something's odd,' he said. 'I've never heard of dwarves living in the Mountains of Doom. All our race for thousands of years have lived in the Western Mountains, with a few groups in the Roof of the World. We all know of each other and are in communication. But none have ever, in all that time, been known in these mountains.'

Fero led the way towards the centre of the cavern. They walked for fifteen minutes but still no one, not even Basalt or Asphodel, could make out the far wall. As for the roof, well, that disappeared high above.

Asphodel could see no sign of life, though. When the travellers got nearer to the centre, they found dim lamps burning around the village on tall posts, giving a shadowy light. Here they noticed a dropped basket, there, a fallen vegetable. They saw dwellings here, in this part of the cavern, all built of stone or carved from the cave walls. The settlement seemed the size of a large village or small town, but where, in a village above ground there would have been a bustling population, here nothing stirred. There remained only the signs they had noticed showing that people lived in the village.

The buildings lay scattered around in seemingly random fashion. A large building with double doors lay on the left of where they entered. Not one of the buildings had any windows. They passed buildings with the appearance of houses. A couple, with open doors, had tables, chairs, and even food left. Some looked like workshops that had been left hurriedly, tools scattered around. Then they found a big open area with a large building at one side, a bit like a square in a town above ground. Even here they saw no sign of life. It looked as if everyone left hurriedly.

'People live here, still,' Asphodel said. 'All these buildings show signs of recent occupation. Very recent. I wonder where they've gone, and why?'

'Perhaps they think something dangerous is about to happen, like an earthquake or a volcanic eruption,' Thadora said.

'Or perhaps we are the danger,' Fero pointed out. 'After all, these people, assuming they are people, have been cut off from outside for thousands of years, if Bas is anything to go by.'

'What do you mean "If Bas is anything to go by." I know my people's history.'

'Sorry, Bas. Of course you do. What I meant is, these people might see anyone from outside as a threat. We should just sit down and wait, to show them we're not going to harm them. A bit like you would with a wild deer. After a while, if you are quiet and still enough, they'll come closer.'

Thadora drummed her fingers. They entered this cave what seemed to her like hours ago, and Fero told them to sit and do nothing. The seventeen-year old was not good at waiting. In her own words she had said, *'I don't do patience.'* when Asphodel admonished her for not sitting still.

The others all sat there with peaceful expressions on their faces, barely moving, and not talking. The girl edged slowly away from the others. No one noticed so she edged some more. Her curiosity burned in her like a flame. She really must take a look around this place.

Through the occasional door, left open, they glimpsed rooms as though they had been hurriedly left and their owners would soon return. A meal in the process of being prepared, a child's toys scattered around, tools left where they lay in a workroom, half-finished handiwork on a chair. The girl decided she must explore this strange place to see if she could answer the many questions running through her head. Who were these people? Why had they left so suddenly? Why did they live completely under the mountains? Why did no one know of their existence?

When they arrived in this square in the centre of the village, Fero had called a halt. He said if their approach had frightened whoever lived here, they must do nothing to antagonise them or give them reason to fear.

'Maybe,' he said, 'If we indicate we are not in anyway dangerous, the people will show themselves and help us find another way out.'

Therefore, they waited. And waited. Then they waited some more. And Thadora got impatient.

Just as she rose to her knees, about to make a dive for the nearest corner, Basalt spotted her. At the same time, a movement came from the northern end of the square.

Basalt reached out and made a grab at the girl, hissing, 'Just what do you think you're doing?'

Because of this, they both missed the entrance of three inhabitants of the village.

The street at the north of the village led straight from another cave entrance, and the figures emerged from here. At first, the waiting friends thought three dwarves approached them, as the trio had a similar build to the dwarves they knew, but then, as the newcomers emerged from the shadows they immediately changed their minds.

The three looked about the size of dwarves, maybe a little taller, but they had very different skin and hair, as well as the fact that they had no beards. They had almost pure white skin and their hair, which they wore in ringlets hanging to their shoulders, had a similar colouring. In contrast, though, their eyes seemed to be the deepest black.

Thadora said afterwards they reminded her of the snowmen children built in winter, with little pieces of charcoal or the burning rock for eyes.

One of the three stood a little in front of the others, and was obviously the leader. He carried no arms and wore a flowing red cloak over his shoulders, covering what appeared to be a brown leather tunic and trousers. The other two wore leather armour and sported no cloaks, but they carried the biggest war hammers the group had ever seen.

The leader spoke. None of them understood what he said. He repeated himself, pointing to them.

'It sounds like an archaic form of dwarvish,' said Basalt, frowning. 'I think he's asking us how we come to be here, and what we want.'

'Can you speak to him?' asked Asphodel.

'I can't speak the ancient form of my language,' Basalt replied. 'I can understand it a bit as many words are similar enough, even though the pronunciation and endings are a bit different. Maybe he'll be able to understand modern dwarvish if I try to speak to him.'

'Do so then,' Fero told the dwarf. 'Tell him how we come to be here, and ask if there is another way out.'

Thadora stared at the newcomers. Why was their hair and skin so white? They looked like ghosts to the girl, but she knew that a trio of real flesh and blood stood before her.

Basalt began to explain, slowly and with many repetitions, how hobgoblins chased them, and that they found the tunnels when the hobgoblins trapped them in a cave. The mention of hobgoblins got an immediate reaction from the newcomers. The leader turned to his companions, who Thadora decided were bodyguards, and spoke excitedly. He gave one of them an order and the guard immediately raced off towards the north.

'This is not easy,' Basalt told his friends. 'There's some understanding, but it's slow. He obviously understands the word for hobgoblin and has the same view of them that we do, though. He's sent his bodyguard off to round up some more men to lead them off the scent. I think he intends to get them lost in the caves.'

Basalt scratched his beard before continuing.

'These people call themselves *"Walchin"*, a very similar word to the dwarvish *"wallin"* which means *"people of the mountain depths."* I think they are distant relatives of dwarves who've become separated from their kin. Their language alone indicates some relationship.'

'Fine,' snapped Thadora, 'We're all fascinated by your theories about how these blasted people developed, Bas, but me, I'm more interested in whether they can get us out of this damned hole in the ground.'

'Steady, Red Cub.' The dwarf laid a calming hand on her arm and used the name the Yeti had given her. 'We must go steadily. These folk are suspicious and wary. We can't go demanding they show us the way out just like that. Diplomacy is what we want here.'

Thadora snorted at the thought of a diplomatic Basalt.

Slowly, the five became aware of people moving back into their homes. Some element of fear had gone, it seemed, but the people still exhibited a great deal of caution. They saw no one clearly, just movements in the shadows. The leader, for so they assumed him to be, then spoke again to Basalt in his archaic tongue.

'My guard has gone to round up some of the younger men to lead the hobgoblins away from here,' he told them. 'This is mainly for our own protection, you realise, and not as a favour to you strangers.'

He waved a hand in the direction of a young man who passed closely and muttered something to him. The young man returned shortly with a chair and the Walchin leader sat down.

Thadora's heart sank when she saw the chair. This might be a long session.

'You seem to be little threat to us,' the Walchin told them, 'but you cannot be allowed to leave with the knowledge of our existence. It only takes one slip and people will know we are here and come seeking us, either to enslave us or to find some mythical treasure. We remember what your kind is like. It is in our stories and myths. Our existence must remain a secret.'

When Basalt translated this as best he could for the others, they erupted in simultaneous speech, each as appalled as the other. Fero held up his hand and they fell silent.

'We *must* get out of here,' he said to this companions. 'We have to carry word of Erian's plans for war, and of this Master person, whoever he is. We must also try to rescue the others. This we will not accomplish without the help of these folk. It seems that the ways out of here are complex. We must convince them they need to help us. Bas, tell them of the war and how it will engulf all the nations of Khalram if we can't stop it. This Master seems to me to want to rule all the continent and his talk of bringing "democracy" is just an excuse.'

After Fero finished speaking, the dwarf began to repeat what the ranger had told him to say.

The Walchin leader listened, then he replied, 'If no one knows we exist, your wars and quarrels will not affect us. We will go on with our lives as we have always done, quietly and peacefully in our mountain caves. This seems even more reason you should stay here. If war breaks out above, we will go on in peace and survive. This is how we have survived so far, unchanged and unchanging.'

Asphodel then spoke, after Basalt had translated. She looked the walchin in the eye as she spoke. Basalt translated her words as best he could.

'I do not know how long your people have lived beneath the mountains,' she said. 'It must be a long, long time for all memory of you to have disappeared from the world above, and for you to have lost all pigment in your skin. The world above has changed, and is forever changing. You said your people did not change, but that is not natural, nor what the gods intended.;

She paused and took a deep breath, her eyes never leaving those of the Walchin, who, in his turn, fixed his own eyes on hers.

'We are here on Vimar to learn,' she said, 'to question and to develop. We live our lives as best we can and hope it's enough for us to be taken to the bosom of Kassila and live with the gods. For most of us, it's not enough, and we must return, judged and sent back by Khalhera to further our education. We must learn to keep the balance. To keep ourselves in balance too. This means confronting whatever un-balances the world and ourselves.'

The others all looked at her as she spoke. As-phodel never preached to them, but here, now, she preached her view of the world and what she knew of the gods and their desires for the people of Vimar.

'The world lives in balance. All nature is one huge balancing act. Remove one part of it and all is up-set. The scales come down too hard one way. The eagle eats the rabbit. This is right and good, and the rabbit eats the grass. When the eagle dies, it decays into the ground and feeds the grass, which in turn feeds other rabbits. So it goes on. But suppose some-one kills all the rabbits in their greed for the meat and fur? What happens then? The eagles have lost their main food source. They have to find another, or starve. They will not produce as many young as there is less food, so there will be fewer eagles next year.'

The Curate of Sylissa paused and the Walchin leader nodded and looked about to speak, but As-phodel began talking again.

'This usually rights itself after a few seasons, but suppose the rabbits did not come back? Ultimately the eagles all die. Their bodies cannot go back into the ground if they are not there, and so the grass will not be fed and will die too. They are all in balance you see. All are needed for the survival of the others.

'This is very simplistic, I know, but the whole world is in balance. The gods created the peoples of the world, and all are needed for it to be truly as it is meant to be.'

The Walchin leader now frowned in thought.

'Maybe you don't need to come out from your hiding places under the mountains, but you cannot keep us here. It will upset the balance between good and evil, and evil will prevail in Khalram. But I believe the world needs you people and you should not remain hidden here.

'You were a creation of the gods, made for a purpose. Discover that purpose and go and embrace it, and in the meantime, help us to escape. Maybe that's the purpose you're here, to help prevent the evil I can feel in Erian from spreading over the whole continent.'

With that, she and the others sat in silence. The Walchin leader stared at her, eyes wide as he listened to Basalt's laboured translation, but he clearly saw the fire inspiring her to make the speech.

When Basalt had finished, Thadora exclaimed, 'Wow! Some damned speech. I can see why you're a cleric now. Great sermon, Curate Aspholessaria.'

It seemed her speech made some impression on the leader of the Walchin and he spent several minutes in silence, pondering her words. At least, that is what they assumed him to be doing.

After several minutes, he turned to them and said, 'I must confer with the council before any decisions can be made with regard to you, and what we should do. Please come with me to the Meeting Hall and we will give you some refreshment.'

He rose, and, beckoning them to follow, he walked towards the large building in the square.

Passing through the door of the round building they found themselves in a large circular chamber with doors leading off all around it. No windows opened through the walls as with all the other buildings in the underground cave. It seemed the Walchin found no need of them, as the caves had little light to let in, and looking out did not seem to be a thing they considered. They had little enough to look out on, e Thadora said later.

The Walchin leader, who told them his name was Zhor, led them to a door on the left which led into a wedge-shaped room. Once they passed the threshold, Asphodel looked around. The large room had chairs and Zhor indicated they should sit.

Then Zhor clapped his hands and a figure appeared at the door, clad from head to foot in a white robe that completely covered it, except for holes cut for its eyes. None of them could tell the sex of the figure, or even if one of the Walchin attended them. Maybe the person had a facial disfigurement and it dressed in such a way to cover it. Zhor saw their surprise, and after he spoke to the figure and ordered refreshment, he turned to them.

'Our young women are modest and often cover themselves when around strange men,' he said. 'Some of the older ones do too, though not as many as in former years. That was my daughter, Khel. She's a good girl, and covers herself when around others not of her blood, and will continue to do so until she takes a mate. Then she will be at liberty to go uncovered if she so wishes and her mate allows it. However, no woman, mated or not, will allow men not of the Walchin to see them.'

Just at this moment, Khel, if it were still she, returned carrying a tray on which sat six cups, a large pitcher and some small round cakes. She poured some water from the pitcher into the cups and, bowing slightly to her father, withdrew.

Zhor stood and handed a cup to each of them before passing round the cakes. They drank thirstily.

The water had a slight tang they could not iden- tify, but that they found pleasant, and its coolness refreshed them. They ate the slightly warm cakes, with relish.

After eating and drinking their fill, Zhor again spoke.

'It is our custom for our unmarried men and women to live separately from their families as soon as they come of age. The young women live in the House of Virgins and the young men in the House of Youth. Are any of you mated?' he enquired.

After hearing they were not, he continued, 'Then you will please follow our customs. It would not do for our young men and women to see you accom- modated together, unwed as you are. Your customs are obviously different from ours. We would never tolerate the close proximity you have, travelling to- gether, without at least one chaperone, preferably more for a twenty four hour watch to be kept on the virtue of the young women.'

He sniffed and looked pointedly at Asphodel and Thadora as if expecting them to suddenly grow horns and tails.

Basalt smiled inwardly as he did his best to trans- late Zhor's speech. He took a perverse delight in watching the expressions on the girls' faces.

'So we're to be separated,' said Asphodel. 'I'm not sure I like that.'

'No more do I, Asphodel,' replied Fero, 'but I don't see we have much choice. We're entirely in the hands of these people, and if we're to gain their help and confidence, which we must if we're to get out of here, we need to comply with their wishes. If that means observing their customs as regards unmarried people, then so be it.'

All agreed, if reluctantly, to abide by the customs of the Walchin and to go to the two Houses. They would, they learned, be able to meet during work hours, but the girls would be expected to dress in the covering robes the other girls would be wearing, due to the presence among them of Fero, Grimmaldo and Basalt. The two young women looked at each other and Thadora rolled her eyes.

Asphodel said, 'I'm not sure I like this talk of but "work hours", Basalt, It implies we'll be here for some time.'

Basalt put this to Zhor.

'I must consult with the Council, as I said,' he replied. 'They may take some time to decide what to do with you. This situation is unprecedented. Usually strangers do not reach the City but become lost and either escape or die in the tunnels.' He shrugged. 'Either way it concerns us not. Whether you will stay here or be escorted out is up to the vote of the Council.'

Thadora gasped at the thought of remaining in the Walchin City for the rest of her days and tears filled her eyes. Grimmaldo noticed and leaned across to her.

'Don't worry, Red Cub,' he reassured her. 'It hasn't come to that yet. We'll keep on trying if the first decision goes against us.'

She sniffed and wiped her eyes and nose on her sleeve.

'Thanks, Grimmaldo,' she told him. 'I'll try not to be such an idiot again. Of course we'll not give up.' She smiled at him, a rather watery, but brave smile. He grinned back at her.

Chapter 4
Separated

Khel escorted Asphodel and Thadora to their accommodation and a young male walchin, called Nhid, showed the others the way to their rooms. Both the Houses had been built on the edge of the City, but at opposite sides. The House of Virgins lay on the east, near to the Meeting House while the House of Youth lay on the west, near the opposite side of the village.

Khel led the way and Asphodel and Thadora followed her. They entered a round building through a pair of double doors, guarded by two men, one on each side. The guards came to attention as the three approached and Khel spoke to them. Asphodel and Thadora found themselves at a disadvantage now, as neither of them could understand a word that anyone said, but deduced that Khel told the guards that the strangers would stay in the House of Virgins until the council decided what to do with them.

'I think the guards are here to protect the virtue of the young women and not because of any other threat,' whispered Asphodel to Thadora as they passed through the large double doors.

'Why are you whispering?' replied Thadora. 'These damned Walchin can't understand anything we say, anymore than we can understand their gods-forsaken language.'

'Force of habit, I suppose.' Asphodel spoke in a normal voice.

Once through the door, they found themselves in a vestibule with stairs running up on each side. Many of the concealing white robes hung on pegs in the vestibule. Here Khel removed her robe and hung it up with the others. More double doors stood before them.

After following Khel through these doors they found themselves in a large room filled with young Walchin girls. The girls laughed and talked much as girls everywhere, while doing each other's hair and all the other things young girls do when together. Asphodel felt at home. This felt similar to the acolytes' hostel in Bluehaven where she had begun her training as a cleric.

She smiled. Khel noticed and smiled back shyly, reaching out her hand to pull Asphodel towards a door at the side of the room. Many such doors ran along the walls and along a balcony running around the room. Presumably the stairs in the vestibule led to the balcony and hence to these rooms.

Khel opened a door and pointed to the room, then to the two girls. They entered, followed by a smiling Khel, and found themselves in a small room containing two beds with a chest at the foot of each. Between the two beds stood a table with a lamp and a flask of oil, as well as a flint to light the lamp.

A washing bowl and a jug for hot water stood just in front of the lamp and a small cupboard hung from the wall on one side of the door. Khel indicated the chests and cupboard, and then their packs, telling them they could put their things in them. She smiled and said something else, which they did not understand, then she left them to their unpacking.

* * *

As Zhor directed, the three men followed Nhid to the House of Youth, although Fero and Basalt both thought it a misnomer in their cases as Fero was twenty-six and Basalt thirty-five.

Like elves, dwarves lived longer then humans, although they did not live as long as the long-lived elves, who could live many hundreds of years. A dwarf could often reach one hundred and fifty, and so Basalt was, in dwarven terms, still a young man, although past the first flush of youth. He considered himself of a similar age to Fero, and much older than most of the others they found in the House.

The Men's House, as they discovered people usually called it, was very similar to the House that Thadora and Asphodel had been taken to. Situated on the opposite side of the City from the House of Virgins, like its opposite number, the House of Youth was circular and had the two layers of rooms for the young men, but there was no sign of guards.

It had a vestibule like the House of Virgins, with stairs running up on each side, but instead of concealing white robes, boots, cloaks, some bows and axes and numerous other tools of various trades lay scattered around.

Passing through the doors, the first noticed the noise that assailed their ears. Young men filled the large round room, laughing and drinking, mock fighting and gambling. The atmosphere felt like that of young men, let out from the control of their parents, determined to have a good time.

Nhid told them the young men could come and go as they pleased, and that no one ever locked the door. Male friends could come and visit at any time, and in any part of the building, but females must never pass through the inner door, and certainly not after the eleventh hour of the day, when it began to go dark outside at the Equinox.

The young Walchin man took them towards the back of the large room, obviously a common room, and showed them into three sleeping rooms. These rooms, furnished with a bed and a chest with a stand for a wash bowl and jug were just like the girls' room. Although the rooms appeared Spartan, they seemed adequate. The three men smiled as they entered their accommodation. They had all been used to living rough from time to time and compared to sleeping on the ground, the rooms were luxury itself.

'Thank you, Nhid,' Basalt said to the young Walchin man. 'We'll settle ourselves in and then come out to join you, if that's alright.'

Nhid agreed and told Basalt he would be with some companions not far away, indicating a table with a group of young men playing cards. The others then entered their allotted rooms and began to try to settle in.

Fero did not unpack his pack, but placed it, unpacked, into the chest. He did not want to think about the possibility of having to stay here and the loss of freedom that would entail. That way lay the blackness of depression. Bramble whined as though he could sense the way Fero's thoughts turned. The ranger patted the dog and sat down on his bed.

'I've not taken much notice of you, have I old fellow,' he told the animal. 'I'm sorry. This is no better for you than it is for me.'

He stood up and crossed to the bowl and jug on its stand. 'Let's see if there's any water for you. You must be dying of thirst.'

The water jug was empty, so Fero called on Basalt in the next room for his aid. The pair went to find Nhid and ask where they could get some water for Bramble.

That mission accomplished, and Bramble's thirst duly slaked, Fero's worried about what the dog would eat. He asked Basalt, who had remained with him whilst he gave the animal his water, if he thought the Walchin would have any meat to give to the dog. Basalt frowned. He had no idea how these people produced their food, living as they seemed to do, completely underground.

'I can't imagine Bramble enjoying vegetarian food, if that's what they eat here,' Fero said, shaking his head. 'I'm not even sure a purely vegetarian diet is good for dogs, either.'

'We'll ask as soon as we get the chance, Fero,' the dwarf told the ranger. 'Maybe when we eat ourselves would be a good time.'

Just then, Grimmaldo appeared in the door, followed closely by Nhid. The young Walchin asked if they would like to join in a game of cards with him and his friends, and Basalt readily agreed, especially when he discovered that they played Rond, a game which involved skill and which Basalt had become extraordinarily good at in the gambling dens of the cities and towns of Grosmer.

The three soon became involved in the games. Basalt found slight differences in the game from that which he knew, but, after losing a few hands, he quickly learned the differences and soon began winning. Neither Grimmaldo nor Fero had been very good at the game, but found themselves roped into playing a strategy board game with other young Walchin. They quickly learned the rules, and enjoyed the game, which involved much thought and bluffing the opposition.

The time passed quickly and soon they heard the sounds of tables being set out for a meal. Half a dozen older Walchin women transformed part of the common room into a dining room, and soon they called the young men to the meal.

Long tables set with water jugs, stood at one end of the room, and trenchers and mugs sat at each place. The young men hurried to the tables, and Nhid placed his charges before seating himself opposite them.

The women began to serve the meal. To the surprise, of the three newcomers, the women placed mutton on their plates along with a type of mushroom they did not recognise and slices of freshly prepared bread.

They ate the meal with gusto. Not only because of their hunger, but they truly enjoyed the food. Basalt managed to beg some of the meat from the women servers for Bramble. They drank a type of ale as well as water, and after a course of fruit and cheese, the Walchin served some type of distilled spirit. Basalt pronounced it good, with the reservation that it was not as good as Dwarf Spirits, of course.

Eventually, after several beakers of spirit and much convivial company, with raised spirits, the three retired to bed.

* * *

Asphodel and Thadora ate a similar meal in the House of Virgins, but here the girls themselves prepared the tables, and some of them helped to prepare the meal under the direction of the older women chaperones.

The girls had round tables arranged in small groups, and not in long rows as in the men's House. This way the girls could sit around them to make conversation easier.

After the meal, where they also drank ale but not the spirits, some of the girls showed Thadora and Asphodel their handwork. The girls seemed to spend the evenings in embroidery and sewing as well as playing instruments and singing. Some of the girls who enjoyed drawing made small portraits of each other, and some caricatures both of each other and prominent figures in the City.

To Thadora and Asphodel, the girls appeared to be gossiping and telling tales with much laughter. Of course, Asphodel and Thadora did not understand any of this, not having the advantage of someone to translate, but they seemed like groups of girls everywhere with the chatter and laughter. Eventually, like Fero, Grimmaldo and Basalt, they retired to their beds.

The next morning, a young Walchin girl knocked on the door. Thadora yawned and sat up in bed, wondering where she was. As she turned to Asphodel, she saw the other girl out of bed and dressing quickly. Once memory returned of their plight, Thadora groaned and got reluctantly out of bed.

Once the pair had washed and dressed, the girl who had knocked on their door returned and beckoned them to follow her. They looked at each other quizzically, but quickly washed and dressed and hurried into the common room.

A long table stood near the kitchen end of the large round room. The delicious scent of warm bread assailed their nostrils as they approached the table. Girls walked along the table, picking up plates and filling them with rolls. Further along the table Thadora saw pats of butter and a variety of conserves. She wondered where the Walchin got the fruit from to make the jams.

She picked up a couple of rolls, and spread them with butter and jam. Before setting off to one of the tables, she poured herself a cup of hot herbal tea, also provided on the long table.

She ate the food with relish,. She had not realised just how hungry she was. They had eaten the evening before, but the food Asphodel and Fero had caught while they ran away from the Erian army had been rather sparse. As she wiped her mouth on a napkin the girl who had woken them beckoned again and led the two young women towards the anti-room.

One of the older women, who acted as chaperones, met them and she indicated they should clothe themselves in the all-enveloping robes hanging on the pegs.

Thadora began to argue, even though the woman would not understand her, but Asphodel whispered to her.

'We should do as they ask, Thadda,' she told the younger girl. 'We want to get out of here, don't we? Try not to annoy them. It's their custom for unmarried girls not to show themselves to any men not related to them, and we should comply if they want us to. You do remember being told that, don't you?'

'Yes,' Thadora pressed her lips together into a hard line, 'but we're not bleeding Walchin girls, I'm human and you're an elf.'

Asphodel shook her head, then, hardening her expression she said, 'Just do it, Thadora.'

The younger girl gave Asphodel a scowl, but she lifted a robe and pulled it over her head.

Asphodel turned away and donned one of the robes. Since she taller than the tallest Walchin girl, the robe came only to her mid-calf, and the one Thadora reluctantly pulled on came a little higher, reaching just below her knees, she being slightly taller than the elf. The chaperone tutted when she saw that, but realised she could do nothing about it, and handed the two girls a hood to cover their heads, leaving only their eyes visible.

'I feel like a parcel,' whispered Thadora to her friend. 'Where are they taking us?'

The doors leading to the main City opened and the chaperone led the pair out into the streets of the underground village, as Thadora preferred to think of it. She could not think of it as a city. She had seen towns bigger than this.

They followed the chaperone who retraced the path they had come the previous day. Thadora looked around. They did not have far to go. Only across the square to reach the Meeting Hall, which appeared to be their destination. Perhaps, she thought, the council would tell them they could leave. Reaching the doors to the Meeting Hall, the chaperone opened the doors and indicated they should enter.

Fero, Grimmaldo and Basalt stood waiting with their escort, Nhid. Thadora called out to them and the three opened their eyes wide to see them so covered. Grimmaldo's face broke into a grin at the sight.

'All these precautions so's we don't see you un-covered. I seem to remember an evening not so long ago when we'd got very wet and dried off by the fire. How shocked these Walchin would have been if they'd seen you then!'

Thadora aimed a punch at the young mage, but the hood hampered her eyesight and so the young man easily avoided her blow. Then Bramble noticed them and came running to greet them. Asphodel felt glad of a chance to turn away, although she knew Grimmaldo could not see her blush. Why did Grimmaldo bring that up? She fussed the dog until she had regained her composure.

When she stood up from patting the dog, she looked around the room. The Walchin had erected a large dais at one end and on it sat seven figures. Zhor sat in a slightly larger seat in the centre, with three Walchin on each side.

'*The others must be the council,*' she thought.

The rest of the room had long benches, many with Walchin already sitting on them. Nhid led the companions to the front and told them to bow to the council before sitting down in the front row. He took a seat immediately behind them.

Zhor stood and addressed the room and Basalt translated as best he could.

'Walchin, we are here to decide the fate of these *"brandin"'* Basalt said he did not know the word, but surmised it meant *"strangers"* or *"foreigners"*.

'They stumbled upon our City whilst trying to escape from hobgoblins and evil men. These have been dealt with in the usual way, and will not be seen again. However, it remains for us to decide what to do with the brandin.'

He looked around the assembled Walchin before continuing.

'It is not our custom to allow brandin to leave our realms lest we are betrayed to other brandin and evils such as war or pestilence come to our people. These, however, seem to be in good faith. One is indeed a sister of the Church of Sylissa, and another a distant cousin of ours. They have spoken to me of many reasons why we should allow them their freedom and show them the secret ways out of the Land Below the Mountains.

'We must decide what to do. Do we grant them their request and show them the way out? Do we keep them here in the City or do we turn them loose as we have done others on occasion, to wander forever in the dark tunnels?'

Here Thadora gave a little whimper, and Asphodel took her hand to comfort her.

Zhor continued. 'There is no precedent, as far as our history goes, for allowing brandin to leave. That is how we have remained hidden all these centuries, but we have sometimes allowed people to remain in our midst, free to walk our city, and also these people have worked to earn their keep.

'Some have brought new ideas that we have adopted when we saw they were good for our people, but never have these people been allowed to leave the mountain tunnels, nor allowed them to have children amongst themselves or worse, to mate with Walchin.'

Zhor paused again and looked around to see what reaction his words had on the gathered people. The Walchin in the audience stirred in their seats, and a murmuring of agreement arose.

'Thus we keep our race pure and safe. These people, however, have powerful arguments for allowing them to go. They will be allowed to speak their arguments in good time, then the council will decide.'

Zhor sat down and waved to one of the other councillors to speak. He sat next to Zhor on his right and wore the orange robe of a cleric of Roth with a silver pickaxe symbol round his neck and he had the black sash of a second rank deacon. He stood and cleared his throat.

Against his white skin and hair, his almost black eyes seemed like pieces of jet. They raked over the five on the front row.

'You all know me except these five brandin.' He looked at them. 'I am Jheg and I am the deacon of Roth in the City.' He took his gaze away from the front row and addressed the rest of the Walchin.

'We have survived only because of our laws, and those laws say that brandin must be kept here or sent into the tunnels alone.

'It is quite clear that if we allow brandin to leave us and show them how to leave the tunnels so they can go back to the World Above, they will bring destruction in return.'

His eyes raked the assembled crowd until they fell on the little group sitting in the front row.

'Brandin are not to be trusted,' he continued 'They give promises they do not intend to keep. These brandin are young and healthy. They are both male and female. I do not see how we can keep them in our midst and prevent them from reproducing themselves, or worse, mating with our own women to produce creatures neither Walchin nor brandin.

'Brandin are dissolute and hedonistic, all know that, and young ones are the worst of all. They will lead our own youngsters into all kinds of immoral practices. There will be sexual excesses and promiscuity.

'Even now, without influences from without some of our young women walk the city streets unveiled. (Thankfully only a few as yet. That is something I am working on, and I hope soon to have all unveiled young women declared outcast, so they will never be able to marry.) I have even heard of young men and women meeting secretly, unchaperoned! I dread to think what goes on in those meetings. 'Our House of Virgins will become a House of Whores if we do not clamp down tightly.'

His voice began to rise as he spoke. Then he paused, seemingly realising that he had got off the subject in hand and onto one of his favourite hobbyhorses.

'So,' he continued, 'we must safeguard our own young people from the evil influences from without. We cannot keep these folk here. I say we turn them loose into the tunnels to die of hunger and thirst—or whatever may get to them first.'

With a smug, self-satisfied look, he sat down. Zhor rose and indicated to the woman on his left. She stood and looked down at the five seated on the front row.

'I am Mher,' she told them, smiling. While her skin appeared the same white as all the other Walchin, her hair had a tiny amount of colour, slightly yellowish. She had eyes of a dark grey rather than the black of Jheg's and she looked more kindly.

'Whilst I have the greatest respect for Deacon Jheg and all he tries to do to keep our people on the straight track, I must disagree with him on this point.

'First, I agree it would be dangerous to keep these young people here in the City with us for many of the reasons given by the deacon. But would it not be an evil act on our part to just simply turn them loose in the tunnels to die? There are many dangers in the tunnels, which make death from hunger and thirst seem pleasant.

'We all know of our own who have been taken by the creatures of the depths. Surely it is wrong to inflict such on innocent and what I believe are good people. Because something has never been done before does not mean it cannot be done now. If these brandin say they will not reveal our existence to any outside, and they take holy oaths saying as much, then I believe they will keep them. I say we should let them leave and show them the way out.'

'Mher smiled again at the friends and sat down. Zhol rose once again to his feet. He looked at Asphodel and spoke directly to her. She looked to Basalt for help.

'He wants you to argue your case as you did with him yesterday. It seems the two councillors who have spoken are the two spokespersons for each side of the argument, and now we have the chance to plead our own case.'

'Please be eloquent, Asphodel,' interrupted Thadora, her green eyes no longer merry, but with a longing look in them.

Asphodel stood, and looked at the girl.

'I'll do my best, Red Cub,' she said. Then she looked to the dais, sweeping them all with her gaze before beginning.

'I am Curate Asphodel,' she began. 'We arrived in your realm yesterday, as you know. It was entirely by accident that we are here. A party of hobgoblins pursued us and we were trying to escape.

'We thought we had lost them and so we sheltered in a cave as there was a thunderstorm. Unfortunately, the hobgoblins found us, but Thadora here,' she indicated the young thief, 'found a crack in the wall at the back of the cave. Hoping to escape via another exit, we squeezed into the crack and eventually stumbled into your City.

'We have important information that must get back to our rulers. The future of our land lies in our hands. If we cannot return with our information, war will come and many will die.

'What is more, some of our friends have already been taken captive by the Master commanding these hobgoblins. He is an evil man and we wish to rescue our friends from his clutches. Already he has tried to capture us once before. It is he who wishes to make war on our land and he spreads false rumours to influence his people.' She paused for a moment and Zhor said something.

'He asks you to talk to them as you did to him yesterday,' Basalt told her. 'About the importance of all races, and the Balance of all things in the working of the world. I think you swayed him, girl.' He patted her on the arm to encourage her.

Asphodel began to talk as she had done the previous day, and as she warmed to the task, the others could see some of the faces on the dais beginning to change.

At least two, though, seemed to be unswayed by her eloquence, and even hardened in their views. One was the deacon, Jheg, and the other a sour-faced woman who sat at the far end on the left of Zhor. These two looked as though even if the sky should fall in they would not change their views.

After she had finished and sat down again. Zhor again rose.

'Thank you, Curate Asphodel,' he said. 'I must ask you now to withdraw. The council will debate what you have told us and come to a decision. It may take some time, maybe several days as we are not used to being hurried, and so I will ask Nhid if he will show you around our City and give you jobs to do while you await our decision. We cannot afford to have people eating our food and drinking our water unless they contribute.

'If the decision is that you will stay and work here, those jobs will continue. If the decision goes in your favour, you will be shown the way out. If it is decided to turn you into the tunnels unguided, we will offer our prayers to Roth for your souls.'

He sat down again and waited while they withdrew, along with the rest of the people who had come to hear the debate.

'Prayers?' muttered Grimmaldo. 'Fat lot of good that will do us when we're dying of hunger and thirst, or being eaten by the denizens of the tunnels.'

On the way out, they again picked up a chaperone and Nhid led them on a tour of the City.

The Walchin called it the City, but Grimmaldo privately thought it more like a large village or small town. It did not seem to have any other name. Nhid told them that other, smaller Walchin settlements were known to the folk in the City, and there some spoke rumours of others much further away.

A few people travelled to trade with the smaller communities, and some people found their husbands or wives from outside the City, too. He himself had not been out of the City though, but intended to go to one of the nearer settlements to find a bride.

He took them past a blacksmith's shop and a metal worker's shop. They saw a bakery and a potter. Grimmaldo wondered where they got the grain to make the flour for the bread. Then Nhid led them into a large building with several rooms.

In the first, to their surprise, women sat carding wool and then passed it on to the spinners in the next room. Not far away they saw a dyer's and when it had dried from the dye, the wool, Nhid told them they took it to a place where some more people wove it into cloth.

'Where do you get your wool from if you don't trade with outsiders?' queried Fero.

'Come,' said Nhid, smiling. 'I'll show you.'

He led them towards the northern exit from the city. They entered a tunnel, which then branched to the left. Nhid indicated the left fork.

'That's the way to the mines,' he told them.

'I wouldn't mind seeing them,' said Basalt. 'Maybe we could go later?'

'You would be a help if you would be willing to work there,' the Walchin told him. 'We are usually short-handed in the mines.'

'What are you mining?' asked Bas.

'At the moment we've run across a silver seam,' replied Nhid. 'We have all kinds of metals in these mountains though, and even occasionally we find some of the burning rock.'

The pair then went into a long discussion that Basalt did not bother to translate. They surmised, correctly as he told them later, that they discussed mining.

Eventually, after a number of turns, Nhid paused and took a hood from a peg hammered into the face of the rock. He handed one to the chaperone too. They donned them, and to the surprise of the others, there was no space for the eyes, just a slight thinning of the cloth.

They walked on until, rounding a corner, Thadora suddenly cried out, 'I can see daylight! Look! That's daylight ahead.'

Sure enough, there before them they could see the end of the tunnel and daylight. They almost ran towards the light, but remembered their hosts and so moderated their pace.

As soon as they exited from the dimly lit tunnels, they knew why their guides had covered their eyes. They all blinked in the brightness, and their eyes watered as the daylight entered them. They realised how it must be for the Walchin who lived all their lives in the tunnels and had become adapted to the dim lighting.

Drinking in the fresh mountain air, they looked around them.

'I thought you weren't going to show us the way out until the council has made its decision,' said Grimmaldo. 'How is it that you've shown us out?'

Nhid smiled. 'I haven't shown you the way out. Look around you.'

This they did and saw steep cliffs surrounding a large valley.

'Those cliffs are an effective barricade and will keep you trapped here. There is no way over them,' he told them. 'This bowl on the top of a mountain is our garden and farm.'

They gazed around and saw a fertile area at the bottom of the bowl. In the centre a lake of the clearest blue gleamed, rivalling the sky in its purity. Trees grew close to the lake, and they could make out the forms of animals grazing the grass.

In other areas, crops grew, and some places had been ploughed ready for next year's sowing. Their eyes opened wide and mouths dropped open.

Nhid smiled again. 'I thought you'd be surprised at this place,' he said. 'Usually we only come here at night as the day is too bright for us, but I wanted to show it to you. You must have wondered where we get our food and wool for our clothes from. Well, here it is. We have animals for milk too, so we make cheese and butter. I'll show you the dairy.'

True to his word, Nhid led them towards another cave in the cliff. Here he showed them the Walchin making the butter, cheese, and another product, which he called 'yoghurt'.

The others had never heard of this new product, but the Walchin made it by allowing milk to become sour, but in some way that made it pleasant to the taste. One of the people working in the dairy gave them a sample, but they did not like it very much. Nhid told them it could be made more palatable by the addition of honey, which they did for children, but that the adults enjoyed it neat. They also served it with fruit as a dessert.

After the tour of the dairy, they once more emerged into the daylight. Screwing up their eyes once more, they looked around them.

'I want to stay out here,' said Thadora. 'I don't like it much in there.'

'I know how you feel, Red Cub,' replied Fero. 'I prefer to be outside too. Maybe they'll find us some work out here if we ask.'

Basalt translated this to Nhid and added the request for outdoor work. He also added that both Fero and Thadora had had a little experience in working with sheep. They had stayed with Grandolin, the old shepherd who took them in when Fero had become sick with pneumonia after Khland captured them the first time when they searched for Sauvern's Sword, Equilibrium.

Nhid promised to put the request to the council. He said he thought that if the council decided to allow them to stay and not turn them out into the tunnels, their request would be met. The faces of the five fell as this reminded them of their possible fate when Basalt told them what Nhid had said.

They returned to the caves the way they had come. They had noticed other caves in the cliffs surrounding the bowl, but Nhid insisted that none of them led to the outside. They had to take his word for it, although for a long time Basalt considered the possibility of trying some of them.

Dwarves could easily find their way underground and he thought that if it came to it, he would stand at least an evens chance of finding the correct tunnels to the outside. The gambler in him felt satisfied with these odds, but he did not know how the others would feel, so he held his own council. Anyway, the vote in the Walchin Council might go their way. He would wait and see.

After returning to the city, Nhid took them round other places and now they could see where the food and raw materials for the industries came from.

They saw potters making a variety of different shaped pots and utensils from clay mined from the caves, jewellers making jewellery and putting gems onto a variety of goods for decoration. The little group passed butchers, bakers, and even candle makers making candles from the fat from the mutton.

They saw clothes being made, vegetables and herbs being dried, ale and cider being made as well as some of the fruit being pressed to make juice. Near one end of the cave the Walchin had built a mill, and a stream running through the cave turned the wheel. Then Nhid took them along a fork that led to the northeast.

Here they came to a large lake fed by a waterfall from the eastern side of the cave, A tunnel left it in the southwest taking the water with it. Nhid explained the City got its drinking water from here. The river flowed from melting snows high up in the range and ran above ground until it sank below the mountains , finishing up in the lake.

'It is very pure and good, also very cold. It is forbidden to bathe in these waters. We consider them to be sacred, put here by Roth for our use as drinking water. To use the lake for anything other than the god's wishes would be blasphemy. We also believe that Roth is often near his lake, watching over us.'

He knelt and prayed briefly to Roth, and Basalt and the chaperone quickly joined him. Although the rest of the group, did not worship Roth, he was a god, after all and this was his realm, so they all knelt beside the lake and offered up their own private prayers to the god of dwarves, miners and metal-workers.

After this, Nhid showed them a fast flowing stream to the southwest, leading into a small lake.

'All the waste from the City ends up here,' said Nhid. 'The stream flows quickly, even through the lake, and carries everything away. As it's lower than the City, there's no danger of unpleasant stuff seeping back, even in times of flood.'

Asphodel nodded her agreement, impressed by the conditions.

'The Clerics of Sylissa, and indeed, Sylissa herself, I'm sure, would have done exactly the same. I'm impressed.'

Nhid smiled in pleasure. All knew of the importance Sylissa gave to hygiene.

Little smell emanated from the stream, although it was, in effect, a sewer, because it flowed so swiftly that nothing remained for long. Asphodel wondered briefly where it came out and if it eventually flowed anywhere near any habitations on the outside. It might cause problems there. She dismissed the idea. Any villages near, would surely have wondered where the pollution came from and investigated.

Their tour of the City ended and Nhid took the men back to their House while the chaperone took the girls back to the House of Virgins. They felt sorry to say goodbye to the men. Basalt asked Nhid if it would be possible for them to meet the next day if the Council had not decided their fate by then.

'If you request at the House of Virgins, you will be allowed to visit your friends. In the company of a chaperone, of course,' he added. 'If you can persuade the chaperone, you may be able to go out of the House and walk.'

He thought for a moment before continuing.

'I don't expect the Council will make any decisions for a sixday or so. They will not be hurried. They must weigh all the arguments properly. If the problem is contentious, then it may take longer, depending on how long it takes to get a majority. If you ask me, this will be a long one.

'I thought, looking at their faces, that the Council was divided equally; three for putting you in the tunnels and three for letting you live. Then of course they have to decide whether to let you go and show you the way out, or to keep you here. No, this will be a long one. I'm afraid.'

Basalt 's face fell. 'I was afraid that might be the case.' he murmured, but he said nothing to the others.

Chapter 5
Decision

The five friends stayed and worked with the Walchin. Asphodel decided to work as a healer and Basalt worked in the mines. The other three worked outside.

They did their outdoor tasks during the day, unlike the Walchin, and so often found themselves the only ones in the bowl. When no other Walchin could see them, Thadora gratefully removed the all-enveloping robes and worked in her breeches and shirt.

The weather felt fine and warm, even so high in the mountains, and all three revelled in the sunshine, watching the birds and animals in the bowl. Thadora picked some of the multitude of flowers blooming there and took them to decorate the tables in the House of Virgins.

She tried to persuade the men to take some for their House too, but Grimmaldo told her he did not think the other young men would appreciate flowers.

They tended the animals and learned to milk the cattle. They harvested crops and carried the grain to the mill for grinding. Bramble had already learned what it meant to herd sheep before he joined Fero and the others. He was an intelligent dog and learned quickly to respond to Fero's whistles, which he found a little different from those he had been used to. He enjoyed the time outside as much as did his human friends.

Occasionally Asphodel joined them, but there many people requested her services as a healer, and so her forays outside were few. As an elf, she did not relish the life in the caves. Elves lived in forests and led as natural a life as possible, but her calling as a healer made her tolerate the conditions. Still, she enjoyed her visits to the bowl.

One day, as they worked in the fields hoeing the inevitable weeds, Thadora paused to wipe her brow.

'It's getting hot.' she said. 'I've lost count of the blasted days since we've been here, but it must be summer by now, even if this heat doesn't suggest it.'

'Not quite,' replied Grimmaldo. 'I've been keeping a note of the days that have passed and it's Zoldar two. Still twenty-eight days 'till the Solstice. With any luck we'll be able to celebrate it in Meridor or Berandore.'

'Oh, I hope so,' said the girl. She looked up to the sky to see the height of the sun. 'The sun looks bleeding high enough for summer to me though, and it's certainly hot enough.'

Grimmaldo squinted up.

'That's because we're further south than Hambara.' he pointed out. 'I don't know how much further, but enough to make a difference.' Suddenly he stopped, put his hand up to shade his eyes and turned to Fero.

'What's that flying up there,' he asked the ranger. 'It looks too big to be any bird I've heard of, unless it's nearer than it looks.'

Fero looked up. He squinted in the bright sunlight, then shaded his eyes. His expression turned grim.

'It doesn't look like a bird, Grimmaldo, because it isn't. At least I don't think so. It's hard to tell at this distance. To me, from here, it looks like a dragon. Probably a blue in these mountains.'

The others visibly blanched.

'A d...dragon!' stuttered Thadora. 'A bloody d...d...dragon! Are you sure, Fero?'

'As sure as anyone can be at this distance. I guess that's why they need their herds guarding. I wondered what dangers there could be in this bowl. Only predators from the sky can get in. That means eagles, hawks–or dragons. Possibly griffins or wyverns might be around too, although griffins tend to prefer dryer places.'

'How can you be so bleeding calm, Fero,' demanded the girl. 'Dragons are bloody dangerous. They like humans, and not for conversation. I don't wish to be dinner for a bleeding blue dragon.'

'I don't think you need worry about being dinner for one,' said Grimmaldo, with a grin. She looked at him quizzically, one eyebrow raised. 'You'd only make a small snack!'

She punched him, hard, and he stepped back wheezing.

'That's for trying to joke with me when I'm bleeding panicking,' she said, picking up her hoe. 'I think the gods-forsaken thing's gone now. Let's get on then we can go back into the caves.'

'I thought you didn't like the caves, Red Cub,' teased Grimmaldo. 'Wouldn't you prefer to stay out here in the sunshine?' He had to dodge another punch before Fero grabbed her arm.

'Stop that the pair of you!' he ordered. 'Grimmaldo, dragons are dangerous and Thadda has plenty sense to be afraid. They are not a joking matter, and Thadda, this is not the time to behave like a little girl arguing with her big brother.'

He released her arm, and the pair looked sheepish. He picked up his hoe and began to hack at the weeds between the rows of beans. Perhaps a little harder than necessary.

Suddenly he stopped, turned to Thadora, grinned and said, 'And, Thadda, watch your language. Your father would be appalled if he could hear you!'

* * *

Two and a half sixdays after they had arrived in the realm of the Walchin, Zhor once more summoned them to the Council chamber. Again, the seats contained some of the Walchin, come to hear the decision.

The girls had to dress in the all-enveloping robes, of course, and the chaperones accompanied them. Nhid came with Fero, Basalt and Grimmaldo, although they did not need to be guided any longer. The young Walchin said he wanted to hear the result and had got permission from his work at the pottery to take a few hours off. The chief potter told him that, as he had become a friend of the brandin, he could go and hear what the council decided to do with them, and bring back the news.

All the assembled crowd stood as the Council ascended the dais. Zhor rose once more and spoke. Basalt again translated.

'Friends,' he began. 'We have debated long and hard on this matter concerning these brandin in our midst. We have prayed with Deacon Jheg for enlightenment from Roth as to the correct way of dealing with them.

'We have, unfortunately, been unable to come to a unanimous decision.' Here he paused and Asphodel felt a sinking feeling in her heart. Then the Council Leader went on.

'We have, however, a majority decision, and fortunately I have not had to cast my deciding vote. The decision has gone two to four. The council has decided that these brandin should not be condemned to the tunnels.'

Asphodel breathed out the breath she did not realise she had been holding. Now, would the Walchin to allow them to go on their way? They had lost much time here in the City. Time t hey all felt they did not have.

It seemed the council had not decided their fate. Zhor went on to say that, although the decision to allow them to live had been made, they still had to make the decision as to whether to release them or make them stay in the City. This would be debated and they would tell everyone of the conclusions as soon as they had made their decision.

He dismissed the people and the Council once more left for the small room to continue its deliberations as to the fate of the five.

'I thought that was going to be the final decision,' said Thadora, her face a picture of anxiety.

Grimmaldo put a comforting arm round the girl and one of the chaperones gave him a slap. She rounded on him angrily, and, although he could not understand her words, her tone told him what she meant and that made him redden with embarrassment. The others, including Thadora, laughed at his discomfiture.

'It seems a reprimand is clear in all languages, whether you understand the words or not,' laughed Asphodel, grateful for the release of humour.

She then became more serious. 'We should be grateful we're to be allowed to live, I suppose,' she went on, 'but I can't help but be worried. We *must* be allowed to leave here. We *must*. We have to warn King Gerim of the plans of this "Master" who rules Erian before it's too late and the invasion begins.'

The others agreed, but Fero pointed out, 'That's out of our hands. We can't do anything except to continue doing our jobs and hope the gods are on our side.' 'I'll pray to Sylissa,' Asphodel told them. 'You might all pray to your own gods too. It may help. It certainly can't do any harm.'

They parted again, and returned to their respective houses. As Asphodel and Thadora struggled out of their robes, the young thief said, 'If we have to stay here, Asphodel, do you think we'll be forced to wear these robes for ever?'

The elf smiled.

'Until we're too old and decrepit for anyone to fancy us, I expect.'

Thadora groaned. 'I don't think I can stand it for years and years to come.' she told her companion. 'And what about you? You'll be young and beautiful for centuries.'

'Remember what Zhor told us when we first arrived and we met Khel? He told us that some of the young girls had started to go around unveiled. Maybe after a time we can join the young "progressive" girls and dispense with the robes. Not just yet though,' she went on as she saw Thadora open her mouth to state that she would join them immediately. 'We still need their good will until this second decision has been made.'

It took another two sixdays for the Council to come to their second decision.

Again they received a command to attend the Council Chamber where as before, Walchin sat waiting to hear the decision. The people of the City seemed as anxious to know the decisions as the members of Wolf.

The friends took their accustomed places at the front, and Nhid, sitting near the back, smiled encouragingly at them, then the council members entered, and all stood.

As the members of the council walked to their places, Deacon Jheg scowled at them and Councillor Mher gave them a smile. The other councillors remained expressionless.

Zhor bade the audience to sit down and began a long speech. Basalt translated as best he could.

It seemed that Zhor decided to give an account of every other time brandin had found their way to the City and what had been done. Most times, the brandin had been condemned to the tunnels.

Zhor gave lurid accounts, which Basalt did not translate too literally, of what happened in the tunnels. (It sounded to Basalt as if Walchin followed at a distance to ensure no one found a way out accidentally, then reported on the happenings.)

The Walchin leader gave descriptions of the bloody ends of most of these brandin, and of the assassinations of any who looked like escaping. Eventually, Zhor described how, on no more than a handful of occasions, brandin had been allowed to live with them.

'Those brandin were those who we considered useful to the Walchin,' he said, 'and trustworthy enough not to be a danger to us in any way. We consider this current group useful and trustworthy. Curate Asphodel has already proved her worth with her healing skills and Basalt has brought some new and useful ideas to the mines.

'Walchin are not usually very open to new ideas, but Basalt's were so helpful we have decided to adopt them.

'The Council has had a very difficult time debating this. Even after all these days we are split. Three members thought we should allow the brandin their freedom and show them the way out. Three thought it too risky and those three wish to keep them here.

'We have discussed it time and time again. We have taken vote after vote, but there was never any change. Not until last night. After much further discussion of the pros and cons of allowing the brandin to leave, a decision was made by one of our number changing their vote.'

'I wish he'd just get on with telling us our fate,' whispered Grimmaldo.

Zhor looked at him pointedly with eyes like black diamonds in his white face. Grimmaldo's face fell. He felt sure that look gave him the answer to his question.

'I could not understand the words of my young friend here,' went on Zhor, 'but I detected impatience in his voice. It does not do to be impatient, youngster,' he told Grimmaldo. 'Things unfold in their own good time. Always.'

He paused and took a drink from a glass of water before him, then he continued.

'The decision of the Council is this. Our young friends here will remain in the City. They will be given all the privilege and freedoms of our own citizens. They will have work and pay, just like our own and have voting rights just as our native-born citizens have. In all respects they will be full citizens of the City and honorary Walchin.

'Thus has the council spoken.'

Asphodel glanced over at Thadora. Although covered in the all-enveloping robes, the elf could see two large tears beginning to roll down her face. This was going to be hard for all of them unless they could find a way to change the Council's mind.

Chapter 6
Plans

After the formal speech, Zhor approached the friends.

'I am very sorry,' he said. 'I argued for allowing you to go, and was just about to call a stalemate and give my casting vote when they came out of the closed room for the sixth time. Unfortunately, the three that thought you should stay managed to persuade one of the others and it went four to two.'

'Who voted to let us go?' sniffed Thadora.

'That I can't say.' Here Zhor raised his hand as the girl opened her mouth to speak again. 'No, I'm not being difficult. I genuinely don't know. It's a secret ballot, you see. Each council member has two balls—one red and one white. They drop the balls into a jar. Red is for 'yes' and white for 'no'. In this case, the question was 'Should we allow the brandin to leave the City?' There were four red balls and two white ones on the last count.'

Grimmaldo looked at Basalt for the dwarf to translate, and said, 'Could we appeal? After few weeks, say, or even a few months?'

After listening to the translation, Zhor shook his head. 'No. Once the council has made a decision, it stands. There is no appeal.'

Asphodel looked at the others.

'I think we should have a meeting to discuss this,' she said. 'Suppose you men come to the House of Virgins later this afternoon and we can talk.'

This they all agreed to and went their separate ways to eat lunch in their respective houses.

* * *

That afternoon, a chaperone reluctantly admitted Fero, Grimmaldo and Basalt into the House of Virgins. They entered the vestibule and a young girl led the three up the stairs to a meeting room on the balcony. Here she left them alone.

Shortly afterwards, Thadora and Asphodel arrived, muffled up in the all-covering robes. They only recognised them by their height and Thadora's unusual green eyes. A pair of older women followed them. At least they assumed they were older, and at least one of them had wrinkles round her solemn eyes.

The old women went and sat on a sofa in the corner of the room and took out some knitting, but they never took their eyes off the five, working without needing to look at their work.

'You must stay over on that side of the room,' said Asphodel quickly as Grimmaldo made to embrace her. She glanced at the old women who had sat up ram-rod straight and glared at the thought that a man should touch one of their charges.

'Well,' said Grimmaldo, walking over to a chair and sitting down, 'at least they won't know what we're talking about.'

When they sat at opposite sides of the small room, Thadora began to speak.

'I can't stand all this bloody wrapping up. That's worse than being inside a bleedin' cave for the rest of me life. I feel like a parcel!'

Grimmaldo grinned. 'You look like one too.'

'We're here to discuss how we can get out,' pointed out Asphodel. 'The Walchin aren't going to help us, obviously. We'll have to do it on our own. Bas, can you remember anything of how we got here? You're a dwarf, after all, and so ought to be the best of us at finding the way underground.'

Thadora squeaked. 'I'm not going that way. I couldn't go through that bleedin' narrow place again. I'd die. I'd rather stay here dressed as a damned parcel for the rest of my days than try to get through there again.'

Basalt looked at the others. 'I could find the way back there easily enough, but if Thadora won't go…'

No one spoke for a few minutes until Thadora suddenly said, 'I could p'raps climb those cliffs round the place where the animals are.'

'Crater,' corrected Basalt absently.

'I could then secure a rope and throw it down for the rest of you to climb up.'

Asphodel rejected that due to the difficulty of both the climb and the possibility of getting a long enough rope.

'Even if we got several and tied them together, I don't think they'd reach. Anyway tying them together is not secure enough,' she said.

Again there was silence.

The five talked around the subject for some while until they felt they were getting nowhere. An hour had passed and the chaperones started to fidget.

'I think we'd better call this meeting to a close,' said Asphodel. 'We don't want to upset the chaperones too much or they may not allow us to meet again.'

Fero rose, his dark head almost touching the low ceiling. He grimaced. He supposed that the diminutive Walchin thought them high and airy.

'We must all continue to think of any way we can get out of here. Don't forget that we need to warn Grosmer of the coming war.' With that, he nodded to the chaperones and made for the door.

Basalt then thanked the chaperones for their time and followed the ranger out. Grimmaldo gave a cheeky grin and trotted after the other two.

Asphodel shook her head. 'I don't know how useful that was.'

'At least we have some ideas that *won't* bleedin' well work.'

'What good will that do? We need ideas that will work.'

The two girls walked slowly down the stairs. Once at the bottom, they disrobed and entered the large common room.

'It means that some things we needn't think about again. Kassilla's tits, Asphodel, I'm not used to doing all this bloody thinking. It makes my head hurt.'

The elf smiled. No, the young thief from the Warren had usually just done the first thing that entered her head. That was how she came to be with them in the first place—running away from possible problems in Hambara to join them on the road.

Asphodel wondered if at any time the girl had regretted that impulse. Life must be more difficult now than it had been before, even if the girl's mother had sent her to Madame Dopari's Emporium, the brothel in Hambara. Thadora had told them that her mother intended to send her there. At least she would have had a warm place to sleep and regular meals.

Asphodel shuddered at the thought of that place and what went on there, but at least it was clean and the girls inspected for sickness every month.

As Asphodel thought these things, a girl came up to her and beckoned for her to follow. She mimed enough for the healer to realise that a woman wanted her to attend a birth and so, saying goodbye to Thadora she left for her duties.

The next day Thadora, Fero and Grimmaldo went out into the crater to look after the animals. Bramble delighted in helping his new owner, Fero, in rounding up the sheep and small cattle. Fero smiled as he thought how lucky this had been part of the animal's training as it meant the three humans did not need to do so much running around after the beasts.

Thadora grinned as they exited the cave, delighted to get outside again. She breathed deeply of the fresh mountain air. The sun still lay below the crater rim and so it felt a little cool, still, in spite of it being almost summer, but as soon as it breached the top, they knew it would get very hot in the hollow. With the high rim all around, the breeze hardly ever reached the bottom.

The animals had been penned overnight. Although no large predators such as wolves could get into the crater the aerial predators had no problems and so they had them to contend with. Eagles, vultures and other raptors flew over by day and a large owl flew by night. Then, of course, there were dragons. The dragons could decimate a flock of sheep or herd of cattle in a night with their prodigious appetites.

Thadora ran over to the cave where the sheep had been penned and opened the gate. She particularly liked the sheep.

'You make such a fuss of those silly sheep,' Grimmaldo told her.

'They're not silly,' responded the girl, stamping her foot. 'They're woolly and I like the way my hands feel after I've handled them. They feel softer than they did when I started helping with them although it's been only a few sixdays.'

Grimmaldo laughed. 'What nonsense. How can your hands be softer?'

Thadora scowled at the mage.

'Say and think what you bloody well like, Grimmaldo. they do feel softer. Here, feel for yourself.'

The young man, still laughing, took her hand in his and ran his thumb over the back of it.

He raised his eyebrows. 'Well, you might be right. Your hands certainly feel soft, but how do I know how they felt before? After all, for the last year and a bit you've been living a life of luxury as a daughter of the Duke of Hambara. Plenty time for your hands to get soft.'

Thadora stuck her tongue out at him and went to get her sheep.

She herded the flock, with Bramble's help, past the rows of vegetables, keeping the animals moving so they would not stop to eat the plants, and then they passed through a gate into the main part of the crater.

Thadora absently scratched Bramble's ears.

'I think I could climb up there, you know, lad,' she told the dog. 'I was always the bleedin' best in the

Warren at climbin'. It's high, yes, but is it as smooth as it looks? I'll bet there are a load of damn hand and footholds for an experienced climber.'

Then Grimmaldo called.

'Hey, Red Cub. Get over here and help with these cattle. They may be small but they're feisty little things. It needs more than the two of us to make sure they don't get into the beans.' He grinned as she turned round. 'They're brighter than your sheep, see. They have the brains to go after the food and not just follow where they're told.'

Thadora rushed back to punch Grimmaldo in the stomach, and as the mage doubled over she said, 'Serves you right for dissing my sheep.'

Fero paused and looked at the pair, but decided not to say anything this time. He walked over and opened the gate to the cave where the cattle spent the night. He ordered Bramble to guard the vegetable garden and then he shooed them out, past the plants and into the crater along with the sheep. Grimmaldo and Thadora, having finished their spat, also ensured the animals went the right way.

A couple of Walchin girls worked in the dairy. They came earlier to milk the cows and now they had finished, they cooled the milk, passing it over a water-cooled cooler. They put the milk in a tank high on the wall. The water ran through metal tubes and the milk ran from the tank over the tubes and into a channel. It then ran out of the channel and into churns.

'Why do you need to cool it?' Basalt asked, on behalf of Thadora, who stood watching.

One of the girls stopped working to explain.

'The milk is warm when it comes from the cows,' she said, 'but warm milk goes sour very quickly. We cool it, then put the churns into a cave that is itself cooled by icy water from a glacier. It keeps longer this way.'

The Walchin allowed some of this milk to stand so the cream would rise to the top and then they skimmed it off to make butter in hand churns. Thadora asked if she could have a go the first time she saw it being done.

The Walchin girls readily agreed and soon the young thief's arm ached with the constant turning and she also found it very boring, even as it fascinated her to watch as the fat globules came together in the churn and formed butter. She supposed if you had someone to talk to it would be alright, but she could not speak the language of the Walchin. She decided that butter churning was not for her.

She had watched the cheese making too. That she also found interesting, but too long-winded a process for her to ask to have a go. At least the cutting of the curds did not seem as boring as churning, nor as tiring. No, she decided she much preferred working out in the fields and so she did not object when Fero set her the task of weeding the rows and rows of peas. She still kept glancing up at the crater rim though and trying to hatch a plan.

Chapter 7
Found

The days passed. Asphodel, being a healer, found herself in great demand. Deacon Jheg worshipped Roth, the god of dwarves, mining and metalworkers and his healing powers were limited. He could heal simple things, but not anything complex. The Walchin kept on calling for Asphodel to do things they would not dream of asking Jheg.

Basalt spent his work hours in the mines, helping dig out the silver from the new seam the Walchin had found. The tools they used seemed primitive to Basalt. He made suggestions for improving them, and taught them new ways of shoring up the mine ceilings. The Walchin had, up until the arrival of Basalt and the others, carried the ore up to the smelters in sacks on their backs. Basalt suggested putting down rails and building carriages to run on them, thus enabling more ore to be taken up in one go.

The Walchin got excited about this, and they commandeered two blacksmiths to work exclusively on making the rails. The blacksmiths complained they had no idea how to go about this, so Basalt left the mines to help the blacksmiths in this new task.

On days when few people needed her healing powers, Asphodel worked outside with the others. She enjoyed this work as it gave her the chance to get into the woods. She missed the wildlife of the outside world, but birds came into the trees, and there were always insects. (Blasted insects, Thadora called them when they pestered her and the stock.)

It so happened that on one of the days when she helped outside, a bell began to ring. The girls in the dairy and cheese room all ran out, fear on their faces. One girl ran up to Asphodel and, saying something rapidly, began to pull the other young woman towards the main cave.

Asphodel frowned, but then turned to the others and said, 'I don't know what's going on, but it seems to me that bell signifies something that has made these girls afraid. We'd better follow. Perhaps one of the monsters from the tunnels has found its way in here.

It so happened Fero had his sword with him. Asphodel always brought her sling outside to use on any predators who might fly over the wall, even though it would only be of use against birds. If the dragons decided to attack the animals, she would be as helpless as the rest of them. Thadora never left the caves without her throwing knives for the same reason.

Entering the City, a girl pointed to one of the tunnel entrances and shouted something. The girl had pointed to the tunnel where they had entered the City. Asphodel looked round. Not a single Walchin could be seen. Everyone had gone into hiding in the labyrinth of tunnels surrounding the City. Then there came a sound from the entrance they had used. Three large dogs entered, baying loudly.

Bramble growled in reply and, hackles standing erect, flew at the three. Asphodel looked around. These dogs could not be alone. With her peripheral vision, she noticed Basalt arriving, wealding a heavy blacksmith's hammer.

'Some men and hobgoblins are close by,' he yelled. 'Some of the Walchin young men have gone to try to head them off, but I think some are going to make it through.'

'Are they after us, do you think?' Asphodel asked him.

The dwarf nodded. 'I rather think so. They must somehow have tracked us down . Be ready for a fight.'

Asphodel became aware of chanting just beside her. She glanced to her right and saw Grimmaldo preparing a spell. When he released it, one of the dogs yawned and lay down. Bramble still fought two, though.

She could do nothing to help the dog. With them moving around so quickly, she would be as likely to hit Bramble as one of the attacking animals. She turned her attention to the cave entrance where some men appeared. They poured into the City, and then stopped. Eight of them. The one in the lead shouted when he saw the five lined up facing them.

'So you are here, after all,' he called to them. 'I thought you must have made it through that crack when you just disappeared. Found a nice little abandoned dwarf town, too, I see. Don't make yourself too comfortable, though. You're coming back with us.'

Basalt replied with a warcry and rushed forward, brandishing his hammer. The men did not expect this and Basalt got in a couple of blows to the head of one man, who fell to the ground.

Asphodel noticed the patrol had a mage as part of it. He had begun to chant. Thinking quickly, the curate of Sylissa prayed a quick prayer and soon felt her god filling her. She threw out a silence spell and the mage looked confused as he could no longer hear his own words. She smiled in triumph, then took out her sling and loaded it with a bullet.

Swinging it round and round her head, she aimed at the man who had shouted at them when he first arrived. The flying bullet found its mark, but not on the head, as she had wished, but on his wrist as he raised a sword to bring down on Basalt's head. Fortunately for the dwarf, the bullet to deflected the blow and he could to block it easily. She did not see what happened next, though because she loaded another bullet and let fly once more.

Asphodel did not see much of the battle. It all seemed one mess of noise and confusion. Silvery darts of energy flashed past her every now and again as Grimmaldo let off a spell. Once she ducked as Thadora yelled at her to do so and the young thief threw a dagger unerringly at the enemy mage. He collapsed in a heap on the ground and she ran towards him. She paused to stick a dagger in the sleeping dog, then ran on to the mage and dispatched him as well.

Soon the fighting approached where Asphodel stood. She could no longer use her sling. Looking around for some weapon, she spotted a mace one of the dead enemy had dropped. A mace. How fortunate. It was one of the weapons she had learned to use She sprinted towards it and scooped it up. As she did so, she felt someone behind her and she rolled away, coming to her feet facing the man who had been just about to stab her with his sword. She batted it away with her mace, then swung it back-handed and caught him on his right arm She heard bone crunch and the sword slipped from his hand.

Standing up and looking around, she saw six bodies lying on the ground, some not moving, others groaning. Fero made a swing at a hobgoblin and there came a gush of blood as the sword cut through an artery. Fero jumped back, but he still got splattered as the hobgoblin fell. Then all became silent.

Asphodel counted those standing. All five of her friends and one man being held, with a sword at his throat, by Fero. What had happened to Bramble? Her eyes went to where the dogs had been fighting. The enemy dog Thadora killed lay where she left it. Of the other two, one was obviously dead, but the other lay whining, badly injured. Bramble lay nearby, trying to crawl to where Fero stood.

First, Asphodel looked towards her friends. None of them appeared badly hurt. A few cuts and bruises, some that would need her attention, but Bramble bled profusely from the bites of the dogs he fought.

She looked at the dog and noticed one of his forelegs looking the wrong shape. She walked over to him and laid her hands on his head.

'Good boy,' she said gently. 'You lie here and I'll try to see how bad it is.'

Bramble whined.

'Yes, I know it hurts. I'll be gentle.' She began to pray again and as the goddess's power filled her, she ran her hands gently over the dog's body. She detected some severe injuries. He had lost a lot of blood, too. As well as the bites he had a broken leg and had received a blow on the head. One of the men must have come over during the fight and hit the dog on the head, she concluded. It did not look good.

She became aware of movement around her as the Walchin returned. Zhor took the man that Fero held at sword point and tied his hands. He then led him away to the Meeting House. Asphodel had no illusions as to what the council would decide should be his fate and she shuddered.

Fero approached. 'Is he alright?' he asked.

She shook her head. 'Not really. I'll do what I can, and with Sylissa's help he might recover, but I'm only a curate and I don't know if I can channel enough of her strength yet.'

The ranger crouched down and stroked the big dog's head.

'You're a very brave dog,' he said. 'Well done. We'll do our best to get you well again.' He turned to Asphodel. 'Can I pick him up to take him back to the Men's House?'

'Let me just do a bit more. I can stop the bleeding, at least for a while, and make sure he doesn't have too much pain, but I really need some herbs. Willow bark is very good for pain, but I don't know if there's any in the crater. It would be better than I can do at the moment until I get more strength to channel Sylissa's power.'

The cleric then approached the others and did what she could. Grimmaldo had received a cut on his face that she told him would most likely form a scar.

The young man shrugged. 'It'll not make much difference to my beauty,' he told her. 'Can't compete with the likes of Carthinal in the looks department.'

Asphodel's eyes glazed over at the mention of the other mage. Where was he? Was he alright? What were they doing to him? Then she brought herself back to the present and her healing duties.

Fero carried Bramble back to the Men's house and laid him on his bed. Under the circumstances, the chaperones allowed Asphodel into the House to tend to the animal. They had been shocked to see her and Thadora without their robes, but agreed that if they had worn them, they would probably not have won the fight. However, they insisted the two girls wear them now, and especially Asphodel if she insisted on going into the Men's House. Thadora had asked to go, too, but the chaperones had vehemently forbidden it. They only allowed Asphodel to go because of her job as a healer, they told her. and even she would be chaperoned.

Asphodel ran her hands over the dog's leg. She found a break but it would cause the animal pain if she manipulated it.

Turning to Grimmaldo, who had come into Fero's room with them, she said, 'Could you put him to sleep for me, please? I don't want to hurt him as I would if he remains awake.'

By way of an answer, the mage began chanting and as soon as he cast the spell, Bramble's eyes began to droop, and he laid his head on the bed and began to snore softly.

'Fero,' Asphodel said to the ranger, 'Do you think there are any straight sticks or something to set this leg? I can't heal it without some help. I will need perform healing on it several times before it's mended properly.'

'I'll go.' Grimmaldo left the room, knowing Fero would want to remain with the dog.

When he had gone, Asphodel manipulated the leg until the bones lined up once more, then she passed her hands over him, muttering prayers to Sylissa. When she finished, she sat back on her heels.

'The bleeding has almost stopped now,' she said, 'but he's lost a lot of blood.'

Just then, Grimmaldo returned followed by Nhid who carried a variety of sticks and also some straight pieces of metal.

'I found Nhid and managed to tell him what I wanted. It wasn't easy without Bas, believe me, but when he did understand, he insisted on coming with me to see Bramble. Where is Bas, by the way?'

Asphodel looked up from sorting through the various splints.

'I think he went with Zhor and the prisoners. Probably to translate so they have some idea of what's going on. Ah, these are just perfect.' She laid two of the metal splints on the bed beside Bramble and reached for some bandages she had managed to find among Fero's things. Placing the splints carefully on either side of Bramble's right front leg, she set about binding them tightly so as to keep the leg straight. Then she prayed once more and held the leg at the break.

As she stood up, she staggered. Grimmaldo caught her just before she fell.

'You are exhausted. I'm taking you back to the House of Virgins right now,' he told her 'and you are to go straight to bed.'

'But there are others to heal. I've not finished with that wound on your face.' Asphodel protested.

Leading the young elf out of Fero's room and across the common room, Grimmaldo left the building with the protesting elf. A scuttling chaperone followed them, protesting all the while about Grimmaldo holding onto her charge. At least, Grimmaldo assumed that was what she said.

Asphodel walked slowly. Truly, she felt drained. All that healing had taken a lot out of her and she felt grateful when they arrived at the House of Virgins. Grimmaldo had to leave her at the door, of course, but the chaperone led her upstairs to the room she and Thadora shared and she tumbled gratefully into bed.

* * *

Basalt followed Zhor and the prisoners. He frowned at the task the leader of the Walchin had asked him to do. Zhor wanted him to act as an interpreter between the Walchin and the prisoners. He told Zhor that he spoke virtually no Erian, but the Walchin leader seemed to think that all Brandin could understand each other. Asphodel could speak Erian. She should be here, not him. Then again, she couldn't speak any Dwarvish, so that would not help. Anyway, she had healing to do. The elf cleric had healed Basalt's cuts and bruises before he left. Fortunately he had received only minor injuries. She had also healed the three prisoners so that at least they could walk.

They entered the Meeting Hall, and Zhor turned to him.

'Can you tell them they will have to stay here, under guard, until we decide what to do with them.'

Basalt turned to the three prisoners. 'Do any of you speak Grosmerian?' he asked.

The leader, who it turned out was the sergeant of the patrol, replied, 'I, a little.'

Basalt took a deep breath and closed his eyes. This 'little' he hoped would be enough.

'You have trespassed on the world of these people,' he began.

The sergeant frowned, then said, 'Please. to say more...gently.'

Basalt frowned. "more gently"? What did that mean. He tried again.

'These people,' he indicated Zhor and the men who acted as guards. 'hate strangers.'

'Strangers?' The sergeant's frown grew deeper.

Basalt shook his head. The "little" was exactly that. Hardly anything, in fact. He turned to Zhor.

'I can't get him to understand,' he said. 'He says he speaks a little of the language of the Grosmerians, one that I speak, but it's so little that he can't understand when I speak to him.'

'You can't speak with him?'

'No. Sorry. Curate Asphodel can speak his language, though.'

'You go get her and bring her here. She can translate to the language you both understand, and you can translate to me.'

Basalt left and crossed the square to the House of Virgins where the guards told him the curate had gone to the House of Youth to tend to the dog. Basalt set off across the City.

Somehow he missed seeing Grimmaldo and Asphodel on their way back to the House of Virgins. When he arrived at the Men's House, and learned

Asphodel had left with Grimmaldo to return to the House of Virgins, he turned to the door to follow.

Fero grabbed his arm and said, 'Bas, there's no way Asphodel can translate now. She's exhausted herself tending to Bramble and needs plenty of sleep. You'd better go and tell Zhor that.'

Basalt set off again to tell Zhor the news.

Zhor did not receive this news well. The Walchin scowled.

'Is healing so hard?' he said. 'It doesn't make Deacon Jheg so tired.'

Basalt tried to explain.

'Deacon Jheg is not a healer. He can only heal small things. What Asphodel has done here is a lot of large healings, especially on the dog. As I understand it, all magic takes its toll. whether clerical or mage. I'm sorry, Zhor, but you'll just have to wait until Asphodel is rested.'

Zhor spoke to the guards and told them to take the three prisoners to one of the rooms and lock the door.

'Bring the key back and give it to me, and then two of you stand guard. I'll see someone relieves you in a few hours.'

* * *

Asphodel opened her eyes slowly. She wondered how long she had been sleeping. Was it morning? Impossible to tell with no windows and no outside letting in daylight. Looking over at the other bed, she saw the shape of Thadora sleeping soundly. So night then, but early or late? Her eyes began to close of their own volition. She fought it, but soon fell back to sleep.

Later on, she woke again. This time Thadora's bed was empty. So it was morning. The elf sat up, rubbed her eyes and yawned. Sounds permeated the walls. Girls getting up and going down for breakfast. Asphodel swung her legs over the edge of the bed and stood. Her legs nearly gave way and she sat back down with a bump. Just a few more minutes rest, then. Her legs did not feel quite ready to jump out of bed. She lay back down and within minutes she had fallen fast asleep again.

She did not hear Thadora come into the room, look at her and go out again. She did not hear the girls returning from their work to have their lunch. The first thing she heard was the sound of preparations for dinner.

Jumping out of bed once again, she quickly dressed. It could not possibly be dinner time. It must be lunch she could hear the girls preparing. She descended the stairs, relieved that her legs now obeyed her. On entering the common room, Thadora rushed over to her.

'Asphodel,' the young thief exclaimed, 'How are you? You've slept all bleeding day today and half of yesterday, too. Are you recovered?'

The elf smiled. 'Yes, Thadda. I'm recovered. All that healing took a lot out of me, but I'll be fine now. How is everyone? Are your wounds better?'

'Thanks to you, yes.'

'What about the others? How's Grimmaldo's face? And Bramble? I should have done more healing today.'

'Curate Asphodel,' Thadora scolded, 'stop worrying about everyone else and take care of yourself. Damn it, just sit down and have something to eat. You must be bloody starving.'

Now food had been mentioned, Asphodel realised she was indeed hungry, and she took her place next to her friend and tucked in to a hearty meal.

Even after her long sleep, the young cleric began to get tired early and went to bed. She fell asleep quickly, but not before resolving to go to the Men's House first thing the next day to look in on her patients.

True to her promise to herself, as soon as breakfast had finished, Asphodel made her way to the Men's House. A chaperone accompanied her, of course, but they admitted her readily. She made her way straight to Fero's room and knocked on the door. The ranger opened it and admitted her, along with her chaperone.

'How is he?' she asked.

'Not too bad. He hates the splint and bandages though. I had a difficult time stopping him from biting them off.'

Asphodel ran her hands over the dog, asking Sylissa to help her find any internal bleeding, then she looked at his leg, running her hands down it in a similar manner.

'That's odd,' she said, frowning. 'He seems to be better than he should be after all the injuries he sustained. It was touch and go that he'd make it.'

Fero scratched his head.

'That's the odd thing. Jheg came yesterday and offered to help us and Bramble. It surprised me after his antipathy earlier.'

Asphodel looked up.

'Perhaps that now we're considered Walchin he thinks he should treat us as he would treat the others.'

'Perhaps.'

Asphodel insisted on looking at Fero's wounds, although the tall man insisted they were healing well. After her examination, she agreed, gave him a poultice to apply to a cut on his arm and left to knock on Grimmaldo's door.

The mage grinned when he saw who stood outside his room. He recognised the clear, grey eyes looking at him from the all-enveloping robes. Even if her height, greater than that of the Walchin, did not give her away, those eyes would. He would recognise them anywhere.

'Let me look at your wounds, Grimmaldo,' she said.

He stood back to allow her to enter and sat down so she could see his face.

'Deacon Jheg was here,' he said.

'I know, Fero told me. Keep still. I need to examine it carefully.'

When she finished, she stepped back.

'It seems to me Deacon Jheg is a better healer than he thinks. The scar won't disappear completely, but it won't be too noticeable.' She grinned at him. 'Anyway, they say young ladies like a scar. It makes a man look brave and strong.'

'Hmmph. What good will that do me stuck here in this gods-forsaken City.'

Asphodel sat down on the bed next to the young mage.

'Don't forget we're going to get out of here. We're going to appeal to the Council again, remember. We won't give up.'

Regaining his usual optimistic self, Grimmaldo replied with a grin.

'Of course we won't. And we'll keep on appealing until they get so sick of us they show us the way out just to be rid of us.'

There came a knock on the door.

Grimmaldo opened it to admit Basalt.

I heard you were here, Asphodel,'he said. 'Zhor asked me to see if you can come and help with the interrogation of the intruders. Only if you're fully recovered, though. They can't speak Grosmerian and I can't speak Erian. It makes for problems'

Asphodel stood and made for the door, saying, 'Of course I'll come, Bas, but before we go, let me have a look at your wounds. You went off with Zhor before I could do anything about them.'

After pronouncing him well, Asphodel and Basalt set off for the Meeting Hall.

Chapter 8
Roth

When the warning bell rang, Jheg went into the tunnels with the other Walchin, hoping the young men charged with leading the brandin astray succeeded. They had failed miserably last time, and now five brandin lived in their midst. He had failed to sway the Council to his way of thinking and now five strangers lived amongst them. What was worse, one of them was a long-lived elf and she would be with them for many centuries.

Eventually he and the other Walchin gradually made their way back to the City. What greeted him there shocked him to his core. Signs of a fight lay around as he approached. The five brandin all had weapons drawn and bodies lay in the ground, some still and some moving and groaning.

'What happened?' he asked Zhor.

'I think the intruders came searching for the ones we have here. Our brandin fought them and won.'

He looked over to where Fero stood, sword at the throat of one of the new brandin.

'I'd better get some of the young men to take this one, and those injured to the Meeting House and we can interrogate them.'

With that, he went about his tasks. Jheg looked around. Curate Asphodel seemed to be coping well with the aftermath of the battle. She knelt on the ground by the dog–Bramble, they called it. It looked badly injured, but Jheg was not a healer and he left it to Asphodel, returning to his home.

His wife, Rhan, welcomed him as he returned. She asked what had happened, and he told her what he had seen as he sat down at the table. Rhan finished preparing the meal she had left when the bell rang. She never got flustered, no matter what. The Deacon thought that if the cave fell in on the City she would somehow manage to continue with her daily tasks. He smiled at her.

'Do you think those new brandin would have come if it hadn't been for those we already have? Some folk are saying they came here searching for them to take them back,' his wife asked.

Jheg stood and took his plate from his wife as she dished up the meal.

'I think there's a good chance they wouldn't. Why did they come looking for these folk? They must want them very badly to brave the narrows and get here. Few do. Perhaps they're criminals. I knew we should have sent them into the tunnels.'

'What will happen to these others?'

'There will be a meeting of the Council and we'll decide. I expect they'll be turned out of the City. Pity we can't overturn the decision about the others, but once a decision is made, it's binding and no further discussion can be held.'

The deacon did not forget his duties, in spite of the upsets of the day, and he told Rhan he needed to go to check everything in the temple was as it should be before retiring for the night. His home lay close to the temple and so it only took him a short while to convince himself all was well. Then he returned home.

After the events of the day, nearly all the Walchin retired early that evening. Jheg and Rhan were no exception. Just before he fell asleep, Jheg decided to pray to Roth to ask for help in the difficult days ahead. There would be the Council Meeting at which he would try hard to get his way this time. He could not consider allowing these brandin to stay in the City. Some of the Council were getting soft. Mher especially. Perhaps he should suggest a vote against her continuing on the Council and a new election take place. He drifted off to sleep with these thoughts running through his head.

The next morning, after a hearty breakfast, Jheg set off to the temple. He had work to do there in his office as well as ensuring the furnace, water barrel and all the tools remained in good order just in case Roth visited, unlikely as that would seem. Although why there should be anything wrong with the tools he did not know. None had ever been used. Still, part of his job was to check them, and he did his job conscientiously.

The temple had been built in the largest of the caves surrounding the City, on the west wall. After walking the short distance from his home to the temple he opened the door to the anti-chamber and donned his robes of office. Then, after igniting a torch with which to light the torches in the temple, he pushed open the door.

As he entered the large space, he stopped. A reddish glow enveloped the room. There should not be any light here except that from the torch he carried. Looking around, he noticed, with a growing anger, that someone had removed some of Roth's tools from the walls. Who dared to steal from a god? Then, walking between the rows of benches put there for worshippers, Jheg saw where the glow came from, The furnace–Roth's furnace–glowed as if with a fire. As he looked, a cloud of steam arose as someone plunged a piece of hot metal into the quenching barrel. But the barrel had been empty last night. Jheg always checked everything before leaving the temple for the night.

Through the steam Jheg saw the shape of a dwarf holding a piece of metal with Roth's tongs. As the deacon watched, the dwarf pushed it into the furnace to heat again. Only then did he turn to see Jheg standing there, furiously spluttering.

'Basalt! How dare you use Roth's furnace and tools.' he shouted at the dwarf. 'They're there for if Roth wants to visit us at any time, not for the likes of you to use.'

The dwarf looked puzzled for a moment, then said, 'Basalt? Ah, yes. I suppose you mean Basalt Strongarm. No, Basalt would not have used these things. He's much too honest for that.'

Jheg's eyebrows came together as he puzzled the words. As the steam dissipated he saw the dwarf was not Basalt. This dwarf looked slightly taller and his hair seemed darker than Basalt's chestnut hair and beard. Also, where Basalt had hazel eyes, this dwarf had dark brown ones. The dwarf put down the piece he had been working on and stepped off the dais where the furnace stood along with the anvil, usually used as an altar, and the quenching barrel.

'Deacon Jheg, I assume.' The dwarf paused by the statue of Roth standing just at the base of the platform. He studied it closely. 'Not bad, I suppose. The nose is a bit long though, but otherwise not a bad likeness.'

Jheg's eyebrows left off trying to get into the same space on the top of his nose, and flew away from each other, each trying to crawl into his hair. He dropped to his knees.

'Y...Y...Your Holiness,; Forgive me for not recognising you.' He bent his head until it nearly touched the floor.

Roth, for it was indeed he, walked to his cleric and raised him to his feet.

'Now stop being silly,' he said. 'I'm just a blacksmith. Well, OK, I'm the gods' blacksmith. I suppose that makes a bit of difference.'

'Not just a blacksmith, nor even simply the gods' blacksmith,' protested Jheg, hardly believing he spoke to his god, 'you're a god in your own right. That makes you worthy of worship.'

Roth laughed as he turned and picked up the metal he had been working on from the top of the anvil. 'Does it, indeed. You'd be surprised at the antics the gods get up to. Poor Kassilla has a job keeping us all in order. There are rules, see, and some of us break them. I'm breaking one now, just being here and talking to you. And we aren't all either good or bad, as people seem to think. Except for Kassilla, that is. She's always good. "Do what's right. Always obey the rules,"' He spoke in a high-pitched voice as though mimicking a woman.

He laughed again. 'Come into your office, Jheg. We need to talk.'

A stunned Deacon Jheg followed Roth into his office where he indicated the god should sit in his chair behind the desk while he sat on a less comfortable chair. Roth declined.

'No, this is your office. You sit where you usually sit. I'm fine here.' He pulled up another chair and sat. Jheg slowly went to his own chair and sank down into the cushions.

'Now,' Roth began, 'I'm sure you are bursting with curiosity as to why I'm here. I'll not beat about the bush. Alright, I probably will. One rule I will stick to is that we should not tell you what to do. People must always make up their own minds.'

The god shifted on his chair before continuing. He held out the piece of metal he had been working on in the temple.

'Do you know what this is?' he asked.

Jheg took it from him and examined it. 'It looks like a sword blade,' he said, 'We haven't used swords in centuries, Nor any other weapons. We are a peaceful folk, but we do have a few rusty swords in our stores.'

'Yes, it's a sword blade. You're right. I've made you a sword blade.' He put it down on the desk in front of Jheg before continuing,

'The prisoners you're keeping here. Why have you kept them?'

'Prisoners? Do you mean those brandin in the cells? We've not decided what to do with them yet. We might very well let them go.'

'No, no, not those. they aren't important. I'm talking about the other prisoners.'

'We aren't keeping any other prisoners.'

'You have five people here against their will. They wish to leave, but your Council told them they must stay. They cannot leave without guidance. What else is that but keeping them prisoner?'

Jheg knew exactly what to say in answer to that question.

'They aren't really prisoners, though. They have free run of the City. They can come and go as they please.'

'Only within the City, Jheg. Only within the City. These five do not wish to live underground. The ranger and elf especially. I would call that being imprisoned.

'Why did you not free them and show them the way out?'

'They cannot be allowed to leave because of the danger to our people.'

'And what danger is that?'

Jheg's eyebrows rose again. They were having an exciting time today, climbing all over his face. The deacon could not understand Roth's question. Surely it was obvious to him why they decided to keep the brandin.

'If we allow them to leave, they might give us away to the folk above.'

'And would that be so terrible?'

Jheg's eyebrows took another trip. This time back towards his nose.

'It's obvious. People would come here for what they can get. Treasure, stealing the metals and gems we find in the mountain depths. They would bring change. We need to preserve the way of life we've had for centuries. It would bring the end of the Walchin.'

'Oh, Jheg, what good are your gems and metals if they only serve you? And this unchanging way of life is more likely to be the end of your race than anything else. Please think about what I said. Those five brandin are important people, you know.'

He stood and held out his hand. Shaking the Walchin's hand he said, 'It's been good to talk to you, Jheg. I must go now in case I'm missed.' Turning to the door, he passed through it leaving a startled Deacon Jheg behind him.

The deacon rushed to the door, following the god, but as soon as he entered the temple he stopped in his tracks. He saw no sign of Roth, even though he could not have got as far as the door. Everything looked as it had the previous day. He walked up to the dais and climbed up. He felt the walls of the furnace. Cold. He went to the anvil. No signs it had been used, He peered into the barrel. Empty and dry.

Slowly, deep in thought, the Walchin cleric returned to his office. Had he fallen asleep and dreamed Roth's visit? As soon as he passed through the door, though, he saw the sword blade on his desk. So it had been real. Roth really had been here. He picked up the blade and, turning it over in his hands, he began to think of all the things Roth had said to him. It would take much reflection before he could understand what the god told him. He took a deep breath and let it out slowly. Gods did not make things easy for people.

The deacon sat there all day thinking. He picked up the sword blade and put it down again on a number of occasions. Why did Roth make a sword blade of all things? And what did he mean by saying that preserving the Walchin would create their demise? Several times he put his head down on his desk, his brain hurting with the difficulty of his thoughts.

Eventually he decided he knew what the god meant. It would mean he needed to call a Council meeting, but before that he had to decide exactly how to put things to them. He rose and, after checking everything twice, he decided to leave for home as all seemed well in the temple.

* * *

Jheg woke. What an amazing dream he had last night. As he ate his breakfast, he said to Rhan, 'Last night I dreamed Roth came to the temple and used his forge.'

Rhan looked suitably impressed. 'That would be a wonderful thing,' she said, serving him a plate of mushrooms. 'A pity it was only a dream.'

Jheg tucked into his mushrooms, and nodded his head, unable to speak with his mouth full of the delicious fungi. Rhan certainly knew how to cook them to bring out their best flavour.

After he had eaten, he returned to the temple. He looked round. Everything looked as it had when he left the previous night, and so he entered his office. As soon as he passed the threshold he stopped dead. There, on his desk, lay a sword blade, just like the one he dreamed Roth gave him.

Turning on his heels, he re-entered the temple and mounted the dais. He ran his hands over the anvil/altar, felt in the barrel for signs of water, then crossed to the furnace. His foot crunched on something. He bent down to see what it he had trodden on and found a small piece of charred wood. As he turned it in his fingers, he closed his eyes. Here was evidence, along with the sword blade, that what he thought had been a very vivid dream when he woke this morning, had, in fact, been real. So those thoughts he had of what he must do must also be real.

This turned the deacon's world upside down. He felt almost sick. He must now do what he needed to do and call the Council together.

As he left the temple to go to see Zhor, he met a youth with a message.

'Councillor Zhor asked me to tell you he's summoning the Council for a meeting. There's to be a trial of the new brandin.'

Jheg nodded and turned his footsteps to the Meeting Hall.

When he arrived, many Walchin already filled the seats in the main Hall. To his surprise, the dwarf, Basalt, and the elf, Curate Aspholessaria, were also present, seated at the side of the platform. He raised his hand to the people seated and made his way to his accustomed seat next to Zhor.

When all the Councillors had arrived, Zhor gave an order to two young men standing near a door at the side of the Meeting Hall. One of them unlocked the door and three men came out their hands tied behind their backs, and their feet hobbled. The three shuffled towards the front of the platform where they sat on three chairs.

The interrogation began. Jheg realised the reason for the dwarf and elf. It became apparent the interpretation was not going to be as easy as he had thought. How much did they lose in this three-way translation? He could not allow this to worry him unduly, though. It was the best they could do.

It transpired these three men had been a part of a group of ten, chasing after the five brandin they kept in the City. Only eight made it through, owing to two of them chasing after the young men sent to try to distract them.

The men told the Council their commanding officer sent them to arrest these five.

'Why?' asked Zhor. 'Are they criminals?'

'I don't know,' replied the sergeant. 'The commander just said The Master wants them. It's not our job to question our orders, just carry them out.'

The questioning went on for some time, the Walchin posing questions, Basalt translating them to Grosmerian, then Asphodel translating into Erian. Then the opposite way for the answers. It made the whole process a long one.

After the questioning had finished, the Council retired to discuss what to do with the men, and the guards took the men back to their prison.

In the small room where the Council held their deliberations stood a round table surrounded by seven chairs, each with red cushions on the seats. Discussions often went of for days, and the Councillors needed to be comfortable.

On the table, in front of each Councillor, one of the girls from the House of Virgins had placed a glass and a water jug as well as a wooden stand with two balls, one white and one black, seated on it. Another door led off this room into the Voting Chamber where the Councillors would go to place their balls in the Voting Urn'

When the Councillors had taken their places round the table. Zhor began to speak.

'We are here to decide what we should do with these new brandin. should we send them into the tunnels or allow them to stay here in the City with the same conditions as the ones already here. Who would like to speak first?'

Mher began.

'I think we should send them to the tunnels. If we keep them here, there would be conflict between both sets of brandin.'

A young Walchin, called Ghim, said, 'That's the opposite of what you said before, Councillor Mher. Why have you changed your mind?'

Mher again explained her position about conflict and went on, 'These brandin came here carrying un-sheathed weapons, intent on a fight, unlike the ones we allowed to stay. Those brandin showed a peaceful intent, sitting patiently waiting.'

'How do we know these brandin we have already aren't criminals?' Ghim asked, looking around. 'Perhaps that's why the others came looking for them, and braved the narrows, too.'

Jheg listened to the discussion without saying anything. His mind churning in turmoil. Everything he had ever thought or believed had been turned on its head in the last twenty four hours.

'Councillor Jheg,' said Zhor, 'you are unusually silent. What are your thoughts?'

Jheg roused himself.

'I think we should take a vote now. I propose the question "Should we send the new brandin into the tunnels." '

The Councillors all picked up their balls and, one by one, entered the Voting Room. Once there, they dropped one of the balls into the Voting Urn. Black for disagree and white for agree. They secreted the second ball as they returned to the Discussion Chamber.

Once all six voting Councillors had returned to their seats, Zhor called for a girl to bring the urn. He walked over to a side table and picked up a stand with six holes for six balls. He reached into the urn and pulled out the first ball. Red. Agree.

When all six balls had been recovered, the vote had gone in favour of sending the three into the tunnels. The Councillors returned to the Meeting Room and sent for the prisoners once more.

Zhor gave the verdict, translated by Basalt and Asphodel.

'You will leave this place by another exit from the one you entered by. You will be given food and water for three days. If you return here again, you will be executed.'

The men heaved sighs of relief when they heard the verdict. They had no idea what lay in store for them in the tunnels. Asphodel shuddered at the though, and wondered how these peaceful people could be so callous.

Zhor gave the men their weapons and the promised food and water, then escorted to an exit in the north of the City. Shortly after they left, six young Walchin men followed them to ensure they did not find any exits and to report back on their demise.

Jheg approached Zhor as the prisoners left the Meeting Hall to request a continuation of the discussions.

'What is there to discuss. Deacon Jheg?' asked the leader of the Council.

'I would rather not say until we are all together in the privacy of the Discussion Chamber.'

'I think some of the Council have left now. I'll call another meeting for tomorrow morning, first thing. It had better be important, Deacon. It's unusual to have two meetings so close together.

* * *

The Council convened the next morning, Jheg arrived early with a mysterious parcel in his hands. The others looked curiously at it, and one or two asked him questions about it, but he refused to say anything.

When Zhor opened the meeting, he called on Jheg to speak. The deacon began to tell of his miraculous meeting with Roth in the temple.

'Are you sure it wasn't a dream. Deacon?' Ghim asked.

Jheg lifted the parcel onto the desk before him and carefully unwrapped it. He lifted the sword blade so all could see it.

'Is this a dream, Councillor?' he asked. 'This is what Roth left behind.'

All the Councillors fell silent. Roth had visited the Walchin. But what had he said?

Jheg began to tell of his conversation with the god. Afterwards, the discussion became heated.

'What did he mean by saying that in preserving our way of life we will destroy the Walchin? That makes no sense. You must have remembered wrongly, Deacon,' Mher said.

'Why did he call the brandin we have here "prisoners"?' another councillor demanded. 'They are not prisoners. They are free to come and go around the City, and have all the rights of true-born Walchin.'

Jheg pointed out that Roth said that the brandin were prisoners because they did not wish to be here. That, in his book, made them so. He also told the Council that Roth told him these brandin are important people.

'Perhaps they're Councillors in their own lands,' mused Ghim. 'That would make them important.'

'Do you think Roth meant that more people would come to find them? If they are important, perhaps their governments will send more search parties.'

Mher thought for a moment. 'It did not sound as if the brandin we've sent to the tunnels were seeking anything other than criminals.'

The discussion went on for all the day, and long into the night. Then Jheg suggested the thing he had been worrying about ever since he met Roth.

'I think Roth meant for us to let them go. Not into the tunnels, but to escort them out. Gods never say what they mean, exactly. I've thought and thought on this, and I've decided that's what he wants us to do.'

It took another day to decide to hold a vote, then a further one to agree the question to ask. All this seemed to Zhor to be very rushed, but after two days, they held the vote.

"Can we allow a previous vote to be overturned."

This had never happened before. The vote went four to two in favour. Then there came the next question. Another day to decide on the question.

"Should we escort the brandin out of the City and into the World Above."

The Councillors went into the Voting Room, one by one as before. Then Zhor began the count.

White, white, black, black, white, white.

Jheg rejoiced His arguments had won the day. The brandin would be allowed to go free.

Zhor approached him as they left the Meeting Hall.

'I hope we are doing the right thing, Deacon Jheg,' the leader of the Council said. 'What has happened here is totally unprecedented. Roth's words are confusing. After your insistence on the dangers of the brandin, I'm surprised you came to the conclusions you did.'

Jheg replied. 'I spent many hours thinking about it, and it pains me to have to change my mind, but I believe that this is what Roth wanted. Wanted enough to come here to talk to me. There will be other things I need the council to discuss, but that will do for a later date.'

Interlude

The Master of Erian sat in his office in the Government wing of the castle in Frelli. He smiled to himself.

Everything was going well. Such a pity the Horselords had not agreed to work with him. Their knowledge of breeding would have been useful in his experiments, he was sure, but they were not the most important people. Now he had them in his dungeons, he could probably get information about Grosmer from them that he could use. His torturers were very efficient.

He glanced at the Sword hanging on the wall above his desk. How easily he had come by it. As long as he had it in his possession it could not harm him and the prophecies could not be fulfilled.

He laughed out loud. How fortuitous that Lady Randa and the mage, Carthinal had been in the group arrested by Khland. The hobgoblin had made up for losing them last year. If he had not been in charge of the battalion sent to join with Ellint's, they might have got away. Fortunately, Khland recognised them and arrested them. The Master decided he had done the right thing in agreeing to allow the hobgoblin to stay on in the army after the Sword had damaged his leg so much he had needed to have it amputated.

Sauvern's Sword had its own protective mechanism if anyone other than its rightful owner handled it. In the case of Khland, it had become so cold it gave him frostbite on his leg when the stupid hobgoblin refused to remove it, out of pride. It cost him his leg, and nearly his career, but The Master recognised the value of the creature and allowed him to remain in the army, with his wooden leg.

Lady Randa had now agreed to break off her betrothal to Prince Almoro of Grosmer and to become betrothed to him. Oh, it took some persuading to get her to do so, but when Branlow turned on the charm, he could persuade a dragon away from its kill. He had turned on the charm with a vengeance and used all his powers of persuasion. Eventually she agreed.

She thought her agreement was her duty. Branlow had suggested that. Not in so many words, just by subtle implications. He was a very clever man, and his unnaturally long life gave him experience in manipulating others. He could easily get other people to think that an idea was their own.

For his ambitions, Lady Randa was the most important part. After all, she would inherit the Duchy of Hambara. As her husband, he would undoubtedly have some influence and he could eventually wrest the duchy from her and become the Duke in reality not just in name.

She had a strong character and it would take a lot of work, and perhaps magic to persuade her to give him the powers of the Duke, but he had time. Somehow, he would get power enough to have his revenge on the people of Grosmer for the way they had treated him. He had only been a child but he had been threatened with death and eventually sold to get the Raiders away from Sendolina where he lived.

Now, the mage Carthinal he found the most interesting of the five that Khland sent to him. Rarely had The Master come across such talent. He thought that the young man could possibly surpass even Branlow himself if he had the time. The young man had shown ambition. He loved magic above everything else and Wolnarb suspected he would do anything to learn more. He must get Carthinal to send for his wife and daughter as soon as possible so he could keep him here in Frelli. He would be useful, and his wife was an archmage too. He thought he could use her in some way. From what Carthinal had told him she was an expert in translating ancient documents. That in itself would be useful to him. He had many old scrolls and books she could work on.

With two such parents, the daughter could hardly help but be talented. He could take on her education and bend her to his way of thinking. Yes, it was all working out just fine.

Even The Cat would be useful, but not in ways that he would like.

Branlow chuckled again.

The Cat (stupid name that) would be able to help him in his experiments. At first, Branlow worried when he found the little thief in the tower room. He had obviously been there before and the magister wondered how much he had told his best friend Carthinal.

It looked as though he had told him little if anything. Carthinal was behaving in just the same way as previously. Now The Cat was in the dungeons, Branlow had decided to do an ironic experiment.

He had long wanted to try a meld of a human with an animal. The name of the cat burglar gave him the idea of trying to meld him with a big cat. He had a panther in his cages. He would use that.

What about getting Carthinal to help.? That would be an idea. That should tell him just how keen the younger man was to learn magic. If he would help in this, with his friend involved as guinea pig, then Branlow knew he had him and could use him in any way he wished. With the young man's talents, Branlow knew he would be immensely useful. He could delegate some of the meld experiments to him.

He needed someone like Carthinal to run the magical experiments. Hammevaro was talented, but nowhere near as talented as Carthinal. He would be better employed where he was, as his emissary in Grosmer.

Branlow then woke himself from his reverie. There was work to do. Running a country and planning for war and revenge was time-consuming.

Part 2
Leaving

Chapter 9
Dragon

When Jheg arrived in the crater to tell the friends of the new decision of the council, Thadora jumped around.

'When can we go,' she exclaimed. 'The sooner the better. I'm fed up with these bleeding caves.'

'Not until Bramble can walk properly, Thadora,' Fero told her. 'He's getting better quickly, thanks to Asphodel.'

At last the day arrived for Asphodel and the others to depart from the City. They packed their meagre belongings and said their farewells to the city Councillors and the few friends they had made.

Nhid would accompany them as a guide to show them the way out. They agreed they would leave by a different exit from the one through which they had entered, as they may still be being sought in the mountains near where they had inadvertently stumbled into the realm of the Walchin. In any case, Thadora refused adamantly to pass through the narrow and low tunnels they had traversed previously.

Just before the time came for them to leave, Deacon Jheg summoned Asphodel to the temple of Roth. She felt reluctant to go at first, as the cleric had been so hostile to them most of the time they had been there. She found herself confused by his apparent change of heart and did not really believe it, but a summons from a higher-ranking cleric could not be dismissed, even if he were of another god. So, with some trepidation she set off for the temple.

Inside, the temple was even darker then outside and smelled a little like a blacksmith's shop, which she did not find surprising as Roth was the gods' blacksmith. She wondered irrelevantly where the smell came from.

Deacon Jhed stood before the anvil waiting for her.

'Asphodel,' he said as he saw her approach with Basalt to translate. 'I'm glad you came. I've been watching you as you worked with the citizens in the City. You are a skilled healer and I believe you are worthy of more than a curate's sash. Your skills are at least that of a vicar. Although I'm a cleric of Roth, it is in order for me to give you the grey sash of a vicar since there are no clerics of your own order here.'

With those words, translated by Basalt, he turned to the anvil and lifted the grey sash that all vicars, whatever their god, wore. Asphodel looked at him in amazement. He had been an implacable enemy at first, and now here he was, promoting her.

'Thank you, Deacon Jheg,' she replied, taking the sash and, after removing the scarlet one showing her to be a curate, she tied the grey around her white robes. The deacon watched her, then spoke.

'I will not let it be said that I failed to recognise talent when I see it. Go with the fires of Roth's forge to warm you and mould you into strong steel.'

With those words of blessing, he dismissed them.

'May Roth bless you too, Deacon,' replied Basalt with a bow, and the pair took their leave.

The others waited outside the Meeting Room along with Nhid, who was going with them, of course, and Zhor. Zhor's wife, Whin, daughter Khel, who now lived in the House of Virgins, and their sons, Lhon and Bhir who had not yet reached the age to enter the House of Youth, also came to see them off.

Others had come, too. Mher, the councillor who had argued for their cause shook their hands firmly. Others whom Asphodel had healed also came to bid them farewell. Many children fondled and patted

Bramble who revelled in the attention. He liked children. He had a vague memory that at some time in his life there had been children who patted and stroked him. He remembered protecting them, even after they no longer moved, against the rest of the dogs, who would have eaten them. He knew they were leaving again, and felt sorry to leave the children, even as he delighted in leaving the dim caves.

Farewells said, Nhid led the way across the City and down a passage leading towards the west. They passed an entrance to the mines on the right, and then Nhid lit the lamp he had brought with him.

By its dim light, they saw a steep passage leading downwards. Nhid began to walk carefully along this passage.

He turned and said, 'Be careful here. the passage is very steep and damp. You can easily slip.'

He held up a lamp, and before beginning to traverse the passage, he said, 'Stay close. You'll easily lose sight of the lamp if I turn a corner too far ahead of you.'

Thadora reached out and found Basalt's hand. She clung onto it tightly. Basalt thought this a good idea and reached for Asphodel behind him, who in turn grabbed Grimmaldo's hand. Thadora, seeing what was happening, reached out for Fero in front of her and held on to him. He in turn put a hand on Bramble's neck. The dog could probably find Nhid by scent if they became separated, but they decided not to take the risk.

In this way they followed Nhid through many twists and turns for seemingly hours.

Grimmaldo held onto Asphodel's hand. It felt good to do so, somehow right. The young man had become attracted to the elf, but he did not know if she found him attractive, though. She liked him, that he knew, but did she feel only friendship or could it ever be anything more?

He knew he was not handsome in any conventional way, although not bad-looking. Not as good-looking as Carthinal by a long chalk, yet he knew women liked him. He had a friendly disposition and an optimistic nature. He made them laugh. That was always good for getting a kiss from a girl.

Carthinal, he suspected never had any trouble with getting girls. Even the shy and timid Olipeca had found him attractive enough to single him out for attention at their tests.

He wished he were more like Carthinal with women, but he felt gauche beside the half-elf. Carthinal did not seem to realise his power. He just remained himself and they flocked to him.

He shook his head. Women were too complicated for him to understand so he shelved the problems and concentrated on keeping from falling and the pleasure of feeling Asphodel's hand in his.

After travelling for what seemed like forever to Grimmaldo in the semi-darkness of the tunnels, Nhid called a halt.

They had entered a largish cave. Here the floor seemed dryer and so they all sat down for a rest and something to eat.

The ceiling of the cave stood only a few feet above Grimmaldo's head when standing, and it only stretched about twelve feet across and about fifteen feet long. It had two exits opposite the one through which they had entered.

Basalt told them that Nhid had said they would rest here for about half an hour before moving on. Grimmaldo wished they could have more light, but assumed that Nhid's eyes would not be able to see as well if it were brighter. He shivered.

'Are you cold?' asked Asphodel.

'Not really, I don't like these caves much, I suppose,' he replied.

'You and me both,' put in Thadora. 'I can cope as long as it doesn't get too narrow or low though. If I can manage, so can you so don't be a wussy.'

'Who are you calling a wussy?' demanded the young mage.

'Don't start that again, children,' scolded Fero. 'We can't cope with arguing infants, can we boy?' He patted Bramble on the head. The dog wagged his tail as if agreeing. 'Anyway, it seems to be time to move on again.'

Nhid climbed to his feet and re-filled the lamp with lamp oil before saying a few words and beckoning to them to follow. With a groan, Thadora rose and followed, again hanging onto Basalt's hand. They seemed to have got themselves into a different order, and to his disappointment, Grimmaldo found himself holding onto Thadora at the back of the group.

The passages continued ever downwards. This puzzled Grimmaldo. He thought they were already deep below the mountain range. He voiced the thought to Basalt, who asked Nhid. When the Walchin replied, Basalt turned to Grimmaldo.

'Nhid says the passages go deep before they begin to rise. We'll soon be at the deepest part, but here we must be very careful because we're very close to the lairs of the denizens of the deep.'

'What are the "Denizens of the deep"' Thadora asked. 'Sounds so bleeding scary to me.'

'I don't think they've got names for the creatures living this deep,' Basalt told her.

The tunnel turned sharply left. As Nhid rounded the bend, the others momentarily lost sight of his lamp. Thadora froze.

'Come on, Red Cub,' Basalt coaxed her. I can just see where he's gone.

They rounded the bend and saw Nhid standing stock still.

'Listen,' he said, 'Do you hear that?'

They listened and Asphodel said, 'Slithering. I can hear something slithering.'

'Come, we need to go in here,' Nhid told them. bending down and passing into a low tunnel.

A whimper came from Thadora.

'Zol's balls, not again. I can't go through any more tight passages.'

Nhid looked back. He had not understood her words, but he did understand her whimper.

He spoke to Basalt who in turn told Thadora, 'That slithering is one of the many denizens. You can choose. Go through here or stay and get poisoned then eaten alive by the creature's young.'

Thadora scooted into the narrow, low tunnel. The others followed as quickly as they could.

'It can't get in here,' Nhid told them. 'It's too big. We can wind round to the exit tunnel through here. I think that's the best way. That way we won't meet it later.'

Thankfully for Thadora, the tunnel got no lower nor narrower, and they soon came to a wider passage.

They had not gone far along this new passage when they heard a scraping sound ahead. Nhid held up a hand for them to stop. Then they saw the pale shape ahead of them. The four who had been on the quest for Sauvern's Sword, Equilibrium, recognised it immediately.

'Carrion crawler,' breathed Thadora.

She had been struck by one of the tentacles of a similar creature when they passed through the tunnels of Sauvern's tomb. This one was a little larger. It had the appearance of a caterpillar, but about ten feet long. It reared itself up on its rear legs ready to strike with the tentacles that surrounded its mouth. Those tentacles contained a poison with which the creature paralysed its prey.

Thadora had been struck by one of the tentacles of the one they had met earlier and backed away a little. She pulled out one of her throwing knives.

'Nhid, get to the back of the group and retreat as we do,' commanded Basalt. 'The rest of you, we attack then move back in sequence. Me and Asphodel, then Fero and Thadora, finally Grimmaldo.'

So saying, he placed a bolt in his crossbow and turned towards the advancing creature. At the same moment, Asphodel put a stone in her sling. Both missiles flew to strike the monster.

It hesitated for a moment then began to advance once more. Asphodel and Basalt quickly moved behind the others and as they did so, Fero and Thadora attacked, Thadora with her throwing knives, managing to get two throws in as Fero let fly with one of his arrows, quickly followed by another, then they slipped to the rear.

Grimmaldo had already got his spell prepared and strings of sticky fibres flew from his fingers to entangle the creature thus preventing any further movements.

'Nice one, Grimmaldo,' called Thadora.

Now the friends could finish off the predator without fear of attack. This they did quickly, still keeping their distance from the poisonous tentacles. Afterwards, Thadora and Fero collected their arrows and knives and they once more followed Nhid along the passageways under the mountain.

'That were a so cool spell, Grimmaldo,' observed Thadora as they passed through the tunnels. 'I've never seen Carthinal do that one.'

'I learned it recently,' replied the mage. 'From a book of spells I bought in Roffley on the way here. I hadn't had a chance to try it out before now though. I'm pleased at the way it worked, but I understand that it's possible for creatures to evade the webs if they're quick enough.'

They traversed the tunnels for a couple of hours when Nhid suddenly came to a halt.

'Ssh,' he said, The Walchin waved a hand for them to stop. He and Basalt went into a whispered conference before the dwarf turned to his companions.

'Nhid says he heard sounds like voices ahead,' the dwarf whispered. 'It seems we're not far from the exit and he thinks something wandered in. If it sounds like voices, they're probably humanoid. Let's hope they're friendly, is all I can say.'

The others endorsed that view and Thadora offered to sneak ahead to see if she could find out anything. She pulled her hood over her head to hide her startling red curls. Carthinal had told her she should do this, since her hair had made her stand out so allowing him to both see and recognise her in their first encounter. It stood out in a crowd rather too easily for a thief, he had said.

She slipped into a darker part of the tunnel and to all intents disappeared as far as the others could see. Nhid looked startled.

'How did she do that?' he asked Basalt in his archaic language. 'Does she have magic?'

'No,' replied the dwarf. 'Just skill in hiding in the shadows and she can move almost silently too. Thieving skills,' he said disapprovingly, but then went on to add, in a tone indicating some pride. 'She's pretty good at it too.'

Thadora slipped along the tunnel towards where she could now hear some voices. They were definitely voices, but not speaking any language she had heard before. She paused in a deep shadow and looked out into a huge cave.

It would have swallowed the City of the Walchin several times over. She could see neither the roof above nor the walls at the far side. The lamps that the eight creatures carried seemed to have their light sucked out by the deep darkness of the cave.

The creatures walked quietly and carefully over towards a number of oval-shaped things near the centre of the cave. The creatures had dark skin and about half way between dwarves and humans in size. They had pointed ears, a bit like elves, but nothing else resembled those beautiful creatures. Their light brown eyes shifted from side to side as they sidled up to the ovoids.

With noses that looked too big for their faces, and large almost lipless mouths seeming to be set in permanent grimaces or snarls, they looked very ugly creatures indeed. One of them bared his teeth and Thadora noticed they had all been filed to a point.

The creatures crept around the cave in a bunch. They kept looking round nervously and shuffling their feet whenever they stopped to listen. To an experienced thief, it became obvious this was a thieving expedition, although what they could be stealing in these caves she could not imagine.

As she started to turn away to return to the others, the creatures reached the things in the centre of the cave. They took out four bags and placed them on the floor, then two of them to each ovoid, they lifted them into the bags and carefully pulled up the drawstrings. Then, picking up the bags, they hurried away into the gloom of the cave.

Thadora slipped back to where the others waited. She described the creatures and what they did.

'I don't know what those things were they put in the bags though,' she said.

'Orcs!' growled Fero, his face looking grim in the dim light of their lamps. 'Those creatures were orcs. A more evil, sneaky, underhand, murderous, corrupt, depraved race does not exist on the face of Vimar. I'm going after them to teach them what it means to face their own deaths.'

And with that he drew his sword and started in the direction Thadora had come back from.

Basalt put out a hand and grabbed the tall ranger, swinging him round.

'It won't help if you to go rushing off, Fero. Fighting needs a cool head, and you know it.'

Fero began to calm down.

'I know it my friend,' he replied. 'I can't seem to help myself when I come across those creatures. I see little Zepola's body, tossed away like old rags. My little sister. Only five years old. Orcs took her, then killed her.' His head sank down and his hair, which had come loose from the tail into which he habitually tied it, hung down over his face. Asphodel approached.

'Fero,' she said, 'we may get the chance to do something about those orcs, but we will do it only if necessary and with cool heads.'

She turned to Nhid. 'How far until we're out of here?' she asked.

Basalt translated her words to the Walchin and then Nhid's back to her.

'It seems we need to cross that cave then go down a long, wide tunnel to the outside,' he said. 'There is a problem though. Those things you saw the orcs taking, Red Cub, are nothing less than dragon eggs. Where there are dragon eggs, there is inevitably a dragon, maybe two. The father often stays around too, with blues. Mother will be returning soon to watch over her eggs and we don't want to meet her in the tunnel, or to be around when she finds some of her eggs are missing.'

'I knew it was too bloody easy,' wailed Thadora. 'The Walchin said there were dreadful dangers in the tunnels, but all we met were a buggering carrion crawler and a bleeding denizen. Now we have to get past a blue dragon, and what's more, one who will be very, very cross!'

Grimmaldo patted her on the arm and said, 'Look on the bright side, Red Cub. It could be worse.'

She rounded on him, temper flaring. 'Explain to me how it could bloody worse,' she snapped. 'Go on, I'm waiting!'

'So are we all,' smiled Basalt. 'Explain away, mage.'

'We—el…' hesitated Grimmaldo, at a loss for the moment. 'We could be lost in the tunnels and starve, or have met something worse than that carrion crawler—you know the Walchins' tales of dire creatures in the tunnels. Or we could have been well away from any escape tunnels when we met the denizen. We're close to the outside, so Nhid says, and anyway, if we get hungry, I'm sure we could live for weeks on an omelette made from just one of those eggs if they are the size you say they are.'

Asphodel gave him a look.

'Don't even think of making omelettes from dragon eggs, Grimmaldo,' she warned. 'Dragons are implacable foes so it is said. If she heard you, you'd be the one for dinner, and not as a guest either!'

'She's not there. Remember?' he replied.

'Was not there, you mean. Listen carefully and even your cloth ears may hear what I heard.'

They all stopped speaking and stood in silence, and sure enough, the sounds of scraping talons on stone came to their ears. The dragon was returning to her lair!

Before any of them had the time to wonder if she had caught the orcs, a terrible, heartrending cry shook the ground and walls of the tunnel in which they hid.

'I guess she just discovered some of her eggs are missing,' said Thadora in a small voice, even forgetting to swear in her fear. The others sweated and they cowered back against the walls of the cave as though trying to push themselves through.

'It's the dragon fear,' muttered Fero. 'All dragons generate an aura of fear around them. Few are immune to it. It gets worse the closer one goes. It means that most are totally unmanned near to dragons and cannot fight. They capitulate or are frozen in terror and so make easy pickings for the creatures.

'That's the reason they are so difficult to fight and kill. Apart from their scales that is. They are like armour.'

Thadora looked at him. He had mentioned dragons before and seemed to know quite a lot about them. She must ask him more sometime. If they ever got out of here.

'Do you know how long she's likely to stay in the cave?' Asphodel whispered to Nhid.

The Walchin looked at Basalt and then answered as he received the translation.

'I know little of the dragons,' he replied. 'I suppose she's just been hunting. It should be nearing dusk now, and dragons prefer to sleep by night, I've been told, so she may be here all night. She will also be protecting her eggs, and if she ate a large creature the meal will last her several days.'

'Great!' muttered Thadora. 'We'll either have to stay here for days or sneak past when she's damn well sleeping.'

They all looked gloomy at the thought of either alternative until suddenly, Grimmaldo exclaimed, 'Of course! She's just discovered the loss of some eggs, hasn't she!'

'So what?' inquired Basalt.

'What would you do if someone sneaked in and took some of your children while you were out?' he asked looking round the group. 'And how would you feel?'

Basalt thought for a moment, then his eyes lit up as understanding dawned.

'Will you bloody explain, please?' Thadora demanded.

Basalt began, 'First, there would be sorrow that they had gone, and mourning; but not for long. Then there would be anger at the perpetrators.

'If the children were known to be alive, or there was a possibility they were still alive, rescue would be the next thing, and revenge on the kidnappers. That would mean leaving to chase the thieves.'

'And leaving the others alone?' said Asphodel. 'She may have decided that she'll sacrifice those taken and protect those left. They are, after all, eggs still and not baby dragons.'

There came another roar from the cave ahead. This time it sounded more angry than despairing, and the sounds of scraping followed, gradually getting quieter as the huge beast made her way from the tunnels.

'I guess we've got our answer,' said Grimmaldo. 'I rather think she's going after those orcs who took her eggs. She sounded sorrowful at first, but that second roar was anger if I've ever heard anger.'

'We'd better wait a bit though, to give her time to clear the tunnel.' Basalt said. 'I'd hate her to mistake us for the thieves. After all, she's not to know it was orcs who stole the eggs, or that they went back outside and not further into the mountain.'

They agreed, and sat down, backs to the walls of the tunnel, waiting until they thought she would be far enough away.

'Let me go first to check. I can be quieter than the rest of you, and I can keep out of sight more easily too,' Thadora pointed out.

'Be careful, Red Cub,' whispered Fero. 'Remember that dragons have a much better sense of smell than you do, or most animals for that matter. She'll be able to smell you even if she can't see you.'

Thadora grinned at him. He could just see her teeth gleam in the dim light.

'Thanks for the warning,' she said, and then, inexplicably ran in the opposite direction.

'What's that fool girl doing now?' grumbled Basalt. 'She'll get herself lost. Well, I for one am not going looking for her.'

Asphodel laughed, 'You'll be the first one down that tunnel if she's gone longer than five minutes,' she pointed out, and the dwarf replied with, 'Humph.'

Before any of them had time to worry, though, Thadora returned. She had covered herself in a dark substance and smelled decidedly unpleasant.

'What in the name of all the gods have you done to yourself. You smell like a midden!' exclaimed Grimmaldo, holding his nose.

'Just a little blood from a certain carrion crawler, and some stuff from its insides,' she replied cheerfully. 'Now the dragon will think I'm just another denizen of the deep.'

Nhid spoke to Basalt then.

'Nhid says he'll leave us here,' Basalt told the others. 'He thinks it'll be safer for him if he doesn't have to traverse the dragon's lair twice. We must take that tunnel ahead.' Bas pointed to a dark entrance between two others. 'It's straight from here now, apparently. We mustn't take any side tunnels though or we won't get out. Well, Red Cub, since you're the scouting party, off you go!'

'Tell Nhid I'd give him a hug, but I don't think he'd enjoy it with me smelling like this. Tell him I'll miss him though. I like the Walchin even though I couldn't speak to them or understand them.'

With that, she sped off across the cave to the tunnel Nhid had indicated and disappeared.

'I hope she'll be all right,' worried Basalt, after passing the message on to Nhid, who smiled and then looked embarrassed at the praise from the young thief.

Fero and Grimmaldo shook hands with their Walchin friend and Basalt and Asphodel embraced him. They watched as he and his lamp vanished into the gloom.

After only a few yards, Thadora began to feel sick. The smell would certainly mask her own, but the others were right. It stank. She had not thought it would smell so bad. However what was done was done and she would have to put up with it.

The girl took a deep breath.

Swallowing, she pressed on towards the dragon's lair. She crossed the cave, empty now, except for the eggs; six of them now, lying together. They had a bluish tinge in the dim light cast by the lamp she carried. Slipping back along the tunnel, she gave the all clear signal to the others.

* * *

After what seemed like hours, but probably only lasted about ten minutes, a light appeared in the exit tunnel. It swung backwards and forwards, in the pre-arranged signal, to show the dragon had gone.

One by one they crossed the lair, passing the eggs, and entered the new passage. Asphodel paused to look at the eggs. They were enormous, reaching almost to her waist. As the light from her lamp fell onto the nearest, she could just make out something inside. It seemed to be moving. Hurriedly, she crossed the remaining space to join Thadora and Grimmaldo. Fero and Basalt quickly joined them, and they made their way through this final tunnel towards the outside.

When the companions emerged from the tunnel the sun had just set. The cave came out half way up the side of the mountain. An open grassy bank ran down towards a stream tumbling down the mountainside. No trees grew here, although woods covered, although the rest of the steep valley. Fero supposed it made a good place for the dragon's den since it gave her plenty of space to land before entering the cave.

'I need a bath,' Thadora stated, wrinkling up her nose. 'I didn't think I'd smell quite this bad.'

'You can't bathe here, Red Cub,' Basalt pointed out. 'Trust me, we're all as anxious as you to get you clean again, but that dragon could arrive back at any time. We don't want to be here when that happens.'

'Sickening as your smell is,' Grimmaldo said, 'I agree with Bas. Let's get going.'

They began to walk towards the stream, meaning to follow it down to the valley they could see below. Mountains surrounded them and, looking around Fero wondered where in the range they had emerged.

After a little discussion, they decided that once in the valley they should head in a westerly direction as much as possible and avoid any habitations until they had left Erian behind.

Then came the sound of creaking, leathery wings and a sudden draught. Fear washed over them and they knew the dragon had returned. A large rumbling voice spoke in Erian from over their heads. Fero looked up and saw an enormous cerulean blue head, similar in colour to the sky. It had two large horns sweeping backwards in graceful arches. A ruff surrounded a long sinuous neck, which descended towards the group. They found themselves rooted to the spot with fear, but Asphodel managed to summon up the courage to reply.

'We do not all speak Erian,' she said in a quavering voice. 'Do you speak Grosmerian?'

The dragon tilted its head to one side.

'Grosmerian?' it replied. 'You are far from home then. Some further than others if my eyes do not deceive me. Two Grosmerians, a dwarf, an elf and a dark skinned stranger. Nevertheless, you are thieves and will pay the price.'

The dragon drew in a deep breath intending to fry them when another dragon landed behind the first.

'No, Pranesh, not yet,' said the second dragon. 'They must have hidden the eggs somewhere. We must find out where before we punish them.'

The first dragon turned and looked at its mate. The newcomer was larger than the one who had arrived first. A slightly darker blue dragon had landed in the clearing. Its shimmering scales caught the dying sunlight in mirror-like silvery gleams. The eyes of the first dragon turned away from this magnificent creature and returned to the group of people cowering before it.

'My mate has saved you—for now. She wants to question you as to where you've hidden our eggs. If I were you, I'd tell her.'

He leaned his head towards them and said in a conspiratorial whisper, 'She can be very difficult if she doesn't get her way.'

He then turned his head towards his mate.

'Question them if you wish, Jerriash, my dear. We can dispose of them later. They will be good eating for the little ones when they hatch.' He turned back to them. 'They should begin hatching any day now. She...' and he nodded towards Jerriash '...is getting excited about it, but then it's her first brood. Decided to stick around for a while to help her, new mother and all that, not to mention that she's so-o beautiful.'

'What's that you're saying, Pranesh?'

'Just that I think you're so beautiful, my love,' replied Pranesh.

Jerriash purred. It sounded to Fero like an overgrown pussycat.

The two dragons changed places and Fero found himself looking into yellow eyes with vertical pupils, like the cat she had sounded like just now.

'Your Magnificence,' he began. 'We know nothing of the whereabouts of your eggs. We are not the thieves. They were stolen by orcs.'

'What are you doing here then? No one comes here—because we're here. This is our territory. No. You are obviously in league with these orcs, if, in fact, there are any orcs.'

Fero spluttered at the thought of himself in league with the hated orcs, but managed to pull himself together to reply.

'We came from the tunnels behind your lair, your beauteous majesty, and saw the orcs stealing your eggs. There were eight of them and they put the eggs into bags, then left. We have no idea where they went.'

Pranesh's head snaked round Jerriash to peer at Fero. His green eyes had a hard look.

'Not a likely story. Those tunnels have only the scum of the land in them—Carrion crawlers, giant spiders, rats, not to mention Walchin! No one could pass through the mountains using those tunnels.'

'We did, though,' said Thadora. Then she remembered how Fero had addressed the dragons and added, 'your magnificences.' She explained how the Walchin had captured them and then released them to be guided out by Nhid. Then she frowned.

'The Walchin told us no one knew they existed. How do you know of them?'

'Those pasty-faced relatives of dwarves are known to us as we know all creatures that dwell in the mountains, inside and out,' spat Pranesh. We see them in their bowl as we fly over. They're out there "guarding" their livestock, but refuse to fight. Namby-pamby creatures they are. Not much better than elves, with their ecology and loving trees and plants and animals.'

'Ehem,' interrupted Jerriash. 'I thought I was conducting an interrogation here.'

She turned to Thadora. 'I think you'll do, although you smell like a crawler.' She reached out a front leg and picked the young thief up.

Thadora screamed once, then once again as Jerriash dropped her into the icy water of the stream.

Basalt drew his battle-axe and strode towards Jerriash, but Fero held him back.

'No use you getting yourself killed, friend,' whispered the ranger. 'What do you think you can do with that against two adult dragons?'

He turned to the dragons.

'What are you doing with the girl?' he demanded.

'Just washing the stink off her,' came the reply. 'Then I'm taking her to the lair. She'll be a hostage to ensure your return. You are going to get the eggs from wherever you, or the orcs, have stashed them. Only then will you get her back.

'You have, let's say, two days. More and they may be hatching—or dead if they get too cool.'

Everyone looked at her in amazement, even Pranesh, her mate.

'How do you know they'll come back for her?' he asked. 'They may just leave her and run. Then we'll not find the eggs at all.'

His mate looked at him as one might a small but not very bright child.

'Pranesh, my dear,' she said. 'these two-legged creatures have what they call "honour". At least many do. They will not abandon one of their number. They'll return, with or without the eggs. Without and they will try to rescue her by force.'

She laughed. 'Pathetic, aren't they. As though they could ever win against one dragon, let alone two.'

She picked Thadora up from the bank of the stream where the girl had climbed and stood shivering.

'Anyway,' she continued to her mate, 'this one will make a good first meal for the hatchlings if they don't return.'

This elicited another squeak from Thadora. Then Jerriash turned back to the others. 'Remember, be here at the same time in two days at the latest, or this girl feeds our youngsters.'

With those words, she and her mate walked slowly back to the cave, carrying a screaming Thadora with them.

Chapter 10
Eggs

'We'd better start to look for the eggs then.' growled Basalt, as they stood looking after the dragons and Thadora. Her screams had faded as the dragon entered the caves, but those who remained stood motionless for several seconds. 'You once said you could track orcs over bare rock, Fero, so you'd better make a start. I think there may be a need to make good your boast. We've not got much time.'

'Nor much of a plan, either.' Grimmaldo said. 'How are we to get the eggs from the orcs if there are more than the ones we saw?'

'Let's cross that bridge when we come to it,' replied Asphodel. 'We have to find the thieves first, then we can decide what to do.'

Fero searched the meadow around the cave entrance. Spotting something, he called out that he had found tracks, and they led into the woods. Bramble, too, sniffed around. He had caught the scent of the orcs from the cave, and soon picked up the trail.

Fero followed the dog, using both his own experience of tracking and Bramble's nose. The others quickly caught up with him. Asphodel decided the creatures could not have got too far across the difficult terrain. They would have had to traverse a very rocky track with a number of steep climbs, but then again, it would take the companions time too. And darkness approached.

'Fero,' she called to the ranger, 'we'll get nowhere in the dark, The orcs will need to rest for the night somewhere. It would be dangerous to try to follow the trail when we can't see where we're going. We could easily end up falling off a cliff or something.'

Fero stopped in his rush to follow the orcs. He took a deep breath and said, 'You're right, of course. We can camp here and leave early tomorrow morning at first light.'

Dawn came quickly and as soon as it became light enough to see, the four, with Bramble running ahead, scenting the trail, set off along what looked like an animal track through the woods. Soon they had to scramble down a steep bank.

The stream had wound round and now flowed to their right again. The tracks led into the water, so they crossed over. On the opposite side, Fero searched again, but failed to find any trace of the orcs' passage. He reported back to the others.

'I thought you could track them "over bare rock".' said Basalt.

'But I said nothing about tracking them along a stream though, did I?' snapped Fero, irritated. 'If you can do better, you try.'

'I'll leave it to an expert.' the dwarf replied. 'You think they've gone along the stream then?'

'Almost certainly. There's no sign on either bank. That's what we'll have to do. Follow along in the stream. Bramble can't track in running water, either.'

'Do we have to get wet?' asked Grimmaldo. 'Couldn't we just walk along the bank until we find where they got out?'

'Several reasons why not.' Fero turned to the young mage. 'One: we cannot keep an eye on both banks if we're walking along one or the other. Two: the path, or what passes for a path, may turn away from the stream. And three: the banks may rise and make it impossible for us to continue along side the stream.' He pointed ahead. 'Just as it does along there.'

They all plunged into the icy water, having first removed their shoes. Fero, Asphodel and Basalt pulled their trousers up as far as possible while Grimmaldo hitched up his robes above the level of the water. The cold of the stream struck them as they entered.

Soon, their feet hurt with the cold, but no one complained as they remembered Thadora's plight in the lair of the dragons, destined to become baby dragon food if they failed their quest.

They followed the stream for some distance. Asphodel estimated nearly half a league, and most of the time it ran between high banks. After traversing a small waterfall, Fero stopped.

'Look!' he exclaimed.

The others saw a very muddy bank on their left. Fero walked over and examined it. Here the bank came a little lower, but still stood about six feet above the water.

'Something has slipped down the bank here,' he told them. 'Look how smooth it is, and I can see skid marks in places, as if whatever climbed it kept slipping. Our friends left the stream here, I think.

'Could it have been otters or something else sliding into the water instead of someone climbing out?' asked Asphodel.

'I don't think so.' replied the ranger. 'Otters don't cling to branches of trees and break them to stop themselves from sliding.'

The others looked and sure enough, they saw broken branches on a tree overhanging the bank, and Asphodel noticed what looked like the imprint of bare toes on one part of the bank near some grass. She pointed it out to Fero.

'Well done, vicar.' Fero praised her. 'We'll make a ranger of you yet.'

They clambered out of the stream with much backsliding. Basalt had the most problem, but with Grimmaldo and Fero heaving him, he eventually made it up onto the top of the muddy bank. Grimmaldo had mud on his face while Basalt's leather armour looked as if he had rolled down the muddy bank, which, indeed, had almost happened. Asphodel's usually immaculate white tabard had become unidentifiable beneath the mud.

'At least we'll blend in with our surroundings.' she grimaced.

In a nearby clearing they found the remains of a fire. Fero noticed other signs that something had camped for the night. They deduced the orcs had stopped here. Or at least Fero did. He also told them he thought the orc party had met up with others here as he saw signs of more than the eight they had already seen.

'Maybe they were waiting here.' he suggested. 'Anyway, I think they probably left at dawn, as we did, so are now only about three hours ahead of us. We should be able to move more quickly than they can as there are only four of us, and Bramble, of course, and they have the eggs to carry. They must take care with them, although they are leathery rather than brittle like birds' eggs. They won't want to risk any damage.

'On the negative side, however, the fact that we have to track them will slow us down a little.'

'Then what are we waiting for?' demanded Basalt. 'Get tracking, Ranger.'

The tracks became clear now, even for the others to see. They seemed to go down towards the valley bottom, following the stream as it tumbled towards a larger one flowing southwards in the valley.

The tracks eventually led out of the wooded hillsides onto meadows. The companions paused before emerging and saw a band of orcs and hobgoblins sitting eating their mid-day repast in the sunlight. The orcs looked pleased with themselves as they pulled open the strings of the four large sacks they had with them.

The hobgoblins peered in. One poked a finger at what he saw inside, and a large hobgoblin, obviously the leader, immediately reprimanded him. This creature turned to the orcs and said, in poor Erian:

'You done good. Master be pleased. Wenkl take eggs. Wenkl tell Master orcs done good.'

One of the orcs replied to Wenkl, also in Erian. This one seemed less in awe of the big hobgoblin than the others.

'Orcs come too. Maybe Wenkl forget orcs' names and Master not know who to reward. Very dangerous getting eggs from dragon. Orcs need reward.'

Wenkl seemed to grow angry.

'Orcs not know place.' he said, drawing himself up and putting his hand on his wicked-looking curved sword. 'Hobgoblins higher than orcs. Orcs obey hobgoblins.'

The orcs drew themselves into a tight group around their leader, who seemed ready to fight the bigger hobgoblin. Fero frowned.

'This is not usual orc behaviour.' he whispered. 'They're usually cowardly creatures. These seem willing to stand up to a much bigger hobgoblin.'

He turned back to watch the creatures as the quarrel continued.

'We not less than hobgoblins. We Special Orcs.' His voice put capitals on the words. 'Master made Special Orcs for special tasks. We brave and strong. Only Special Orcs can get dragon eggs. Other orcs too afraid and weak. We go with you to Master.'

The hobgoblin, Wenkl, growled.

'Special Orcs!' his voice made it sound like an insult. 'No orcs special. All orcs scum.'

The dozen orcs and about ten hobgoblins started to fight. Ordinarily, it would have been no contest, the hobgoblins being able to defeat the smaller and weaker orcs easily, but when the fight started, it became obvious to the watchers that these orcs. had definitely got something different about them. They fought with a fierceness more akin to humans, and did indeed seem to be stronger than usual. Basalt turned to the others.

'This may be our only chance. We must act now while they're distracted. What spells do you have available, Grimmaldo?'

'I can put invisibility on one person.' replied the mage. 'It will not work if the person attacks or is bumped into. The spell simply bends the rays of light so they go around the person. This means that the person who bumps will know someone is there and …'

'We don't have time for a lecture, Grimmaldo.' scolded the dwarf. 'Just do it. Invisible me, then I can sneak in to grab the sacks.'

'Not you, dwarf.' replied Grimmaldo. 'You're not quiet enough. You'd be as obvious as that mountain over there. Fero or Asphodel should go.'

Basalt then said Fero should go as Asphodel should be protected. The elf became angry then.

'Are you suggesting I can't take care of myself, Basalt Strongarm? I'm no weak woman in case you've not noticed. I am in need of no protection.'

Fero turned to them, anger making his black eyes look like thunder. They recoiled.

'Are you all as mad as that lot?' he indicated the now fighting orcs and hobgoblins. 'Grimmaldo, just cast your spell on Asphodel and we'll cover her from here. She's the one most likely to manage to get by those fighting creatures without a collision as she's the smallest. Except for our noisy dwarf here. Now get on with it!'

Reprimanded, Grimmaldo spoke the words of his spell and wove the mana to bend the light rays. Asphodel vanished from their sight.

They noticed a slight movement in the bushes as she left the cover of the wood and then some incongruous movements of the grass. No one would have noticed if they had not been watching for them though, and the orcs and hobgoblins were too busy fighting to notice.

Already two orcs and a hobgoblin lay dead, and another hobgoblin seriously wounded. Asphodel wanted to stop to try to heal the injured creature as her vows had made her promise to aid all, regardless of allegiance, but the thought of Thadora in the clutches of the dragons made her ignore its cries and to reach out for the first sack.

She managed to put her hand on it, and then she paused before reaching out for the second. As she touched them, the sacks vanished from view and she slowly dragged them back to the waiting group in the wood. When she got there, she released her hold, and the sacks reappeared.

Breathing a sigh of relief, she again crept as quietly as she could to the remaining two sacks. Her breath came quickly as she reached out for the sacks. Just two more of the heavy. sacks.

By the time she reached the edge of the battle again, another two hobgoblins had fallen and three more orcs. Five orcs, three hobgoblins dead, and one hobgoblin wounded. The remaining seven orcs and six hobgoblins fought around the last two sacks.

She found it difficult to get near without being bumped into. This she knew must not happen. What should she do? One of the orcs collided with a sack and went sprawling, rolling towards Asphodel who only just managed to jump out of the way. The orc rolled to its feet and ran back into the fray.

Asphodel reached out. She managed to get her fingers onto the third sack. She tugged gently. The sack moved. Slowly, she moved the sack to where she could get a proper grip on it, and then she ran towards where the others had hidden.

'I could only get one this time.' she panted. 'How long have I got before the spell wears off?'

'You should have time for the fourth.' Grimmaldo whispered back, 'But be careful, Asphodel, you were nearly caught just then. My heart was in my mouth.'

Asphodel did not reply, or ask how he knew, but crept back to try to retrieve the final sack. She just began to carry it back to the others when one of the hobgoblins noticed they had vanished. It called out and the fighting stopped as the protagonists turned.

Immediately another argument began as to what had happened. The hobgoblins accused the orcs of hiding the eggs so they could get all the credit from the Master, while the orcs in their turn accused the hobgoblins of trying to take the glory away from them. This argument threatened to turn into another fight and in the confusion Asphodel rejoined the others in the woods. They each took one of the sacks and, hefting them over their shoulders, began to pick their way back the way they had come.

Eventually, the hobgoblin, Wenkle, managed to regain control of the fighting orcs and hobgoblins and pointed out some small footprints, too small for either orcs or hobgoblins, leading towards the woods.

'While you lot fight, thief steal eggs.' he roared. 'We follow and get back, or we face anger of Master. Come. We follow tracks.'

No one bothered to point out that Wenkle had been fighting just as hard as the others. They sheathed their weapons and made to follow and one or two of both orcs and hobgoblins grinned and said:

'Good fight though, wasn't it?' and the others agreed.

In the woods, Fero indicated that the others should go ahead.

'I'll obliterate our tracks as best I can.' he told them, handing his sack to Basalt. 'They're only a few minutes behind. I'd rather not fight them unless we must. The odds are still in their favour.'

He slipped back into the trees while the others pressed on back along the route they had followed on the way out. It was getting towards evening again, but they dared not stop. Grimmaldo took a turn with the fourth sack that Fero had been carrying, taking it from Basalt, but they all found it tiring work as the track they followed became narrow and overgrown in places. Soon Fero re-appeared.

'I've done the best I can.' he told them. 'I've tried to indicate that we went a different way. Usually, orcs and hobgoblins are none too bright, but these orcs, at least, seem more intelligent than most I've come across before. Bigger and braver too. It may not work with them.'

When after a half-hour they heard no sound of pursuit, Fero called a rest. They sank down onto the ground in relief. The dusk grew deeper with every second and they all felt very tired. Basalt asked Fero if he thought his trick had worked and their pursuers had gone a different way.

'Maybe, friend.' replied the dark man. 'Perhaps we should rest and have a little sleep if possible. I will keep watch.'

'No you won't.' Grimmaldo told him. 'We'll all take our turn. You need rest as much as the rest of us, and we need you.'

They agreed to take turns at watching. Fero and Basalt took the first watch. Asphodel watched with Grimmaldo in the second part of the night.

'I wonder where the others are?' she asked the mage as they listened to Basalt snoring. 'Do you think they are all right? What if this "Master" tortured them or had them executed as spies?'

Grimmaldo reached out and took her hand.

'Asphodel, I wish I knew.' he said. 'You've known them longer than I, but even so, I worry too.'

'It was only about a year and a half ago that we all met.' Asphodel went on. 'But I feel I've known them all my life. They, and you people here, are the best friends I've ever had. It's more like being with family than simple companions.'

Grimmaldo made a sound of agreement. A wolf howled in the distance and another answered to the left.

'Wolf!' smiled Grimmaldo. 'A rather romantic idea that, but I feel we are something like a wolf pack. Close knitted and looking out for each other.' He grinned at her. 'Also feral and dangerous too. Yes, we are!' he said at her surprised look. 'We have all killed to further the causes we believe in, and we're different from other people. We all have minds of our own and are independent, but nevertheless we work well together. Something of an enigma that.'

At this point, Asphodel seemed to realise that he still held her hand and she gently withdrew it. She stood and looked up at the sky through the branches at the gibbous moon, Lyndor, which hung over the treetops towards the west. Ullin had not yet risen. She wondered just where Carthinal and the others were now, and was he looking at the same moon? She sent a thought towards Lyndor.

'*Look down on him. Give him my love.*' But she did not voice her thought aloud. Instead she said, 'I pray Sylissa guards them well.'

'I, too. May Majora guard them.' replied her companion.

Chapter 11
Thadora

In a cave in the Mountains of Doom, far from any known tracks, a young girl sat looking at the enormous bulk of a huge blue dragon. She shivered, but not with cold. The cave was, in fact, quite warm. She had slept fitfully during the night, dreaming terrifying dreams involving dragons and carrion crawlers, orcs and hobgoblins.

How long had this dragon given her friends to find and return the eggs? How long had passed anyway? She realised the allotted time had not yet passed, or she would be dead. Or had the dragon–Jerriash was she called?–decided to keep her alive so she would be fresh meat when the young hatched? She shivered at the thought.

'Awake are you?' boomed Jerriash. She uncoiled herself from around the remaining four eggs, took hold of the girl's shirt in her teeth and picked her up. Thadora screamed. The dragon deposited her on the ground next to the eggs.

'Don't start that again,' the dragon scolded. 'It's not good for me, you or the hatchlings. They can hear in the eggs, you know.'

'Why should I care about them?' demanded the young thief. 'They'll probably grow up and eat the people around here.'

'Probably,' replied Jerriash looking at the eggs with a gentle expression in her large eyes, 'but *I* care about them, and I have *you* in my power. You are an insignificant little insect as far as I'm concerned. Apart from the nourishment in you, you're nothing at all. Your death will change nothing, except your friends and family will grieve, I expect, for a while. Then they'll put you to the back of their minds and carry on their lives without you.'

Thadora looked at the dragon, her shivering stopped as she became angry at this huge beast before her.

'You're trying to make me afraid,' she said. 'You needn't bleeding well try, I'm afraid already. Those eggs were stolen by bloody orcs. My friends'll 'ave to fight 'em. Supposin' they get killed? Then they can't come back and you'll kill me for food for your damn babies. Gods, even if they do come back, there's no telling you'll keep your promise. Bloody evil beasts like you are treacherous.'

Jerriash smiled in a dragonish way, showing huge teeth like the tusks of the beasts called elephants. Thadora had heard of them, but privately wondered if they really existed.

'What do you mean, "evil beast"?' she queried. 'And, by the way, a young girl like you should not be using such language!'

'You sound like my father!' retorted Thadora. 'An' it's well know you're evil.'

'By whom, might I ask?' the dragon replied. 'And I don't like to be called a "beast"'

Thadora thought. 'Everyone always says dragons are evil. I've never 'eard anyone say anythin' else. The term "beast" is used in an insultin' way, I suppose. Obviously you're an intelligent creature.'

'Much more than you are, my dear,' replied the dragon. 'Yes, very much more than you, or any of your friends out searching for my eggs.'

'I bet you're not bleedin' cleverer than me friend Carthinal though. 'E's the cleverest person I know.'

'Which of them is Carthinal?'

'Oh, 'e's not with us. We was separated somewhere t'wards Frelli. I'm not sure exactly where we was.' She paused for a second, and looked thoughtful. 'For that matter, I'm not at all sure where we are now, either.'

'Since I do not know this "Carthinal" of whom you speak, and cannot meet him as he is not with you, the point seems rather academic. However, I very much doubt if he's as clever as any dragon. No humanoid is.

'Now let's consider "evil." Why do people say we dragons are evil?'

Thadora thought for a moment, then said, 'I s'pose because you kill and bloody well eat 'em an' steal their animals leavin' them without food.' replied the girl.

The dragon thought for a moment then said, 'What would a man, or woman for that matter, do if a rogue wolf had taken to attacking and killing not only their food supplies but also people too?'

'I guess they'd get up a huntin' party an' go in search o' the buggerin' beast an' kill it.'

'So, it's fine if people do so but not if we do the same?'

Thadora wrinkled her brow. 'What do you mean?' she asked.

'Well, if we hunt down people because they are killing our young, stealing our eggs and taking our food in their hunting of the game in the mountains, or wherever dragonkind lives, that makes us evil, but not when you do the same?'

The girl did not answer, having no reply to give. She had to think about it for a while.

'Ha!' said Jerriash. 'Got you there, little one.'

'I just need time to think.' muttered the "little one". 'It's not the bleedin' same, I know it, but I need to think about it some.'

Just then, the egg against which Thadora had been leaning rocked violently. She jumped to her feet.

'I'm sorry, I'm sorry.' she exclaimed to Jerriash. 'I hope I've not hurt it.'

Jerriash looked at her hard.

'No.' she replied. 'The membrane outside the eggs is very tough for all it feels soft. You cannot harm it by leaning on it. I think that egg is about to hatch.'

The dragon began to croon to the young dragon in the egg, encouraging its struggles. The sound seemed to soothe the girl and she thought it sounded as though words hid somewhere in the sound, but Thadora could not make any out.

'*Probably Dragonish,*' she thought.

Thadora watched in fascination as the young dragon first broke through the tough membrane surrounding the egg and began to struggle out. Suddenly, Jerriash pushed her back with her tail.

'Get behind me.' she told the girl impatiently. 'Stay clear of the hatchling. Don't let him see you.'

Thadora peeped over the tail of the dragon at the baby now nearly out of its egg.

'Why? Will it eat me?'

'No! That wouldn't matter.' said Jeriash, offhand-edly. 'No, he will imprint on you if he sees you first.'

'What d'you mean, "imprint?"'

The mother looked at her offspring finally clearing the egg and turning to eat the remains.

'Ah! A little male. Just as I thought from that one.' she exclaimed and began to lick the remains of the egg from him. 'He'll be called Grennish I think.'

The newly named Grennish looked at his mother and crooned to her in a piping little voice. Jerriash answered in her deep musical voice. She turned to look at Thadora and then replied to her previous question.

'My father, who came from a land far to the east, once told me of a human who did some experiments. Apparently, according to my father, the man, whom I think was called Radcon Renzlor, took some eggs, I think they were either wyvern or dragonet, but some relative of we dragons anyway, and hatched them. When they hatched, he ensured that he was the first thing they saw. The youngsters decided he was their mother and followed him around just as they would have done with her. That is what I meant by "imprinting".'

'You mean that if he'd seen me first, before you, Grennish would 'ave thought I were 'is mother and followed me everywhere? Cool!'

'Yes, exactly that.' replied Jerriash. 'Don't think of trying it with any of the others or I'll eat you myself!' she warned, seeing a gleam come into Thadora's eyes.

'Wouldn't dream of it!' said the girl innocently.

During the course of that day, another egg hatched. A little female, this time After she hatched and Prannesh had been in several times to admire his youngsters and bring some small creatures for them to eat, Jerriash curled around the hatchlings and again faced Thadora.

The huge creature was as gentle as a pussycat with her babies, the girl thought, and began to amend her thoughts about the evil of dragons. Maybe they were not evil. Maybe they were not the creatures of the goddess, Allandrina, god of persuasion deception, as she had been taught. Thinking these thoughts, she drifted off to sleep.

Chapter 12
Double-cross

The edge of the sun's disc had just begun to appear over the tops of the mountains as the group, carrying the bags containing the eggs reached the bank of the stream. They had still not seen or heard anything of the pursuit, but slid down the bank and into the water with alacrity.

Again all of them gasped at the coldness of the water. This stream must have its source under the mountains not too far away from the dragons' lair to still be as cold as this in Zoldar. It would soon be Candar and the Solstice, thought Asphodel.

Summer began with the solstice celebrations on Candar 1. The people on the world of Vimar dedicated that month to Candello, the god of weather and the sea, fishermen and farmers in particular, celebrated it, both relying on the vagaries of the weather for success.

Hefting the bags high above the water to prevent the eggs from getting wet and cold and harming the little dragons growing inside, the four, and Bramble, struggled along the stream until they reached the place where they had entered the previous day.

Asphodel glanced at the sky again to see how long they had left before the time the dragon had given them ran out. The sun had past its zenith long ago, but they did not have much further to go. They would be back well before dusk and then Thadora would be safe. Asphodel hoped her optimism was correct and the dragons would honour their part of the bargain.

Sure enough, they soon emerged onto the open place before the cave and gratefully put the bags down.

'Do we call or wait?' asked Grimmaldo. 'I don't know anything about the etiquette of dealing with dragons.'

'Not many do!' mumbled Basalt. 'Most people end up dead and cannot pass word on.'

'A fine cheerful soul you are.' replied the mage. 'And not much help either. Well, do we call, or what?'

'I think we'd better let them know we're back. The female, Jerriash, will want the eggs as soon as possible to prevent any damage.'

Just then, in a rush of wind as Pranesh landed in front of them.

'So you've come back then, and with the eggs I see. I'll just go and tell Jerriash and then come and tell you what she wants you to do with them.'

With that, he disappeared into the cave. With his disappearance, all four, five if one included Bramble, let out their breaths. They had not realised they held it, but the dragon fear had held them. After a few minutes, the blue dragon returned.

'Come and bring the eggs. The other eggs have hatched and Jerriash says she cannot leave just yet. These will be a day, maybe two, later as they've probably slowed development being taken out into the cooler air. I hope it doesn't mean they'll be much smaller and weaker.'

They followed Pranesh into the cave and deposited the eggs in the centre. Jerriash crooned over them and wrapped her tail around them, holding them into her body for warmth. The others looked round.

'Where's Thadora?' demanded Basalt. 'You promised to let her go when we'd brought you the eggs.'

'Over there, feeding those who've hatched.' replied Jerriash, inclining her head towards the far end of the cave. 'She's very good with them, and they seem to like her. Maybe I'll keep her to help rather than feed her to them.'

'What do you mean, feed her to them?' Basalt put his hand on the hilt of his battle-axe. 'You promised to let her go if we returned the eggs before dusk today. It's not yet dusk, so let us have her and be on our way.'

The dragon laughed softly.

'You didn't really believe that did you?' she asked the dwarf. 'No, I've got what I wanted. My eggs back safely. Now I've also got four, no five with the dog, extra "meat on the hoof", so to speak. No, none of you are going anywhere, so sit down near your friend and sleep. The youngsters don't need any more food today.'

They walked over to where Thadora sat scratching a hatchling behind its ear. The youngster crooned with pleasure.

'Isn't she sweet?' the young thief asked. 'Her name's Yellerinish. I think she's my favourite although that darker blue is also cute. He's called Grennish and he hatched first.'

The girl seemed to have got over the dragon fear. She sat down, back against the wall and shooed the four youngsters away. Her friends sank down next to her, Bramble whining in pleasure at seeing her again. She stroked his black head.

'Thadora,' Asphodel spoke gently to the girl. 'It seems the dragons are not going to keep their part of the bargain. They mean to keep us prisoner here to be "food on the hoof" as Jerriash put it. They mean to feed us to their hatchlings regardless of the fact that we've kept our side of the bargain.'

Thadora looked at her in horror.

'I can't believe that.' she said. 'Jerriash and I have had some long talks and I find it hard to imagine she's as evil as they say dragons are. She persuaded me that dragons are a bit like the yeti, killing only as a kind of self-defence.

'She said it was like a man going out to kill a wolf who had killed his child. The man wouldn't be evil, would he? I was really confused at the time, but have decided that it isn't evil to kill those who menace your family and livelihood.'

Asphodel looked at the girl speculatively.

'Remember, Thadda, that dragons are Allandrina's creatures. She's the goddess of deceit and persuasion and is evil personified. Her creatures, whether human, elf, dwarf or otherwise are gifted with the powers to deceive. They have smooth and persuasive tongues. Trust me, girl. Dragons are evil.'

'What's evil about protecting your own?' demanded Thadora. 'People do it all the time. Anyway, I can't believe those little ones are evil!' She sounded a little sulky.

Asphodel gave a sigh.

'Is going back on your word an honourable thing to do?' the vicar said.

'This isn't the time for a debate on philosophy,' interrupted Grimmaldo. 'We're in a pretty pickle and need to decide how to get out of it, so shut up and think.'

The remark was so out of character that the pair immediately obeyed and turned to look at him.

He blinked and said, 'Don't look at me like that! I've no ideas. We can't fight these beasts, but we must get away if we don't want to end up inside them.'

'A fat lot of help you are.' grumbled Basalt. 'It's no use telling us what we can't do. We all know that. What we need to know is what we *can* do.'

'Will you *all* be quiet.' said Fero, looking stern. 'I'm trying to think! Anyone with any positive ideas at all may say what they are, but negative thoughts keep to yourselves please.'

They all fell silent and after a few minutes, Thadora spoke again.

'I don't want to bleedin' die here.' she said in a small voice. 'I can't believe the dragons would go back on their word. I had such an interesting conversation with Jerriash about evil and what it is.'

Fero's eyes flashed.

'Will you all be quiet!'

He almost shouted, but then quickly looked at the dragons. They seemed not to have heard him. Another egg rocked back and forth, on the verge of hatching, and both adult dragons crooned at it in encouragement. Fero frowned at his own impatience.

'I'm sorry for getting annoyed.' he told them. 'I don't want to end up as dragon fodder any more than the rest of you, but I'm afraid I can't think of any way out of this one. We'll have to play it by ear and take any chance we can get. Just hold yourselves ready for my word if the slightest opportunity presents itself.'

Five people and one dog leaned back against the wall of the cave and tried to sleep. Sleep, however did not come easily in their present predicament and they passed a long, slow night. Partly, Thadora said afterwards, she felt glad the night seemed to go so slowly as it meant that their lives seemed to last that much longer, but part of her wanted it to go quickly to get the seemingly inevitable out of the way. They lost track of the time completely.

Eventually the baby dragons began to stir and to make little noises. A third hatched in the night and she whimpered. Pranesh and Jerriash woke up and soothed her. They spoke to each other in that crooning language and Pranesh raised his head to look at their prisoners.

'The babies are hungry,' he said. 'I think the young red-head would make a good breakfast for them, Jerriash.'

As Thadora tried to sink into the wall, Jerriash replied, 'I did think of keeping her as a pet for the babies as she's so good with them, but as you see fit, Pranesh. Kill her if you wish. She will be a nice tender first meal for Haammish.' With that, she began to groom the newest hatchling.

Pranesh raised his head and prepared to snap his jaws over where Thadora sat, eyes squeezed shut, trying not to cry. Just as he was about to deliver his killing blow, a small blue shape, flapping its wings leaped in his way. Yellerinish. She did not want her friend made into food.

Unfortunately Pranesh could not pull his stroke in time and as he bit down, he took off the hatchling's head. Blood spurted from the severed arteries showering people and dragons alike. Then all hell broke loose. The baby dragons all leaped onto Yellerinish's remains and began to tear her to pieces. Fighting broke out which the two adult dragons did nothing to stop. They both stood watching as more blood flowed. Fero whispered to the others who watched in horrified silence.

'Come! This may be our only chance. Quickly whilst they're occupied. But be as quiet as you can.' He gave Basalt a hard look, which the dwarf returned in kind. Then all five companions crept slowly towards the exit, Fero's hand on the scruff of Bramble's neck to keep the dog from growling.

As soon as they reached the daylight, they ran as quickly as they could towards the path through the woods. Suddenly they heard sounds approaching. Ducking into the nearest cover the five waited. Two hobgoblins, one being Wankl, and four orcs entered the clearing before the dragons' lair. They paused and looked around. One of the orcs pointed to the cave and said something Fero could not hear. Wankl replied.

Before Fero, who spoke some hobgoblin, had chance to tell the others what he said, there came the rush of wings as Pranesh hurtled out of the cave.

'Come back, thieves.' he called. 'You cannot escape. We will find you.'

Immediately the hobgoblins and orcs threw themselves onto the ground and began to wriggle backwards towards where Asphodel and the others lay hidden. At that moment, Jerriash came out of the cave, a blue tail disappearing down her throat.

'Who was that?' queried her mate.

'Haammish.' she replied. 'He was too weak to stand up for himself. The others were all full, and it seemed a pity to waste good meat.'

'How many left?' asked the male dragon.

'Three dead, including Haammish. Not too bad. And they didn't break any of the unhatched eggs either.'

'Mmmm!' replied the other dragon. 'Best the weaklings go early. What was that?' He looked towards the side of the clearing, opposite to where the friends had gone. 'I think breakfast's waiting in those bushes. I look forward to killing our friends. The bloodier the better.'

'I think the little ones will sleep for a long while after their fight and all that blood's made me want to kill something too, dear. Let's go get them.'

Unfortunately for the orcs, what Pranesh had heard one of them shifting his position. When they realised the dragons had decided to come after them, they rose and fled along the path they had arrived by. The dragons, now full of bloodlust, forgot about the others and gave chase to the newcomers, not realising they were, in fact, chasing the real egg thieves.

'We should go this way I think.' Grimmaldo indicated a narrow pathway leading away from the stream and in the opposite direction from the path the orcs and hobgoblins had taken.

It looked little more than an animal trail, but no one was about to argue and so, in single file, they walked carefully away from the dragons' lair, all the time hearing the crack of lightning and screams of the dying, and hardly daring to breathe themselves.

When they thought they had covered enough ground to put them sufficiently far from the dragons, and all the sounds of violent death had faded, the five friends stopped to catch their breath.

Fero went back for a short distance to try to obliterate any signs of their passage and to see if the dragons had followed them. When he returned, he told them that he saw no signs, but since the dragons could fly and he could not, he could not say if the creatures would be able to see any signs of their passage from above.

Asphodel assured him they knew he had done the best he could and that he should rest and get his breath back.

They had no idea where they were, having taken little notice of where they went, simply wanting to put as much distance as possible between themselves and the rampaging dragons'

After giving Fero fifteen minutes rest, which he claimed was sufficient, the little group continued following the track in what they hoped was away from the dragons' lair. The sky had become overcast, and with the tree cover, they found it difficult to see the position of the sun. Shortly, light drizzle began to fall.

'Just our luck!' exclaimed Thadora. 'Now we get wet as well as running for our lives.'

'Again!' Basalt replied. 'Running for our lives again while getting wet.'

'We do seem to be doing rather a lot of it, don't we?' This came from Grimmaldo. 'Is that all Wolf does? Do we ever get to sit in one place for more than a few minutes together?'

'We manage a few hours each night, don't we?' responded Basalt.

Grimmaldo laughed.

'Yes, we do, then we're off running again. I've forgotten what a bed feels like.'

'What's a bed?' asked Asphodel, smiling.

Just then, Fero stood up.

'We'd better be off again, though. If you don't want to move for a day or two, you're welcome to stay here, Grimmaldo. I'm sure the dragons will find a permanent place for you—in their stomachs, or that of their hatchlings!'

'I think I'll come with you,' grinned the young man. 'Sitting in one spot too long gets very boring and I need to keep fit. I'll tag along.'

The others laughed. Even Bramble looked as though he shared the joke, looking at Grimmaldo with his mouth open, tongue lolling.

They slowly got to their feet and picked up their packs, which they'd managed to grab as they fled, and followed Fero along the game path.

The path did indeed head away from the dragons' cave. It twisted and turned, continuing in a generally downward direction, but sometimes it turned back on itself. When this happened, Asphodel felt her heart begin to pound as she thought they would end up just below the cave, but the track soon turned again and once more headed away from the dragons' lair.

After one of the backtracks, she thought she heard the sounds of crunching bones and chewing, but it quickly faded and none of the others made any comments about hearing anything. She made herself believe she had imagined it, but she knew her elven hearing was superior to that of the others.

Chapter 13
Farm

After hours of travelling, the trees came to an abrupt end. Everyone in the little group felt damp, although under the trees. The light rain seeped down through the canopy and ran down their necks. Water clung to skin, even inside their boots and lank hair hung down dripping water into eyes.

Asphodel blinked to try to clear her vision. When she did, she found herself looking down at a valley surrounded by high mountains. A river ran along the bottom, and she could see snow fields still lying on patches on the heights.

Flowers bloomed everywhere, of many types. She could identify some, but many she had never seen before. Gentians and saxifrage, edelweiss and mountain bluebells, flowered in every space. Reds, pinks, yellows, blues and whites. Every colour imaginable.

As she drank in the sight, the rain stopped and the sun broke through a gap in the clouds, its beam of light slanting down like a floodlight to pick out a small hut in the direction of the river, just as though pointing it out to them. With one accord, they moved quickly towards it.

When they got to the hut, they found a small one-roomed stone building. It looked abandoned. The door hung on one hinge, swinging in a slight breeze and the shutters had gone, but it had a sound roof and walls. The remains of a garden surrounded the house, and Asphodel spotted some carrot leaves as well as a variety of herbs. She said she would investigate.

Dust covered every surface in the sole room, but it contained a wooden table and four rickety chairs. A stove stood to one side, its chimney a metal tube poking through the roof, with a stack of wood standing by the side of it. Grimmaldo knelt down and peered into the stove.

'There's a chance the chimney's blocked.' he told the others.

He stuck his head right into the stove and craned his neck trying to see up the chimney, but to no avail.

'I can't tell.' he said. 'It's too dark. I could form a small flame and send it up, but if there's something dry there, it may catch alight.'

'Try anyway.' muttered Basalt. 'I, for one, need to get dry. It may be nearly Candar, but I feel cold as Bramardar being so wet.'

Grimmaldo looked at Fero for confirmation. Somehow he had become the leader of this half of Wolf, although he did not quite know how. The tall ranger smiled, and Thadora nearly exploded in laughter.

'All right, Grimmaldo. Try it. Then try getting some water from the river and washing your face.'

Fero started to laugh, as did the others. Grimmaldo had black smudges on his face from the inside of the stove. He scrubbed his face with his hands, making the situation worse.

Thadora's sides and stomach ached from laughing. The now black faced mage grinned, his teeth gleaming white in contrast and he knelt back down and began to mumble words of magic and weave the mana to gather the energy to create a small flame. In a few minutes, his head re-appeared and he said he thought he had cleared the chimney and he would light the stove.

Soon a bright fire burned in the fireplace and their clothes steamed in front of it, the little group sat round chatting.

They had changed into the clothes the Walchin had made for them during their sojourn in their caves. The sun had not yet set and there was plenty of daylight left for Asphodel to find any edible food in the garden, which she proceeded to do. Fero said he would go out to hunt and Thadora and Basalt offered to go too. Fero accepted the offer of the young thief, but refused the dwarf's offer as he said Basalt could not be quiet enough.

Grimmaldo drew some water from a well Asphodel found in the garden and then he began to cut up vegetables, with some help from Basalt. Asphodel had found some flavouring herbs growing just outside the door and they put some into a pot they found, along with the vegetables, and placed it with some water next to the fire in readiness for Fero and Thadora to return with some meat.

After about an hour and a half, the two hunters returned carrying a small deer. A roe deer, Fero said. He expertly dressed it and in next to no time a haunch simmered in the pot along with the vegetables and herbs.

Fero cut up the rest of the carcass and hung some strips of meat near the fire to dry and placed some more in the smoke from the fire to smoke as a change. The liver and kidneys he put to one side to eat fried, and then he gave some of the lung to Bramble. The dog wolfed it down. He felt very hungry, not having eaten during their stay in the dragons' lair. He would have pounced on one of the dead or injured hatchlings if he had dared, but the dragon-fear affected him too and he had cowered away in a corner.

Soon the smell of cooking filled the small room and also the sound of rumbling stomachs. As darkness fell, Asphodel announced the meat to be cooked and the others cheered loudly.

After lighting some rush torches, they sat round the table on the rickety chairs and tucked in to the venison and vegetables. Basalt discovered some preserved fruits in a small cupboard in the hut and this they had for dessert. Everyone declared it as good as any banquet they had ever had. They spread blankets on the floor, doused the lights and fire, and prepared to sleep.

The next morning dawned bright and clear. Grimmaldo woke first and he brought water in from the well, and lit the fire in the stove to heat it for washing. By the time the others all woke up, he had washed and begun to prepare some of the left over venison for breakfast.

'About time too!' he exclaimed as the others slowly opened their eyes when they smelled the warming meat. 'You've missed the best part of the day lying abed. The dawn was beautiful over the mountains and the birds are singing and the butterflies fluttering by! It has the making of a warm and sunny day.' He nodded towards the stove. 'There's hot water for washing there and by the time you're all ready, so will breakfast be.'

Even after the good meal the previous evening, Thadora felt hungry and she quickly washed, dressed, and sat down at the table before the others had hardly got out of their blankets.

Asphodel took out a brush and brushed her black hair, which had groan long again after the Daughters of Sylissa had cut it nearly all off. The Great Father of the Temple in Hambara had condemned her to a life with that order as a punishment for disobedience. The Most High of the Church of Sylissa had withdrawn healing from all who he deemed evil. A man had come to the Temple in Hambara for healing, but as an assassin, he was one of those who had been declared evil.

Asphodel felt this went against the vows she swore when she first took holy orders and she had healed him in spite of the order. For this transgression, the Great Father, leader of the temple of Sylissa in Hambara, told her that she would remain as one of the Daughters for the rest of her life.

The Daughters of Sylissa was an order of priestesses who had vowed to live a life of poverty and hardship, forgoing speech except for one hour after the evening meal and when they healed the people who came to the infirmary.

While Asphodel had great respect for the women of the order, she had not felt the calling to become one of them and she walked out of the church, thus estranging herself from the Hambara Temple. This act condemned her to the life of a wandering healer, never being able to rise above the level of curate.

While she stayed with the Daughters, they had cut her long, lustrous black hair. The Daughters all cut their hair as they said long hair made them vain, and they deplored vanity. They also slept on wooden cots with little in the way of mattresses, ate poorly cooked food and washed in cold water. They never took baths. They thought this too much of a luxury.

Asphodel, while respecting those who had a calling for that life, knew in her heart she could not live like that. She believed the goddess did not want her to live such a life, cut off from the world, except for the healing.

Her character was not that of an obedient daughter; she questioned far too much. She smiled as she combed her hair and tied it back. Her temperament suited this life, with all its dangers, much more than a life with the Daughters, and even though the Great Father had intimated she would never progress beyond curate, she felt her strength grow and she knew deep within herself that mortals could not to designate rank. That gift lay in the hands of the gods and she knew herself the equal of any minister, the next level in the hierarchy of the priesthood, after vicar.

Asphodel looked at the open door and went outside to breathe the fresh mountain air. The cottage lay quite high up, but the sun promised a warm day. She her gaze fell on the surrounding mountains and she heaved a sigh. Then she heard a movement beside her and looked round. Grimmaldo had come outside as well. He followed her gaze.

'Yes, it's beautiful here.' he said, as though she had spoken.

She looked up at him.

'I could be happy living here.' she replied. 'I'd clear the garden of weeds and grow all my own vegetables and herbs. Maybe plant a fruit tree or two.'

Grimmaldo smiled down at her.

'A goat or two for milk as well, and maybe a pig. Useful animals, pigs.'

'And spend all summer gazing at the view. I'd learn to make butter and cheese, and to spin and weave too. No need of a flower garden with all these beautiful wild flowers around, and just look at the butterflies!'

'I wonder why the people left? It seems idyllic.'

'Are you two going to stand there all day looking at the view?' The voice that interrupted their musings was Basalt. 'We're ready to move on now. We do have somewhere to go you know!'

Grimmaldo suddenly thought of something.

'Wait, Bas, Fero! I've just thought. We may still be wanted out there. There's a village or something down the valley. You can just make it out.' He pointed to where some buildings could just be made out next to the river. 'Suppose our descriptions have been passed to that village and others. We're not exactly inconspicuous—a black-haired elf, a Grosmerian mage, a dwarf, a young Grosmerian redhead and a tall, dark foreigner. Not exactly a common combination to be wandering the countryside.

'I think we should make a few plans before we go from here. What do we do if we should be recognised, for example, and what, if anything, can we do to prevent recognition?'

'He's right, Fero!' Asphodel agreed with the young mage. 'We shouldn't be rushing off.'

Therefore, they all sat down in the sunshine to make some plans.

Chapter 14
Family

'Keep still, Thadora.' scolded Asphodel. 'I'm going a quickly as I can.'

She rinsed the girl's hair with a concoction she had made from some walnuts she found on a tree in the garden. It would, she said, turn it brown, or at the least, a little less red. Grimmaldo cut Thadora's hair with his dagger to a rough crop like that she had worn when they first knew her.

When she ran away from Hambara to catch up with the rest of Wolf, she had posed as a boy. She did not object to becoming a boy again, but did not like having her hair dyed, especially by Asphodel's smelly concoction.

The little band spent a lot of time discussing what they should do to disguise themselves, and eventually decided to become a small family, leaving their farm because of persecution by a pair of dragons higher up in the mountains. Their current abode, an abandoned farm, gave Thadora the idea.

Thadora, they decided, should pose as Grimmaldo's younger brother and Asphodel, his wife. A dwarf and a tall dark foreigner gave them a bigger problem. They found some clothes, or rather Thadora did when she rummaged around in the house. Good serviceable peasant clothes, they would be ideal for their purpose.

Asphodel, as a cleric of Sylissa wore a tabard, showing the goddess's holy symbol over her leather breastplate. As it would not be appropriate for a peasant woman, she folded it neatly and stowed it, along with her armour, in a cart Fero found in an outbuilding.

When she tried on the skirt and blouse, Thadora and Grimmaldo laughed. The clothes drowned her slight figure.

'May I borrow your dagger, please, Grimmaldo,' she asked the mage.

Puzzled, he handed it to her and watched as he split a seam in the skirt. Then wrapping it round her waist one and a half times she fastened it with a serviceable belt.

'Tuck the blouse into the skirt, Asphodel,' suggested Grimmaldo, 'and pull it down as low as you can.'

The elf did as he suggested.

'That's better. Doesn't look too bad. I don't suppose peasant women wear perfectly fitting clothes, anyway,' Grimmaldo told her.

'This blouse is very low-cut, don't you think?' Asphodel said, peering down at herself. 'I think I should look for something a bit more decent.'

Grimmaldo looked her up and down.

'You looked just fine to me,' he said, grinning, 'and if that's what the peasants around here wear, you shouldn't try to look too different or someone will notice.'

;And we don't want that, do we¿Basalt put in. 'We don't want to draw attention to ourselves.'

Asphodel looked down at the blouse once more.

'And showing so much flesh won't draw attention?' she queried.

'Not the wrong sort, though,' Grimmaldo said.

'That's alright for you to say. It won't be you getting the stares.'

'But not the wrong sort of stares,' Grimmaldo responded. 'Not stares of suspicion.'

Asphodel eventually gave in, seeing the sense in what the others said.

Then Fero told Thadora to remove her armour, as a peasant boy would not be wearing it.

'What will happen if we're attacked?' she asked him. 'I'll need some protection.'

'We're more likely to be attacked if you wear it,' Fero told her. 'A peasant in armour will arouse suspicion. Did you have armour in the Warren?;

She shook her head.

'I didn't think so,' he responded. 'You managed well enough there. I can't believe you didn't get into any fights then. If there's a fight, use your skill and wits like you did in the Warren.'

The girl could not argue any more and so, with a frown on her face and a pout on her lips, she did as he asked. As she already wore trousers and shirt she did not have to try anything else.

'Come here, Bas!' called Asphodel. They had made no decisions as to how they could disguise Basalt and Fero. The dwarf strode over to where she stood next to the wagon.

'Sit on the driver's seat,' she told him. When he had obeyed, she wrapped a blanket around him, then stood back and thought.

'Hmm,' she said, scratching her head. Then she said, 'Bas, take your boots off and give them to me.'

'What?' asked the dwarf. 'My boots did you say?'

'You heard.' she replied. 'Get on with it.'

The dwarf muttered under his breath. Something about "women and their strange ideas," but he removed his boots and passed them to the elf. She then re-arranged the blanket and placed his boots on the footboard just poking out from under the it. She stood back again.

'Almost there, but your hair and beard are wrong. They're the wrong colour.'

Basalt nearly had apoplexy at the thought that Asphodel might get to grips with his hair and beard.

'You're not touching my beard!' he spluttered. 'Nor my hair either! I'd rather die first.'

'You might if you don't look a little more like my grandfather!' Grimmaldo told him as he came out of the house carrying a pail of ashes from the stove. 'Now keep still while I rub some of this in to make it a bit greyer.'

That done, they all looked at Basalt, still sitting on the wagon, boots poking out from beneath the blanket where a normal human's feet would be. All declared it would pass unless someone decided to look too closely.

'People tend t' see what they expect t' see.' Thadora told them. 'I learned that in th' bloody Warren as a thief. You c'n 'ide in full sight if you seem t' be what people think should be there. Keeping bleedin' still 'elps too, as does wearin' sommat nondescript. A grey blanket on an old man is not too out o' place. Just try t' look like a bloody, old man and not an angry, bleedin' dwarf!'

Basalt sighed. The girl made sense. He slumped in his seat and cast his eyes down, trying to make them unfocussed.

'That's it, Bas!' exclaimed the girl. 'You look just like an bleedin' old man.'

The dwarf gave her a hard stare.

'Now Fero.' Asphodel turned to the ranger. 'Your height is as much, if not more, of a problem as your dark skin. I propose that you be Grimmaldo's mother.'

The tall ranger spluttered.

'Grimmaldo's *mother?*' he exclaimed. 'How on the face of Vimar am I to pass as a woman, let alone his *mother*! Even if I were small enough, try explaining why our skin's so different.'

Asphodel looked at him patiently.

'You will be his *sick* mother. You will be lying in the back of the wagon, covered in blankets. You can pull your feet up, or we can cover them with our packs and some provisions. Either way your height won't be noticeable, and if you're covered, your skin won't be noticed either. You only need to worry if we see anyone though. When there's no one around you'll be able to emerge.'

She thought she heard him mutter something like *"So kind of you to allow me to come out."* but she made no comment beyond a look.

By the time the disguises had all been decided on, much of the day had gone. They decided to rest at the cottage for a further night rather than setting off late in the day.

During the evening they discussed a few other problems.

'What happens if we're stopped?' asked Thadora. 'Only Asphodel can speak their damned language. What happens if someone wants to talk with one of the rest of us?'

Grimmaldo came up with an idea.

' "Thad" can be a painfully shy boy who hates speaking to strangers,' he suggested. 'He's been brought up far from contact with other people and is not used to them.'

Basalt suggested a solution his problem. 'I'm going to be an old man,' he said. 'Old people are often deaf. I'll be stone deaf and unable to hear anything. I can't answer questions if I can't hear, can I?'

' "Mother" won't be a bleedin' problem 'cos she's too sick to talk to anyone.' said Thadora, 'but what about my brother Grimmaldo? He should be able to damned well talk Erian. And most bloody folk would expect him, as Asphodel's husband, and a supposed Erian, to speak. Probably rather than her.'

That silenced the discussion while they all thought.

'Got it,' Grimmaldo exclaimed, banging his fist on the table. 'I'm a man of few words, who says as little as possible. A bit like Davrael, you know. He doesn't say much, leaving most of the talking to Kimi. I can give the occasional grunt if required, but I'm generally content to allow my wife to speak. I hope that'll be enough to put off anyone,' he continued. 'I'd be in real difficulty if asked a direct question.'

Asphodel thought for a moment before saying, 'You should learn a couple of sentences to mutter if necessary. Mutter is important because we don't want your accent to give the game away.'

Then she started teaching him a few sentences in Erian, just in case he needed them. She taught him to say "Good Day." That took a while. Asphodel insisted he repeat it often to improve the accent. Then she taught him, "My wife is better with words than I am," after which she sent up a quick prayer to any gods who may be listening that that would suffice.

Then another problem arose. Thadora looked out of the cottage window and said, 'Who is bloody well going to pull that cart?'

Fero looked at her, puzzled. 'We'll all take turns, of course.'

'Well I'm not bleeding well pulling no cart. We need a horse or an ox or something. If we pull it ourselves it'll take forever. We'll need to keep stoppin' for rests all the time. We might get back to Grosmer in time for Bramadar and the winter solstice.'

'She's right, you know,' Basalt said. 'We'd get on much better with a draught animal of some kind.'

Fero reluctantly agreed. He wanted to leave as soon as possible. He suggested one of them go to the village they could see from the cottage and see if they could find someone willing to sell them an animal.

Asphodel would, of course, have to go as she could speak the language. Thadora agreed to accompany her, and so the pair set off.

They walked along a track until it came to a wider road, then turned towards the village. Soon, the road down which they walked entered a narrow street with houses on each side. It forked after about fifty paces and they could see a hostelry at the end of the left-hand fork.

They approached the hostelry, which had a sign hanging outside saying "The Goatherd and Goat", and pushed open the door. Inside, they found a long, clean room with sparkling tankards hanging up from hooks on the ceiling. Herbs and straw covered the floor and a number of tables stood scattered around the room. At the far end of the room stretched a long bar, and a fireplace stood on one of the long sides No fire burned there, owing to the heat of the day, but someone had put a vase of wild flowers in it. The colours made it look cheerful and inviting.

At this time of day, no one drank in the tavern, all being at work. Then, while Asphodel and Thadora waited, a girl bustled in from a door behind the bar, picked something up, gave a bold, coquettish smile to "Thad" and bustled out again.

From a door behind the bar a large woman emerged. She wore a blue dress and white apron, and began to needlessly polish the already shiny surface of the bar. She smiled a welcome at them and spoke.

'Bremer, gar y to gom hiloner?'

'Kren to.' replied Asphodel. 'Gare me hanor do farends on ager, of in prise to?'

The woman took down two of the sparkling tankards and poured some ale into them. Thadora tried to look shy as she took hers, and took a swallow. The woman turned again to Asphodel and said something, glancing at the girl.

Thadora got the impression the landlady, she assumed she was the landlady, asked Asphodel about her. She looked down and scuffed her feet as she had seen boys do when under too much scrutiny. Indeed, she did not find acting as a boy difficult. Less so than acting as a girl.

She had been running wild in the Warren, Hambara's poor quarter, all her life, and passing as a boy for four years, only acting as a young lady for just under one year. The conversation went on and so Thadora became bored. She wandered over to the fireplace and looked at the flowers. She did not recognise most of what the landlady had put in the vase. She drank her ale, looking around her in what she hoped was a shy way. Yes, she had acted as a boy before, but not a shy one. Shyness had never been one of her traits. Therefore tried to keep out of the way as much as possible, pretending to be listening to what sounded like so much gobbledegook to her.

Soon, the landlady pointed to the south. Asphodel smiled and thanked her, then beckoned to

"Thad" to come with her, punctuating her gestures with strange sounding words. As soon as they left the inn, Thadora spoke.

'What did she say? Is there anyone who can sell us a horse or ox?'

'Shh!' whispered Asphodel. 'Don't say anything. Someone may hear you speaking Grosmerian.' She said something louder in Erian that Thadora did not understand and pulled the girl back to the main street and along it to the south until they left the village.

Asphodel's eyes blazed as she berated Thadora, almost dragging her along the road.

'You risk blowing the disguise if you don't stick to it all the time whilst we are in places where we might be heard. Anyone could be listening round a corner, or may hear through an open window. Don't forget that.'

'Yeh! All bleedin' right. Stay cool.' replied the girl.

'It wouldn't be very "cool" to get us caught again, would it?' Asphodel could not be pacified.

Thadora pouted. Asphodel so rarely lost her temper she did not know how to react. She decided the tension of the situation had got to Asphodel and wisely, for once, kept quiet.

'Now, as to what we said,' went on the cleric. 'After the greetings, I introduced us. I told Amari (that was her name she said) that we're a family driven from our lands in a distant valley by a pair of blue dragons. That was what we decided, and I told her, again as we decided, that you're my brother-in-law, only fourteen, and very shy, having never had much to do with people, living as we did, in a remote place.

'I said my mother-in-law, your mother, had been taken ill and as we'd found an abandoned farm, she and your grandfather are resting there. My husband, I told her, had stayed there to give any protection needed, and you and I came to the village to enquire if anyone had a horse or ox they would sell us to pull an old wagon we found in the farm buildings.

'Your "mother" is too sick to walk and your "grandfather" is also feeling the effects of our long journey.' She paused.

'I know all that, Asphodel.' the girl replied. 'Just tell me what she came up with and where we're going now!'

'I thought you wanted to know what we said?' Asphodel said, rather acerbically, Thadora thought.

'Only what I don't know all ready.'

Asphodel looked at her and in spite of herself, she smiled.

'All right. She told me there's a farm about half a league to the south, along this road, where the farmer, a young single man apparently, had been talking recently of selling up and going to join the army. "To fight those evil Grosmerians" she said. Her words, not mine!' Asphodel added, seeing Thadora bristle. 'He may be willing to sell us a draught animal. Amari said if he's really going to leave, he'll need to sell all his animals. It's worth a try.'

The two of them trudged along the road for about half an hour until they saw some buildings in the distance. Soon they came to a farm, not particularly well kept. Asphodel whispered to Thadora.

'Roles now,' and she turned up the lane leading to the buildings.

The farm appeared deserted at first, except for a few chickens pecking in the yard, then a small dog came barking and growling round the corner, followed by a young man. He was a very ordinary looking young man, average in every way.

He had mid-brown hair and light brown eyes, and was of average height. He wore a pair of grey breeches and a shirt, which might once have been white, open to the waist to reveal the chest of a man used to hard physical work. He carried a scythe in his hand.

'What is it now, Bim? Bloody dog!' grumbled the man. 'Another bleedin' rat? Or maybe there's actually a soddin' person? Although fat chance...'

He noticed Asphodel and Thadora, (although he gave only a cursory glance at the latter, but his eyes nearly stood out on stalks when he looked at Asphodel.)

'Oh! Sorry, lady! I...er...I didn't expect... that's to say, no one comes near usually. I apologise for my language. I...didn't think there would really be anyone...usually barking at the wind, bleed...er...stupid creature.'

Asphodel smiled at his confusion and replied:

'Please, don't apologise, sir. We take no offence at language not directed at us, especially as you had no idea we were here. I've heard worse in my time. My husband is a farmer and I know something about the frustrations that can make one swear. This is my young brother-in-law, Thad.' She indicated Thadora. 'I'm afraid he's extremely shy and you won't get a word from him until you've known him for at least a year. I'd lived in the same house as him for almost two years before he spoke more than one-word sentences to me.'

She went on to explain the situation they had agreed and then told the now smiling young man that the landlady in the tavern in the village said he might be willing to sell a beast of burden. They wanted one to pull a wagon they found on a deserted farm further up the valley, beyond the village. The young man's smile grew wider.

'Come indoors, and I'll make some tea while we talk business,' he said, indicating the house, his eyes never leaving Asphodel's face. 'Are you an elf?' he asked. 'I've never seen and elf before. I was told they're beautiful, but never would I have imagined... You are truly exquisite...'

He blushed bright red as he realised he had spoken his thoughts out loud. 'I'm sorry, lady. Too much on my own, I think. I'm only twenty-two and never been much further than Hellikeron down the valley. That's only five leagues away. I want to see more of the world, or at least of Erian, before I settle down, so I'm thinking of joining the army. A young man can't have much fun round here, and now my parents are both dead, and my sister married, there's not much to keep me here.'

'No sweetheart?' inquired Asphodel.

The young man blushed.

'Not really.' he replied as he filled a kettle and put it to boil on the hearth. 'My parents hoped that Gerrinda and I would marry one day. She lives on the next farm, but I don't really want to marry her. Oh, she's pretty enough in a *large* sort of way and would make an excellent farmer's wife, knowing the business and being strong, and, well, I like her well enough, but *marriage*?' He paused while he filled a kettle and put it on the stove.

'So you think you would like to join the army?'

'I am going to join.' the young man replied. He sat down and indicated that Asphodel and Thadora do the same. After they sat, he went on:

'I need the adventure. I need to get away from here and meet girls other than Gerrinda. I need to be with other young men and drink and gamble and fight. The army seems to be a good place for all of those things, as well as the Glory of fighting for one's country.'

His voice seemed to put a capital on the word "glory". Asphodel thought she would perhaps disillusion him, but then decided against it. She wanted that horse or ox he may have for sale.

Instead, she said, 'I believe you will have a long way to travel. The army, I heard, is near Frelli.'

'It's moving in this direction, so they say,' the young man replied. 'They say we're to invade Grosmer. Possibly before the summer's out, or if not, early next spring. I want to be with them and trained so I can take part in that.'

Asphodel smiled inwardly at the information, inaccurate though it may be, being based on rumours. Still, they said each nut contains a kernel.

The farmer rose as the kettle boiled and after putting some leaves into a pot, he poured on the boiling water.

'We need to let it brew for a few minutes, he said as he reached into a cupboard and pulled out three cups, obviously rarely used. He wiped each one out with a cloth and poured milk from a large pitcher into a smaller jug.

'Do you have honey with your tea?' he asked, looking at each in turn. Thadora looked down as his eyes met hers. Asphodel smiled and answered for both of them.

'Not for me but Thad likes his tea sweet, so I'm sure he'd appreciate some.'

She crossed her fingers hoping she was right in her estimate of Thadora's taste. The girl likely had not had the opportunity, except rarely, for honey in the Warren, and so may well have taken to it. They had not drunk much tea on their travels and she had not taken much notice when they had.

The farmer poured the tea and handed a cup to each of them. Thadora reached for the honey as the farmer passed it to her and Asphodel breathed a sigh of relief.

After taking a sip of her own tea and complimenting the maker on how good it tasted, she said, 'Now to business. We want to buy a horse or ox, as I said. My husband's mother is sick and we want to get her to a healer. We cannot carry her. Not over such a distance, and so finding the wagon seemed to be sent by the gods, except for the fact that there's nothing to pull it.'

She looked into her mug, then back at the farmer.

'My husband is strong, but not that strong, and the boy here can't do it, even if they both pulled. There's my husband's grandfather too, you see. He's deaf as a post and somewhat infirm. Both would need to ride in the wagon, along with our provisions and other goods. We are desperately in need of an animal.'

The young man looked at her and smiled.

'I think I can help you.' he said. 'Are you sure you wouldn't like to buy the farm? I really want to sell up completely.'

'No,' replied Asphodel. 'We can't afford it, and we want to get my mother-in-law to the nearest town with a healer. Maybe you shouldn't sell the farm though. It would be a place to come to when you retire from the army. And girls like a man of property.'

He thought for a minute and then replied, 'You may be right at that, but if I'm not here I still need to get rid of the animals.'

Putting down his teacup, and seeing the others had finished theirs, he stood and said, 'Come and look at the animals. Do you prefer horses or oxen? I have a horse broken to both saddle and to harness, and also a pair of oxen that I use mainly for ploughing.'

'I prefer horses, myself. I have little knowledge of oxen, although my husband always swore by them for ploughing.'

She extemporised, hoping that farmers in general thought oxen better plough animals than horses and that this thought of her "husband" did not sound strange.

It appeared a correct guess, for the young man went on, 'A wise man, and a knowledgeable one I see. Yes, oxen do better with the plough. You've obviously picked up something of farming. I don't believe you were a farmer yourself. How did an elf

254

come to marry a man in such a remote valley in Erian?'

Asphodel thought quickly. They had not thought about that. Of course, seeing an elf here would appear strange, and a farmer like her supposed husband would not have done much travelling. Stay as close to the truth as possible she had learned in her early days before becoming a cleric.

'I'm afraid to say I ran away from Rindissillaron because my parents wanted me to marry an old man. I've always been too keen on getting my own way, so I ran away with a young elf whom my parents thought not good enough for me. It went wrong of course, and I left him. It so happens that we had been living in a town that Gr...' she checked herself before she gave Grimmaldo's real name. 'Grollo was visiting with goods for sale in the market.'

The young farmer smiled. 'I wish I'd been there instead of Grollo,' he said.

'We met in an inn,' continued Asphodel, ignoring the comment, 'and then several times after. My elf lover threatened me and so Grollo took me to his home to escape. We fell in love and married.'

'What a lucky man to have found such a beautiful wife. I hope I'm so lucky. Here's the stable.' He opened the door for Asphodel to go in first, following her and almost tripping Thadora up. He had forgotten all about her, with eyes only for the young elf. 'And there's Monella. She's not much to look at, I grant you, but she's strong and willing.'

A shaggy grey mare turned her head and regarded them with sad eyes, then turned away to continue eating hay from a hay net suspended from the side of the stall. Asphodel looked at her and tried to look knowledgeable. She had picked up a bit about horses from Kimi and Davrael, but her knowledge was strictly limited. She looked into the animal's eyes, and then at her feet, much as she had seen the Horselords do when examining an hors, then she turned to the young man.

'How old is she?' she asked.

'Six years,' came the reply. 'My father bred her himself. Her dam died last spring. Her sire belongs to Hamm, Gerrinda's father. He and my father were always good friends. The stallion was a riding horse, not a carthorse. My father thought we could breed an animal that we could ride as well as use to pull carts and wagons, so she's a little smaller than the usual cart-horse and less wide. Easier to straddle. But she's strong.'

Asphodel looked again at the mare. She did indeed seem smaller than Asphodel had expected.

She had the feathered fetlocks of a carthorse and a strong muscular build, but a much more delicate head and a slimmer build. Asphodel thought the horse would do and she asked the farmer his asking price for the animal.

'We-ell!' he replied thoughtfully. 'Until you came along, I hadn't thought as far as prices on anything. She's not a magnificent animal, but is strong and willing, and she has a placid nature. Intelligent too. She learns what is wanted of her very quickly.'

The pair of them haggled as to the price and eventually came to an agreement that suited them both. Asphodel paid less than she thought they might have to, and the farmer got what he thought was a fair price for his horse.

While Asphodel waited with Thadora in the yard, the farmer prepared the horse for them to take.

'What's her name?' whispered Thadora.

'Monella.' Asphodel replied. 'It means "Brave One" in Erian.'

Soon the farmer came out leading the horse. To their surprise, they saw two crates hanging, one on either side of the horse. On further inspection, Thadora found the crates to contain three chickens in each.

'If I'm going to leave here, I'll have to get rid of them.' explained the young man. 'They won't bring much, but they will provide a few eggs and the odd meal for you on your travels. I still have a dozen of the things and they lay far too many eggs for me to eat. I don't really like chickens. Stupid creatures.'

He peered into the cages, then turned back to the pair.

'The chickens will be happy enough in the cages. There's straw there at the moment. You can replace it with dry grass or moss when it gets too fouled. They've been fed mainly grain, but will eat scraps too. There's one sack of grain on Monella's back too.'

He handed the rein over to Asphodel and patted the horse affectionately.

'Goodbye, old girl.' he said. 'Work hard for your new owner.' He turned away then and wishing them well, hurried back to the farmhouse, calling his dog.

'Monella, come on,' Thadora said, and the mare turned her head to look at the girl, then rolled her eyes and the three (plus six chickens) plodded back the way they had come.

By the time the weary travellers reached the abandoned farmhouse and the rest of their "family" the sun had just begun its descent towards the west. The others had prepared a meal with some more of the venison Fero had caught. They had roasted a haunch in the oven attached to the stove and the smell reached Asphodel and Thadora as they approached the doorway of the hut.

Basalt had been ferreting around and he had found a store of ale, much to his pleasure and the amusement of the others, while Grimmaldo dug up some potatoes from the vegetable garden attached to the farm. Along with some early peas that had been overgrown with weeds, they had a delicious meal ready.

The two girls felt ravenous, having eaten little all day except for a few dried rations they took with them. They had decided not to stop in the inn on the way back for both safety and because they did not want the others worrying. They had been gone far longer than they initially thought, hoping just to find where they might buy an animal. The cheers of the men reached them along with the scent of the cooking venison as they plodded up the lane towards the abandoned farm.

When they reached the small cottage, Thadora immediately set about settling Monella into the stable alongside the cottage and brushing her down.

'Davrael and Kimi told us to always see to our horse first,' she told Basalt as he came to see what kept her. The girl then found a hay net and stuffed it full of hay from the loft.

After hanging it up where the grey mare could reach it easily, she scooped a few handfuls of grain for the chickens and threw it into the cages to them. After that, she went to the well for water for the animals. Only after she had ensured they had all settled, and with a growling stomach, did the girl go into the cottage for her own meal.

Asphodel told the others what had happened and how they had luckily found a farmer who wanted to sell up and move on. She explained about the chickens too, and although she thought it was rather a lot to carry with them, she felt reluctant to leave them to fend for themselves as they would very soon be food for predators.

'They'll be able to ride in the wagon in their cages.' pointed out Grimmaldo. 'So they won't really be much of a problem. Maybe we'll be able to sell them at the next town if we decide we don't need them.'

Having agreed this, they all settled down for the night ready for an early start the next morning.

The next morning dawned bright and sunny, promising a warm day ahead. The five friends and one dog rose with the sun.

Thadora, who had put herself in charge of the horse, went out to the barn and brought the mare out. She backed her into the shafts of the wagon while the others loaded their few possessions, including two cages of hens, onto the wagon bed. The hens had laid four eggs, which Thadora proudly brought out for them to see, as if she had laid them herself. She packed them in hay and put them in a bag, warning everyone not to tread on them. Soon, they had everything ready and Grimmaldo went to Monella's head and took the reins in his hand.

'Right, girl.' he said to the horse. 'Lets see what you're made of, shall we?'

And the little party set off in the direction of the village.

Chapter 15
Farmers

Each of the chickens laid, nearly one egg a day and the fugitives enjoyed them as a change from their diet of dried venison and whatever roots and herbs Asphodel managed to find or game Fero hunted. They had used up the small stock of flour they took from the farm and they debated buying some more from one of the farms they passed, but, in the end, agreed they would be safer not being seen at all.

As Asphodel drove the wagon, and Basalt sat on the driving seat beside him, she saw signs of people ahead. They travelled for two days and successfully passed a number of small farms without anyone seeing them. When she noticed the dust cloud on the road ahead, she called to the others.

Fero walked alongside the wagon with Grimmaldo, and Thadora while Asphodel and Basalt took turns to drive Monella. At that moment, Basalt sat smoking his pipe and gazing at the passing fields, deep in thought. Asphodel called out her warning and on her word, Fero and Thadora climbed into the wagon, Fero tripping and nearly falling headlong into the wagon bed. He cursed the skirts he wore as the sick "mother" of Thadora and Grimmaldo.

He lay down, covering himself with the blanket and with his head on Thadora's lap. He had his sword to hand below the covers, although he wondered how he could wield it efficiently, if needed, in his skirts.

Similar thoughts passed through Basalt's mind. He held his axe beneath the blanket that covered his legs, and he pondered what it would be like fighting in stocking feet. Both expressed their thoughts in not too polite words.

'Be quiet, both of you.' scolded Asphodel. 'If you leave it to me we shouldn't need to fight. Just don't say anything, and Fero, remember you're sick and keep covered as much as possible.'

'Don't worry, Asphodel.' Thadora told her with a grin. 'I'll make sure "mother" keeps herself covered. After all, we don't want her to make herself worse by exposing herself to the elements, do we?'

This earned the girl a glare from "mother", who then lay down and covered "herself" up almost completely.

Bramble jumped up onto the wagon and proceeded to try to get under the blanket with Fero.

Thadora gave him a sharp slap and earned a baleful look in return.

'Either sit over there or get down.' the girl told him, indicating a space next to the chickens' crates. The dog obeyed and lay down panting in the shade of the crates. The cockerel looked daggers at him and tried to peck at him through the crate's bars. He moved away slightly.

By now, the others could make out the shape of people, and as they came nearer, they could pick out uniforms.

'Typical!' grumbled the dwarf. 'Just our luck to run into an army patrol.'

It was indeed an army patrol. The usual ten, comprised mainly human but with a couple of hobgoblins. The patrol comprised three women and seven men. The sergeant, one of the women in the patrol, approached them. She held up her hand and stopped the group.

Asphodel warned the others not to speak with a look, and, halting Monella, she descended from the driving seat and approached the other woman, leaving Grimmaldo to hold the reins.

'Just a routine check, Ma'am.' the sergeant told her. 'We're not about to harass any legitimate travellers, but we have our orders, especially about foreigners, and I see you are an elf. May I ask what you're doing in Erian at this time?'

Asphodel took a breath. She did not like lying, but in this case, she had little choice.

'I live here, with my husband and his family.' she told the sergeant. 'We're travelling to Hellikeron. My mother-in-law is very sick She's in the wagon, now, resting. We hope to be able to get help for her from the clerics of Sylissa there. My husband's grandfather is the old man sitting on the wagon seat.' She pointed towards Basalt, who, noticing the attention raised a hand. 'My husband is holding the horse, and the young man in the wagon is my brother-in-law, Thad.'

The sergeant looked at her.

'How come an elf is married to a farmer of Erian?' she asked. 'Elves don't often come this way.'

Asphodel told her the same tale she had told the farmer who sold them Monella, and then had to respond to a query as to why the whole family travelled, leaving the farm untended.

'We've been plagued by a pair of dragons these last few years.' replied the young elf. 'Eventually we could no longer support ourselves. The beasts ate all our cattle and oxen, and although we tried replacing them, we could not afford to keep on doing so indefinitely, so we've decided to try our luck in the city.'

'I've heard of dragons up in the mountains. If it weren't for the preparations for war we'd send some troops up there to get rid of them for you,' said the sergeant. 'I must get my people to search your wagon though, just to make sure you're not transporting any spies or fugitives. There's a warrant out for the arrest of a group of spies that escaped from near Frelli, although it's unlikely they'd be round here.'

She turned to the patrol and beckoned to them to come forward and for a couple of them to search the wagon. then she turned back to Asphodel and continued speaking.

'Personally, I think the fugitives will have perished in the mountains by now, but the Master's still looking. There are five of them. Funnily enough, one is an elf with black hair, similar to yours. A cleric of Sylissa I understand. A curate so they say. The others are all fairly distinctive. There is a mage, a dwarf, a very tall dark-skinned foreigner and a red-haired girl of about sixteen. Oh, yes, and a large and fierce black and tan dog.'

Asphodel forced a smile. Her heart pounded in her chest. She drew a deep breath to try to quieten it. The other woman must be able to hear it. What if they decided a black-haired elf and large black and tan dog were too much of a co-incidence? What if they pulled the blanket back and saw Fero's dark skin and obviously masculine features? What if...?

'We have a large black and tan dog too, isn't that a co-incidence?' she forced herself to say. 'But we have no dwarf, tall foreigner or red-haired girl.'

Asphodel realised she was babbling and shut her mouth quickly, forcing herself to mentally go through some of the acolyte disciplines to aid calm.

The other woman smiled as the patrol began to search the wagon.

'It's just a formality.' she told the elf. 'Every patrol has been told to search every wagon they meet. It seems these people are very important to the Master, although why beats me. Then again, who am I, a mere sergeant. Tell me again about yourselves and where you've come from.'

She reached for a scroll and began to write as Asphodel told their agreed story once more.

'Dragons, you say? Two blues? A mated pair no doubt so that means more in the future, although not many survive to adulthood they say. Too fond of eating each other, the youngsters are. So you left.

Did your mother-in-law become sick before that or on the journey?'

'She's been sick for quite a while now, but getting worse.' Asphodel improvised. 'That's why we've decided to try and find some healing for her in the town ahead. If we like it there, we may decide to stay.'

'Life is not easy in towns either. What will you do to earn your living, simple farmers as you are?'

'I can read and write, so I can perhaps get a job at a clerk's office, and the boy can find an apprenticeship of some sort. He's young enough, even though painfully shy. I've no idea what my husband will do though.'

'He could think about a career in the army. We're recruiting at the moment. I'll tell him.'

She began to walk across towards Grimmaldo who looked panicked for a moment, then he turned to speak to Monella in a low voice. Asphodel caught up with the sergeant. Grimmaldo looked at her and murmured "good afternoon" in passable Erian. His accent could easily have been put down to a country drawl. He flashed an anxious look at Asphodel.

'My husband isn't very good with words.' she said. 'He prefers silence. The strong, silent type, you know.' and she laughed. 'I usually do the talking. I talk more than enough for both of us, he says.'

She turned to Grimmaldo. 'The sergeant says have you considered joining the army? You could, you know, the pay's good and then we could buy a little inn or a new farm when you retire.'

'Grimmaldo muttered something incomprehensible almost under his breath, and Asphodel laughed.

'He said he'd think about it,' she replied.

'Hmm,' said the sergeant. She then turned to her men.

'Get on with it.' she called. 'There's another wagon coming. We need to check that one too, remember. Every wagon. Thoroughly!'

The soldier who had climbed up into the wagon pushed the chickens' cages to one side, jostling Thadora in the process. She shrank further away from him, looking for all the world like a shy boy in reality.

The man spoke and she averted her eyes. He spoke again, and she cringed. She felt herself begin to tremble and had no need to pretend the fear passing through her. The man started to get angry. He repeated himself.

Just then, Asphodel came up. She had seen the man speaking to Thadora and she answered him in Erian.

'The boy's very shy.' she told him. 'You'll not get any answer from him. Why, it took nearly a year for him to speak more than two words to me after I'd married his brother, and I was living in the same house all that time! What is it you want?' She repeated the tale she had told several times already.

The soldier looked at the pretty black-haired elf and he leered. Asphodel could almost hear his thoughts and she did not like it.

'I wants ter see behind yon woman.' he said in a coarse voice, speaking in Erian. His accent made it difficult for Asphodel to understand him, but she just about managed. 'I asked th' lad ter get 'er t' move.'

Asphodel shook her head as though in exasperation at the 'boy' and replied in the same language.

'I told your sergeant that my mother-in-law is very sick and we did not want her disturbed.'

'Serge's not telled me t' leave 'er. She telled me t' search th' wagon good. I tells yer t' move 'er.'

Fero could not tell what anyone said beneath the blankets that covered him, not that he would be able to understand if he had, but he recognised a threatening sound to the voice. He had too much experience as a fighting man not to so do.

His hand went instinctively to the sword lying at his side. Basalt, too, nonchalantly laid his hand on his axe beneath the blanket covering him. They were all ready for action in the instant. Thadora placed her hand close to her throwing daggers, and Grimmaldo readied a spell.

The soldier roughly pushed back the blanket covering Fero and began to shout when he saw an obviously male face with dark skin.

He had no time to complete his warning as Fero surged to his feet, sword at the ready and swung it at the man's head. The soldier did not expect this and consequently did not manage to duck in time. The sword clanged against his helmet and he fell to the ground, not dead, but stunned. Fero dealt him a blow with the hilt of his sword and knocked the man unconscious.

'Don't kill unless you have to.' he called.

In his fall, the soldier landed on one of the crates of hens and it splintered. Now chickens and a cockerel added to the confusion.

Bramble snarled as another soldier, a hobgoblin, climbed onto the bed of the wagon and he leaped to the defence of the man he saw as his pack leader.

He had not understood the order not to kill unnecessarily and went for the creature's throat. At the same moment, the cockerel decided that his harem was in danger and also leaped into the fray.

Feathers ruffled and neck ruff raised; the creature flew into the air, claws at the ready and sank them into the hobgoblin's right leg. The hobgoblin did not expect this and it distracted him from Bramble's attack. As he roared, sharp teeth fastened on his throat and his roar turned into a gurgle as he fell dying from the wagon with his throat ripped out.

Fero leaped from the wagon and tripped on his skirts. As he stumbled forwards to regain his balance, a third soldier rushed round the wagon with a war-hammer raised to crush his skull. Fero thought his end had come when the man crashed to the ground, a dagger sticking out from his eye. He clutched at it as though to remove it, but it was little more than a reflex action as he was dead before he hit the ground, the dagger having penetrated his brain. Thadora then followed her dagger, short sword at the ready and stood beside Fero.

'Curse these skirts.' the ranger said. Thadora grinned. 'How do women manage?'

'Beats me. I'm still learnin'.' she retorted as she swung her weapon at yet another soldier, this time a young woman. Then she had no time for any more talking as staying alive became her main occupation.

Grimmaldo released his spell as soon as he realised they had been recognised. He had already prepared a simple spell to put some of the soldiers to sleep.

Four had gone to the wagon and he heard Fero's shout about not killing as he released it. Four of the remaining soldiers yawned and then fell down where they stood, leaving the sergeant dealing with Basalt who leaped down from the wagon in his stocking feet to attack.

Asphodel wielded her mace, which she had somehow managed to get hold of. She had become quite an expert with it, he thought. She appeared to be holding her own with the young girl she fought, so Grimmaldo felt in his pockets for something to tie the sleeping soldiers.

Soon he heard a thud and Grimmaldo realised that either Asphodel's or Basalt's adversary had fallen. He looked round. Everyone breathed heavily, but there all sign of an enemy had vanished.

The cockerel looked warily around him, and as Thadora approached, he eyed her carefully, then when she took her eye off him to look at one of the chickens, he launched an attack. The air turned blue as Thadora swore loudly and colourfully.

Basalt looked at the girl. 'Didn't know you knew those words, gal.' he said.

'I know every swear word there is, and some there aren't, even if I don't use 'em all,' she grinned. 'At least, I'm trying not to use the worst. Asphodel, Randa and Father don't seem to like it.' She came towards Monella in order to soothe the horse. The animal trembled. She had not seen any fighting before and the whites of her eyes showed as Thadora approached. She had been solid during the fighting, though and although frightened had not bolted as many horses unused to such activities would. Thadora patted and soothed her until she calmed down.

Asphodel came up to Grimmaldo.

'There's some more rope in the wagon to tie these others up.' she told him, eyeing the ones he had already tied. 'We'd better get moving. That other wagon is nearly here.'

Grimmaldo complied and went for the rope and proceeded to tie the hands and feet of unconscious patrol, while Fero and Asphodel fetched the patrol's horses. They decided to take them as they did not want to leave the means of a fast pursuit or even a fast return to the city for help.

'Come on,' called Fero. 'Mount one of the horses and let's get out of here. that wagon won't take long to arrive.'

'What about Monella.' Thadora replied, starting to undo the horse's traces. 'We can't leave her.'

'Thadda,' said Asphodel, 'It'll take too long to unharness here. Fero's right. That wagon will soon be here. We don't want any more questions.'

'She waited, even though she was bleedin' terrified.' the girl argued. 'We do so owe her for her patience and bravery.'

Seeing that Thadora would not be swayed, Basalt, now with boots back on his feet, helped unharness the mare, but in spite of her protests, they left the chickens and cockerel behind as they ran in all directions and did not want to be caught. The other farmers in the approaching wagon would catch them and save them from being eaten by predators, Fero pointed out to a distraught Thadora.

None too soon, they mounted the horses they had appropriated. The smallest, a dappled grey mare just under fifteen hands, Asphodel designated as the most suitable for Basalt.

Grumbling about great mountains of horse, and with the help of a leg-up from Fero, the dwarf, became ensconced on the animal's back after three attempts, during which his mount tried to bite his backside, and once he found himself propelled completely over the animal.

He gripped her reins and mane as though he thought she would gallop off over the low hills surrounding them, but having failed to prevent him from mounting, she stood waiting for her orders to move. The army trained their horses well.

Asphodel chose to mount a chestnut gelding with a light mane and tail and a blaze down his face. Thadora chose an iron-grey solid-looking animal that looked as though he could run for miles. Grimmaldo mounted a bay with a black mane and tail and Fero chose a tall, glossy black stallion. The five held Monella and the patrol's other horses by their reins as they kicked the animals into a steady canter and rode away towards the west, at right angles to the road.

As they cantered away, the approaching wagon came in hailing distance, and the driver called out, then, seeing the unconscious soldiers, reined in his wagon and descended cautiously to see what had happened.

The five fugitives never knew that the farmer turned to his companion and said, 'Best leave well alone. Those may be bandits, but if so, they've left their wagon and chickens. Not like bandits to be sure. I think we'd best not interfere. Never did much like the army. 'Specially those regiments as use hobgoblins and the like. Catch those chickens though, and we'll be on our way to the city. They should bring a good price. We can tell the guard what we've found when we get there.'

'Yes,' replied his son, for it was indeed a father and son. 'And if we hitch the wagon to the spare horse, we can take it with us. Good job we brought him. It should fetch a good price too.'

They collected the chickens and wagon, and left the soldiers to come round and free themselves, and make their sorry way to the city and help.

Interlude

Randa sat in the dark and squeezed here eyes shut to prevent the tears from escaping. Soldiers had dragged her down to the dungeons, thrown her into a cell and left without leaving a torch. The darkness was complete.

At first she thought it completely silent, but then her ears began to pick up sounds. There came a steady drip, drip, drip of water from somewhere in the far corner; a scurrying sound of little clawed feet on the stone floor. Rats! She could now hear the occasional squeak as one rat spoke to another.

Randa instinctively pulled her feet up from the floor as her eyes began to adjust and she realised she could see a little light. A torch hung on the wall a little way down the corridor that ran along between the cells. A tiny bit of its light penetrated the gloom and reached fingers through the bars set in the door. Randa could now pick out the shadowy shapes of the rats as they scurried around the cell.

She thought she could see two of them. She tried to make herself smaller, but for a tall girl she found it difficult. Curled up on the bench she could no longer prevent the tears from coming.

She cried for some time, but then pulled herself together. Crying would not change anything. She was here in a cell in the castle at Frelli and it was all her own fault.

Should she have become betrothed to Branlow, as it turned out the man she had known as Wolnarb was really called? Carthinal had proved that. Should she have listened to Carthinal when he persuaded her she must assassinate her betrothed? Was she so very gullible that she could so easily be persuaded?

These questions circled through the girl's head as she sat in the dark and tried to avoid the rats.

She had committed a crime. She had tried to assassinate the ruler of Erian. She could not argue her innocence in a court of law. Wolnarb had caught her red-handed.

Randa stood and paced the small cell,. She nearly fell when she stumbled in a hole in the centre of the floor. A foul smell emanated from it and the cell floor around it was slightly sunken.

This was what the cell's occupants should use for calls of nature, she supposed, and where the rats came from. She shuddered at the thought of using it and a rat coming out.

Her thoughts went back to her predicament. She had no idea of what sentence the Erians gave for attempted assassination. As she had attempted the life of the Master himself, she had no doubt it was death.

She shuddered at the thought. She had only lived for just nineteen years. Far too young to die. She had only just begun living since joining Wolf and getting to know the others. Prior to that, she had been the spoiled and pampered only daughter of the Duke of Hambara.

Perhaps in Erian they beheaded traitors, or maybe they hanged them. Certainly before that happened, she would be tortured. Now there would certainly be war between her country and Erian.

Grosmer did not expect prepared war. She thought of her hometown of Hambara. There had been peace for so long that people now lived outside the walls. Roffley, where they had stayed on their way to find Sauvern's Sword, had poorly kept walls in a sorry state of decay. So many would die and all because she made a wrong decision.

Which of her decisions was worse she could not decide. She felt sorry for Prince Almoro, to whom she had been betrothed before breaking it off to become betrothed to Branlow. She had genuinely thought this was her duty at the time, in order to stop a war between the two countries. She felt suspicious of Branlow when he was not there, but the man had great charisma and in his presence she felt his undoubted charisma and thought his words genuine.

Carthinal had come to her and told her that for some reason Branlow wanted to get revenge on Grosmer and that the prophecy said he could only be killed using the Sword. That he was the Never-Dying Man of that prophecy had now been proven. Since the Sword would allow no one else to handle it he told her it fell to her to perform the deed,.

She agreed, but only after deep deliberation. She had a duty, she decided. To kill the threat to her country. She went to Branlow's chambers the night before and tried to kill him. Unfortunately for her, he slept lightly and had woken, put a spell to freeze her and then put her in the dungeons.

Tears once more falling, the heiress to the Duchy of Hambara lay on the narrow bench in her dark cell, and, now oblivious to the rats, tried to sleep.

Part 3
Home

Chapter 16
Smugglers

The girl guarding the goats and sheep watched with some consternation as five riders cantered over the hill. Her immediate thought was "*Bandits*", and she scrambled into a nearby thicket of gorse. Gorse bushes abounded here on the rolling foothills of the Mountains of Doom, and she did not heed the scratches she was getting.

The riders pulled up near the small stream running away from the mountains towards the bottom of the wide valley. She saw two women and three men with eleven horses. One of the men, or rather, boy, she amended, as he seemed very young, lead two animals and the other four had one each. They had a dog too, a rather fierce-looking black and tan animal. She cowered low in her thicket praying to the gods that the animal did not scent her.

The first thing the group did was to water the horses. As she watched, she observed some strange things.

First, one of the women was spectacularly tall. Well over six feet, she estimated. Her skirts barely reached her ankles, and she had very dark skin. Black hair fell to her shoulders but she did not seem to be very comfortable in the clothes she wore.

The other woman also had black hair of just below shoulder length and from her vantage, the girl could see she was spectacularly pretty.

The second strange thing was the elder of the two men. He scrambled down from his horse in a most undignified way, but, in spite of his grey hair and beard, he did not in the slightest comport himself as an old man would. His stature was very small and stocky. She had heard of dwarves, although she had never seen one, and decided that this must be one of that race.

The final member of the group, a normal young man in his late teens, probably, had a kind face and he seemed to have a ready smile. She immediately liked him. But the final oddity came when they began to speak. She could not understand a single word they said.

The tall woman came round the thicket with a pack and proceeded to withdraw a set of clothing from it. The girl then realised this person meant to change, although she could not understand why.

As she undressed, the shepherdess realised it was not in fact a woman, but a man undressing there before her eyes and she quickly squeezed them shut.

She tried hard to understand their words but it was useless. She had heard that in other lands they spoke differently, but had not fully appreciated how different it would be. She thought, if she thought about it at all, that it would be possible to understand if you concentrated hard enough. Not that the words themselves would be so different, and the intonation of the language so alien. Not that she thought in those words. She was just a simple girl and not too bright and those concepts she did not know or understand.

These people could not be bandits, she quickly realised. The horses looked much too good, and they had no loot, nor means to carry it either. She cowered in her hiding place and tried to decide what to do.

Soon she had no choice as to what she should do. The dog snuffled around and as it came near her bush, it pressed in and soon it both smelled and saw her. It began to bark.

The tall dark man gave a shout, but the dog continued barking. The man walked over to the bushes talking to the dog in his incomprehensible language, and then he saw why it was barking. He spoke again and she tried to get further into the bushes, but was getting very scratched by now. Blood began to ooze from several cuts. She ignored the stinging and closed her eyes tightly.

'*When I open them again,*' she thought, '*I'll be at home in bed and this will have been a dream.*'

However, when she opened them, it was no dream, and as the tall man reached out a hand towards her, saying something softly she let out a little whimper. She was too afraid to scream, and no one was near to help her anyway. The man turned away and called to the others. The black-haired woman came over. She looked into the bush and spoke to the man. She must have told him to go away as he slowly withdrew his hand and backed out of the clump of bushes.

Then the girl noticed the slanting eyes and pointed ears of the woman. An elf, she thought She had heard of elves, just as she had heard of dwarves, but she had never seen one before. Few elves came to this part of Erian. Her eyes nearly popped out from her head. Then the elf spoke to her in Erian.

'Come out,' said the elf. 'We'll not hurt you. We'd like your help. I'm Aspholessaria, but people who are not elves call me Asphodel.'

The girl made no response. The elf called Asphodel continued, sitting herself down on the ground just inside the thicket.

'I see you're scratched and bleeding. I'm sorry we frightened you into running into those bushes and causing your injuries. I may not look like it, but I'm a cleric of Sylissa and can heal you. I'm sure you must hurt.'

The girl shifted in her hiding place and glanced around. She would have nothing to fear from a cleric of Sylissa, as those people were good, so she had been taught, but suppose this elf only pretended? She had also been warned about strangers not always being what they seemed. They might kidnap her and make her uncle pay lots of money to get her back. Or more likely they may take her as a slave to the lands from where they had come.

She knew little of the habits of elves and dwarves, of how both abhorred slavery of any kind, and she knew nothing at all of the land from where the tall dark-skinned man was from. She furrowed her brow as she tried to decide what to do.

The other two might be Grosmerian, and people had said bad things about that land recently. However, her scratches and cuts *did* sting, so she decided to take a risk and let the elf try to heal her. Slowly, ready to bolt at any second, she crept from her hiding place.

'That's better.' said the elf called Asphodel. 'Now you must let me place my hands on you.'

The elf matched her actions to her words and felt the girl trembling. She muttered a few words of prayer, and the girl felt a warmth flow from Asphodel's hands to her body. She watched in amazement as her cuts closed and the blood flow stopped. The stinging vanished in an instant.

'Thank you, sister.' she said, breaking her silence. She bobbed her head as she said these words. 'Thank you.'

'Now come and let me introduce you to the others.' Matching her words to her actions, she took the girl's hand and led her over to where the others watered their horses at the small stream that ran gurgling down the hillside towards the valley below.

The introductions finished, the girl told them her name was Marin, and she lived with her uncle in a house in the village below. She looked after the village sheep and goats for him as he was getting old. It had been his job for many years.

She puzzled about Fero, not understanding how there could be places as far away as they indicated, and decided she must have misunderstood. As to the idea of the Great Desert, a place with no vegetation and only sand and rock, where it almost never rained she could not comprehend. They must have been lying about that to impress her, she decided.

Marin had mousy brown hair and muddy brown eyes. She was slightly plump in spite of climbing up the hills with the sheep, and she did not appear to be very bright. Her eyes opened wide in surprise to find that the boy was in fact a girl, and wondered why she had dressed in boy's clothing. In fact, with the man, Fero, having been dressed in women's clothing and the girl, Thadora, in boy's clothing, Marin was completely confused. She heard Asphodel speak again, so she refocused her attention and listened.

'We need to cross the Mountains, Marin.' Asphodel said, 'and without going onto the main pass. Do you know if there are any other ways across?'

Marin did not, but maybe her uncle did. He had been in these hills forever. He was very old and was wise and knowledgeable. They should ask him. She would take them to him if they would wait while she rounded up her animals. She dare not go back without them.

The five friends found themselves helping to round up sheep and goats, and keeping Bramble away as the animals did not know him and reacted by scattering as soon as he approached.

Basalt grumbled about stupid animals, and did not make it clear if he meant the dog or the sheep and goats.

Soon they had the flock in a bunch and Marin led them down the hillside. She told the others to follow the sheep and goats because the animals would be anxious if they remained too close. This they did and soon found themselves in Marin's village, if village it could be called.

The village comprised of only six houses each surrounded by a tidy garden and a paddock with a shelter for the goats. At the entrance to the village the travellers noticed a large enclosed area into which Marin herded the sheep. The goats seemed to know this was not their place and few attempted to enter, but plodded onwards each to its own paddock where they waited until Marin opened the gate for them.

A few folk greeted Marin with comments as to her early return, but then saw the strangers and went silent, returning to their houses, putting their own animals into the pens or simply turned away puffing at their clay pipes.

Shortly, Marin returned. 'Come with me and I'll take you to Uncle.' she said.

"Uncle's" house was the second one from the village entrance. It was much like all the others, a single storey with a thatched roof, built mainly from stone. It had thick walls which kept the interior cool compared to outside. Asphodel supposed that the opposite would be true in winter, and the walls would keep the cold out and the warmth in.

The house had two rooms. The main room of the house, into which Marin took them, had a fireplace at one end, and a table and a couple of chairs in the centre. A cupboard graced the opposite wall in which a small window overlooked a paddock at the back. Either side of the fireplace, Asphodel noticed shelves with cups, plates and other utensils and a few books. An elderly man, seated in a chair next to the fireplace, rose as they entered.

'What have you brought me this time, Marin? This is a little different from an injured bird or a mouse you rescued from the cat.'

Marin introduced them while Asphodel translated for the others.

'I met them on the hill, Uncle.' the girl said. 'They want to know how to get over the mountains without going through the main pass. The girl's an elf, and she's a cleric of Sylissa. She healed me. You see, I'd got all scratched going into a thicket to hide when I saw them. I was frightened, you see. But I was ever so brave, Uncle. I didn't cry one bit. The big man was dressed like a lady. I was frightened when he came to change behind the bushes. I hid my eyes though, Uncle, like a good girl. I didn't see him change. The boy isn't a boy either. He's a girl. The little man's a dwarf. I've never seen a dwarf before. Nor an elf either…'

'Whoa, Marin.' her uncle held up his hand. He turned to the others.

'I see you speak Erian' he said to Asphodel. 'I apologise for my niece. She's a good girl and good with the animals too. Seems to understand them, but then maybe it's because she's not too bright. I took her in when her parents died as I was the only relative she had left, and though she was fourteen, she could not have looked after herself.

'My name is Georgic, by the way. You want to know if there's a way over the Mountains do you? Why not use the main pass like everyone else?'

Asphodel hesitated, but then decided she would tell the old man the truth. After all, their disguise of a family of refugees fleeing a dragon had been blown completely.

She also needed to give an explanation as to why Fero had been dressed as a woman, at least, and also of lesser importance to her, why Thadora was dressed as a boy. More lies would only complicate things, so she began with their recruitment by Grnff to rescue his cub, referring to him only as a friend whose baby daughter had been stolen by trolls and their efforts to save her.

She went on to tell how they had been "recruited" into the Erian army and then the capture of five of their number. She told how it seemed the Master wanted them, but they did not know why, and as relations between the two countries appeared strained at the moment, they decided to make their escape through the mountains.

She omitted all reference to the Walchin though, in respect of their vow, but told of the encounter with the dragons and their narrow escape. Then she went on to complete the tale of the last few days culminating in their escape from the army.

The idea of leaving the soldiers asleep and tied up without their horses seemed to amuse Georgic and he chuckled. Asphodel looked at him in surprise.

'I'm no great lover of the army.' he explained, 'and I know nothing at all of this man who is our Master. We have a vote, of course, here in Tellin, but we don't have our own representative. Our votes are with a group of villages who send a representative to Hellikeron. Many folk hereabouts don't bother to vote.

The goings on in the towns and cities have little impact on us here, so what does it matter who's governing. We go on in our own way and only see any authority when they think there's smuggling or some such going on. Very good wines come out of Grosmer, as well as some of the best wool on the continent. Good profits to be made from smuggling. At least, so they tell me,' he added quickly.

Asphodel looked at him sharply. *'He's been involved in smuggling in his lifetime.'* she thought. *'That's why he doesn't like the army, and other authority by the sound of it either.'*

Georgic continued, ignoring, or not noticing her glance.

'I have no idea where Marin found out about it, but there is a way over the Mountains. It's hard, mind, and not for the fainthearted. Only a few know of it. It's called "Free Trader Way" as that's what it was.

'The entrance is hidden and you would never find it if you didn't know it was there. I should really hand you over, but it would be difficult to take you to Hellikeron and equally to keep you here locked up while we send for help.

'I'll help you because you made fools of the authorities, and I believe your story. No one would make up a tale like that as a lie. And what's more, we here in this village have no quarrel with Grosmer, nor wish one. Always good people to do business with.' He looked at her shrewdly. 'One final thing though. Those horses won't make it over. The free traders use small hardy animals. You may stand some chance with that sturdy mare of yours, but the army horses, no chance.'

'We had no intention of taking them.' Asphodel replied. 'It was our intention to send them back to the army. We'll leave them here and you can either keep them or send them back, although they are not truly ours to give. We have some little gold left, and would gladly let you have it in payment for your services.'

The old man shook his head. 'I'll accept no payment.' he said. 'I'll arrange to "find" the horses roaming loose much closer to the main pass than here, and they can go back to their rightful owners—eventually. Maybe in a sixday or so.' He again chortled. 'Asleep and tied up! That's good that is. I like that.'

While Asphodel and Georgic talked, a knock came at the door to the cottage. Georgic rose stiffly and went to open it, a woman came in carrying a small child. The child was crying loudly. Asphodel immediately rose and went towards the mother and child asking, in her gentle voice, what seemed to be the matter.

'Oh, Sister,' the woman said, turning to her. 'My son has had a nasty accident, He's only four and thinks he can do the same as his big brothers—they're eight and ten—as a result, he fell from a large tree the others were climbing. He's damaged his arm. Is it broken, Sister? Can you help him? I came to ask Georgic as he's good with injuries and seems to know what to do in these circumstances, but if you can help, I would be grateful. He's such a little boy to be hurt so.'

Asphodel smiled at the woman and gently took the boy from her. She carefully laid him down on the bed that Marin used and spoke to him to reassure him. The boy stopped crying and looked at her through big blue eyes.

'Hurts.' he said, and his eyes filled with tears again.

'I'll try to make it hurt less,' Asphodel told him, kneeling beside the bed and then silently praying to Sylissa for relief of the child's pain. Then she felt along the injured arm to assess t he damage.

'You have, in fact, broken your arm,' she told the child, 'I'll have to try to straighten it first and that will hurt again, but it won't be for long.'

As she prayed, she felt the power pass through her to the child, easing his pain. He managed a watery smile as he felt the pain pass away, but then cried out once more as Asphodel quickly re-aligned the bones.

She once more asked for pain relief from her god, then, as the boy's cries stopped again, she turned and asked Georgic if he had anything she could use as a splint and bandages. The man quickly provided the required objects and Asphodel fastened the splint and bandages so that the bones would knit back in their proper place. Then she prayed again, this time for pain relief and healing.

That done, she turned to the mother and said, 'He should feel much easier now and the pain shouldn't return. The arm will take time to heal though. I've done what I can to speed it up, but I'm, as yet, not strong enough to heal it completely. The healing process has begun, though, and it won't be as long as these things usually take.'

Asphodel got to her feet and said, 'I think Georgic will be able to rebind the splint when it requires and tell you when you can leave it off altogether.' Then she turned to the boy. 'And you, young man, must learn to know your limits. You're much younger than your brothers are, and not as strong. You cannot do exactly as they do yet awhile.'

'He won't listen,' said his mother. 'I'm always telling him that. My thanks to you, Sister. I hope I can somehow repay this debt I owe you sometime.'

With those words, she nodded to the others, took her boy's hand and left.

Chapter 17
Dispute

They sat around a table in what was the meeting room in the hamlet. The five travellers and a representative from each of the six families that lived there had met in this room where the villagers took local decisions.

The previous night, each of the five had been taken in by one of the families living in the tiny community, because no one had a cottage large enough to accommodate all five, one dog and the family who normally lived there. Thadora did not like being split from her friends at first, but a few gentle words from Asphodel, and some more jocular ones from Grimmaldo, soon settled her fears. Now they once more sat around waiting for a decision to be made on their behalf.

'Ever had a feeling of déjà vu?' whispered Grimmaldo to Fero.

'Yes, but I don't think this will take as long as with the Walchin.' Fero whispered back. 'And we're allowed to listen to their deliberations this time.'

'Ssh,' hissed Asphodel. 'I'm trying to listen.'

The two looked chastened.

'What are they saying, Asphodel?' queried Thadora. She got a black look from the cleric.

After a few minutes, there came a lull in the speeches and Asphodel took the chance to tell her friends what the people had said.

'There's some dispute as to whether they should reveal the secret pass over the mountains. Some of them, the large man to my left for one, seem to think it would be dangerous to them if the knowledge were known further than this village.

'They do in fact smuggle between Erian and Grosmer, although those words have not been actually used.

'Georgic is on our side. He points out that we would be unlikely to go to the authorities in Erian as we are ourselves wanted by them, and there's no danger to them from Grosmer.

'They all need to have their say though, and it seems that, unlike the Walchin, a decision to reveal the pass has to be unanimous. However, Georgic doesn't think it will take too long and that it will eventually go our way.'

'Let's hope so,' interjected Basalt. 'I, for one, am getting anxious to be out of this country.'

The talk resumed, and Asphodel again had to concentrate on what the people said, but eventually, after another hour of arguing, even the large man agreed, if reluctantly, that the pass could be revealed to them.

On returning Georgic's home, Asphodel thanked him for his help in persuading the other villagers to allow them the use of their smugglers' pass. (Although she did not use the term "smuggler". "Free Trader" seemed so much more acceptable she thought.)

They all agreed they should make haste to leave as soon as possible and they decided to stay for one more night before their journey in order to prepare.

They would need food and water, said the old man, and as the pass was not as easy as the main one, they would need plenty of rest before setting off.

The next morning at dawn, the hosts of each member of the party woke their guests and packed a pack of food for them to take on their journey.

Asphodel stayed with the family of the boy she had helped, and his mother had made no bones about the fact that Asphodel's helping her youngest son had gone no little way in swaying the opinions of the rest of the hamlet.

She had gone round and told everyone that as result of Asphodel's intervention her boy suffered no more pain and would have a perfectly whole arm in a sixday or so. As she gave Asphodel the package of food and a skin of water, she again thanked the cleric.

'I cannot thank you enough for what you did for my boy.' she said. 'Without you, he would have continued to suffer pain and would perhaps have had a crippled arm.'

'Thank Sylissa, not me,' replied the elf. 'I was merely the channel the god used.'

'But you could have refused, or not been so considerate in stopping the boy's pain before you worked. Some other clerics I've seen have not been as good as you, Sister. Others of a much higher rank too.' She looked to where her youngest child sat happily playing with a wooden horse. 'I used to live in the city, you see, before I married my man and came out here, so I've seen many clerics at work. You will become a great healer one day, if I am not much mistaken.'

Asphodel thought back to her last encounter with the Holy Father of the Hambara Temple of Sylissa. At that encounter, she had spoken words he had not enjoyed hearing; how Asphodel felt about the edict from the Most High that forbade healing for those of evil leanings.

She told him it was not for mortals to judge others and that she had sworn an oath to heal wherever it was needed, and not pick and choose only those she felt worthy.

That had been when the Holy Father condemned her to join the Daughters of Sylissa, Asphodel had stood up to him and told him he could not force her against her will to take the vows and she was leaving the temple immediately. The Holy Father had then condemned her to a life of a wandering cleric, forever to remain a curate, the humblest rank in the fully trained clergy.

She smiled to herself. The Holy Father, in his curse, had not taken into account that other clerics had not heard his words and some would raise her rank. Anyway, she thought. It didn't really matter what she was called—curate, vicar or archbishop—she would, no was, gaining in strength and could already do things only a minister would be able to do, so what if she was just a vicar in name?

It was not long before Georgic told them to make ready to leave. They agreed to be blindfolded and to ride the horses they stole from the army patrol until they came into the pass. Although the people had agreed to allow them the use of the pass, they were not willing to allow them to know its whereabouts.

They sat passively on the horses and allowed themselves to be led by Georgic and a couple of the other men.

They had loaded Monella with their few possessions. The villagers agreed that she was probably hardy and brave enough to make it through the pass, but they warned the little band of travellers that even she may have to be abandoned if the going became too tough for four legs.

Thadora had been upset and said that no way would she abandon the mare after her stalwart service to them.

Seated on the horses, and blindfolded, a couple of men, one of whom was Georgic, led them away from the small hamlet. Thadora had a good sense of direction though; a necessity for a young thief who wandered the sewer system in Hambara in the dark.

She was aware of travelling in a roughly north-easterly direction, away from the mountains at first, and deduced, correctly, that the men decided to take them in a roundabout way to try to confuse any direction sense any of them had.

Basalt, too, being a dwarf, had a good sense of the way they went. The villagers led the horses in this direction for about a league then they turned south-west for another league. From here, they moved in a more or less westerly direction. The travellers, sitting passively on their mounts, became aware of the terrain becoming more hilly and after another league, they stopped to eat. At this point, their guides removed the blindfolds and they saw surrounding them the foothills of the towering Mountains of Doom.

After a brief stop, they remounted, had their blindfolds replaced and then set of again.

This time, after only about a league and a half, they began to wind around. Thadora heard a stream rushing down the hillsides to their left judging by the sound of the water and she decided that the path was following the stream's twists and turns, but always going in a generally westerly direction.

Then they began to climb in earnest. Their companions from the village now breathed heavily and the sound of the stream had retreated.

Then Thadora heard the rushing sound of a waterfall somewhere ahead, and soon the spray made them all damp.

'A pity you can't see this.' Georgic said to his charges. 'It's a truly beautiful sight. The water comes from high above and falls in an almost vertical drop to the stream beneath. We call it Parador's Wedding Veil because that's what it looks like—a wedding veil, but fit only for a goddess.

'The story goes that when she wed Grillon, after he had rescued her from Barnat, she tossed the veil away in her pleasure at being with her true love and it landed here, turning into the fall before us. She then said that it would remind all to come of what true love really means.'

'A lovely story, Georgic.' Asphodel, riding just in front of Thadora, replied. 'I, too, wish we could see it, but we don't wish to compromise your 'free trader's' path.'

In a short while, the companions heard the water very close to their right ears and they became very wet from the spray. Their guides kept them close to the cliff at the left-hand side and Thadora deduced the path passed behind the waterfall. Suddenly they turned left and the young thief became aware, from the sound of the horses' hooves, that they had entered a cave. The roar of the waterfall slowly retreated as they rode on through the cave.

'*The cave must be behind the waterfall,*' thought the girl.

The path through the cave that they followed slowly rose. Basalt said that he thought the cave went up to the top of the waterfall. It had perhaps been a passage cut by the waterfall itself at some distant time, but something had diverted the water and so it now rushed over the cliff top.

Soon they felt the sun on their faces and a change in the sound of their horses' hooves. The free traders drew to a halt. The friends dismounted and Georgic removed their blindfolds. Now they found themselves in a valley surrounded by the high mountains of the Doom range.

The sun slowly sank towards the west, but its rays still managed to reach towards them through a gap in the mountains. The cave they had traversed lay behind them, and in front stretched a long valley. Summer flowers dotted the green of the grass and a few trees had sprung up, mainly birch and alder.

As Thadora had thought, the river flowed through the valley and tumbled down over the edge of an enormous cliff. She frightened them all by going to the very edge and looking down.

'It's well high,' she exclaimed. 'Come and have a look. How high do you think it is?'

'Come back here, Thadora,' called Asphodel. 'No one is going to come to look over that drop.'

As she returned to the group, Thadora giggled.

'I was just thinking how Davrael wouldn't go within twenty yards of that drop.'

'Don't make fun of him, Thadda,' admonished Asphodel. 'It's a very real fear he has. Remember how you felt in the tunnels? Well that's how Davrael feels about heights.'

The girl looked abashed at this reminder.

'Sorry, Asphodel,' she said. 'I wasn't thinking.'

'Well, think in future.'

Then Georgic spoke. We'll sleep here tonight. Tomorrow we'll return and leave you to go on alone. I'll direct you as to the path to take in the morning.'

After a meal of flat, unleavened bread and a stew of mutton the men accompanying them had carried, they all lay down to sleep, the companions hoping it would be their last night in Erian, but thinking it would take more than a day to reach Grosmer.

Chapter 18
Pass

Georgic, true to his word, gave them detailed instructions as to the way over the mountains. There were, he said, many twists and turns and paths to avoid.

Thadora privately thought they would never be able to remember it, but Grimmaldo reassured her, saying he had a very good memory.

'Mages need a good memory,' he told her. 'We have to remember spells, both the verbal component and the gestures to go with it. And phases of the moon, and History of Magic, and reading and writing, and…'

'All right, Grimmaldo, You've made your point,' Thadora laughed, somewhat mollified by his reply.

After the goodbyes and thank yous, the free traders turned back through the cave, leaving the companions to start the last leg of their journey back to Grosmer.

Fero looked around. 'It's not going to be an easy journey across these mountains,' he said, 'so we'd better get going. The more distance we can make each day, the sooner we'll be out of Erian and safe.'

'Statin' the bleedin' obvious,' muttered Thadora.

Asphodel gave her a sharp look but the girl was oblivious to it.

'I remember the last bleedin' time we crossed these buggerin' mountains,' she told them. 'We nearly died, Grimmaldo,' she said, turning to the mage, who had not been part of Wolf at that time. 'We only survived because we was rescued by Grnff and Zplon.' She smiled. 'I thought they were goin' to damn well eat us.'

'They didn't though, Red Cub,' put in Fero, calling the by girl the name that the yeti had given her.

'No, but you were the one who said they was dangerous. "Like the flesh of human, elf and dwarf," I think you said. Zol's balls, Fero, after that, who wouldn't be afraid?'

The tall ranger smiled at the girl. 'I was mistaken. I'm sorry. No one had ever thought that yeti were sentient and not hostile unless attacked first.'

'You're forgiven. I only hope we can cross more bloody safely this time. At least it's summer now. Not so much snow as early spring I suppose.'

'Still snow high up,' put in Basalt. 'We don't know how high this pass goes, do we? It may well go into the snow.'

A little whimper escaped Thadora as she remembered falling asleep in the snow and not wanting to wake up; remembered how easy it had been to simply drift off; remembered the cold and the hard climbing; remembered the fear.

Asphodel put a hand on the girl's arm. 'It won't be like last time,' she said, reassuring the girl. 'It's later in the year. The smugglers, sorry, 'free traders', wouldn't take this path if it were dangerous. You heard Georgic when he said they regularly cross in the summer.'

'Wouldn't have done him any harm to have escorted us across,' grumbled Basalt. The dwarf was as unhappy as Thadora to be crossing a high pass in the Mountains of Doom again.

'I suppose he had his reasons,' responded Asphodel.

'Hmph,' replied the dwarf. He stomped off along the path that followed the river away from the cliff.

The others followed and caught up with the grumpy dwarf. The path followed the river for about a league then it veered northwards, crossing the flow at a ford.

Here Asphodel balked remembering the flash flood that had come down from these very mountains and swept away the entire caravan except for Carthinal, Mabryl, his mentor, and herself. Mabryl did not survive to get to Hambara for the healing he needed after being injured in the flood. Asphodel partly blamed herself for not being able to do enough to save the man, even though she was just a novice at the time.

She paused at the edge of the water.

Basalt came up beside her.

'I know what you're thinking, lass,' he said. 'About that flood on the Brundella. I was in it too, remember. It swept me downstream and I was lucky to escape with my life. We survived, though. You, me and Carthinal. I believe, and you must too, being a cleric, that the gods have saved us for a purpose. We're unfolding things that are a danger to Grosmer. Perhaps to the whole of the continent. The gods can't mean us to die just yet.'

Asphodel, gave an anxious glance upstream, towards where the river left the mountains. After a moment's hesitation, she stepped into the water. This time there was no roaring sound, the river just babbled on its way. She heard no screams or cries for help, this time. Just the mewing of buzzards wheeling overhead.

Asphodel breathed a sigh of relief as she exited the water, closely followed by Basalt. Fero, who knew about the flood, looked in sympathy at the last pair to cross, but Grimmaldo and Thadora wondered why the dwarf and elf had hesitated.

Once across the river, the little party stopped for a brief rest before continuing on the path that was to lead them home. The valley was wide, and by the time they reached the base of the mountains on the other side, the sun neared its zenith Fero called a halt and all sank down onto the rocks intending to eat and drink. The sun beat down on them all morning, making them feel sweaty and uncomfortable. They felt grateful for the chance to sit. Just before they started eating, Thadora noticed a small grove of trees.

'I think we'd feel better in the bloody shade,' she said, standing and making her way towards the trees.

The others followed and sat under the slightly less hot shade. After resting for around an hour, Fero once more said they should move on and, gathering their things together, they reluctantly left the wood and came once more into the full glare of the sun.

Grimmaldo looked up at the mountains. 'Georgic didn't say how high up we'd have to go, nor how far it is to the border. Still, they gave us plenty of food. Come on, Monilla,' he said to the horse, taking her rein. She seemed reluctant to leave the cool of the trees and he gave her a little tug. Bramble, seeing the mare did not want to leave gave a sharp bark and that got her moving.

'We should give Bramble the charge of Monilla,' laughed Thadora. 'He seems to be able to control her better than you, Grimmaldo.'

The mage turned to the girl and stuck out his tongue, which made her laugh louder.

Up and up they went. The path was not too steep and it passed through a deep gorge that gave some shade from the sun. All the travellers felt grateful for this small respite from the heat, but by the time Fero called a halt for the night, they all felt sticky once more, having come out of the gorge, back into full sun.

The night brought some relief from the heat of the day. Grimmaldo expressed surprise that it was so hot high in the mountains.

'It's because we're so far south,' Fero told him. 'It'll get cooler if we go higher up. Remember we're very much further south compared to Frind, where you come from.'

Frind was near to the northern mountains known as The Roof of the World for their height and position in the far north of the continent.

The next day Monilla started to become distressed. She was not a mountain pony, and although she had great stamina, she found it difficult to cope with the rarefied air.

She was not alone. Thadora, too found it difficult. She stopped suddenly and said, 'Please can we rest. I've a bleedin' bad head and am so tired.'

Asphodel laid her hands on the girl but for all her healing powers she could do little to relieve Thadora's suffering.

'It's because we're so high,' said Fero. 'The air's thinner up here and so you're finding it more difficult to breathe. Therefore, you're getting tired and having those headaches. You should begin to feel better as we descend. There's one good thing though. It's getting a little cooler here. At least we're not roasting to death.'

'But we're not bleedin' descending,' Thadora replied, holding her head. 'We still seem to be goin' higher.'

Grimmaldo turned round from his position near the front of the group. 'I don't think this pass will go much higher, Thadda. If it did, even the mountain ponies of the free-traders wouldn't be able to make it. I think we should turn Monilla loose though. She'll find her way back down the mountain to the valley where someone will find her.'

Thadora saw the sense in this, even if she did not want the horse to be left behind.

They all took their packs off the mare's back and removed the halter and lead rein. Thadora flung her arms round Monilla's neck and said into her mane, 'Thank you, Monilla, for your faithful service. I hope you'll find a good owner. Be safe and watch out for predators.'

The girl pushed the horse round and gave her a slap on the rump. Monilla trotted a few steps then turned to look back at them with a baleful look in her eye.

'Go on then, shouted Basalt, and ran towards the animal, who began to walk away down the slope.

'I'm sorry she had to go too,' Asphodel said to Thadora, who wiped away a tear. 'You're right. She has been a faithful friend, but we can't take her with us if she's suffering.'

'I know,' sniffed Thadora, 'but I wish we didn't have to treat her like this after she's been so good to us.'

The girl shouldered her pack and set off after Grimmaldo who walked in the lead. He remembered what Georgic had said, word for word and Fero told him he should walk in front.

The track still climbed steadily and gradually, and Thadora's head got worse. They passed a track leading off to the left, heading westwards and down but Grimmaldo plodded onwards.

'Georgic said to ignore the first two paths and to take the third. They're dead ends, apparently.'

When the sun disappeared behind the mountains, the friends decided they must camp for the night. A small amount of snow lay in a gully and they melted it over a fire that Fero built and Grimmaldo lit with his magic. This gave water for their water bottles, and some left over to soften the dried meat over the fire. They ate a miserable meal. All had begun to experience something of the headaches Thadora suffered and they gratefully lay down to sleep, wrapped in their blankets and as close to the fire as they could safely get.

During the hours of darkness, Asphodel woke to hear sounds of someone approaching. She sat up and listened intently. She shook Fero who also listened.

Then they saw a pale shape in the darkness, heard a harumph and the sound of a creature shaking its head.

Fero laughed. 'I do believe it's Monilla,' he said. 'She must have decided she likes our company more than she dislikes the discomfort of the height and the difficulty of the terrain.'

Rising from his blankets the ranger went over to the mare. He patted her and gave her a drink before getting back beneath his blankets to finish his interrupted sleep.

The next morning, Thadora welcomed Monilla with a shriek that nearly spooked the mare. She ran to her and flung her arms around the animal's neck. Monilla whickered a welcome and stood while Thadora replaced her harness and their packs onto her back. After eating a meagre breakfast, they moved off once more.

The night had been cool and so they shivered as they walked. Their movement soon warmed them up again, even Thadora, whose headache had not eased in the night. Asphodel suggested she ride Monilla. The girl was finding the going harder with every step. Fero unloaded some of the packs from the horse and helped Thadora to climb onto her back. The young thief slumped forward with her head on Monilla's neck and stayed like that for the rest of the morning.

The pass ran along fairly level ground at this point and that made the going easier. The sun climbed in the east and long before it reached its zenith, Grimmaldo indicated a rough track to the left.

'Georgic said the third path and this seems to be it,' he said, pointing down the track.

'Are you sure?' Asphodel asked him, peering along the narrow way. 'It doesn't look much like a path to me. More like an animal track.'

'It's the path alright,' said Basalt. 'Often the best paths look as if they go nowhere. And,' he went on, 'what better way to hide a secret way over the mountains than to make it look like an animal track that goes nowhere?'

They took the path, even though some followed reluctantly. It narrowed as they went along, giving Fero and Thadora some doubts as to Grimmaldo and Basalt's conviction that it was the correct path.

In places they had to negotiate the many rocks strewn around, as if thrown there by battling giants. The narrow path clung to the mountainside and the mountain fell away on the right in a steep drop.

Then it narrowed even more so that Monilla, with the packs and Thadora on her back, had difficulty in keeping her footing.

Thadora screamed as the horse's foot slipped over the edge. Fortunately, the animal managed to scramble her foot back onto the relative safety of the track, and Thadora clung to her mane as if her life depended on it, which, maybe, it did. At one place they had to remove the packs, and Thadora climbed down so the horse could stay on the path.

The mountains soared on each side, but it now was going downwards. Thadora's headache began to decease she no longer felt the need to ride and she dismounted.

Then the path sharply left and the mountains that had previously stood on their right now lay behind them. In place of the mountains, they looked down on a narrow valley and the path dropped steeply away to a stream far below.

Thadora and the two animals were the only ones completely comfortable with the steepness of the path. Monilla plodded on behind Asphodel, who led her, and Bramble ran on ahead sniffing for any game that may have passed that way.

The path became less and less defined as they ap-proached the stream in the valley.

'I didn't argue with you earlier, Grimmaldo,' Asphodel suddenly said, 'but are you quite sure about this? This path doesn't seem to be going anywhere. In fact, it seems to be petering out. Perhaps this wasn't to be counted in the paths Georgic said to count. It didn't look much at the beginning.'

Even Grimmaldo was beginning to have his doubts. He was a confident young man, but truly, this path did seem suspect.

'Let's go just a bit further, Asphodel,' he said, his accustomed smile being replaced by a frown. 'What do you think. Basalt? You are a mountain dwarf so should know a bit about mountain tracks.'

The dwarf stopped and looked round.

'I agree, Grimmaldo,' he said. 'If there's no obvious change in half and hour, then perhaps we should go back.' He looked at Fero for confirmation.

The tall ranger thought for a moment.

'Look,' he said. 'We have a problem here. If we go back and try another path, and this one was the correct one, then we've wasted a lot of time. Similarly, if this is the wrong one, we're not only wasting time but are in danger of getting lost.'

'Let's vote on it then,' suggested Asphodel.

The vote went three to two in favour of continuing along the current path for a league. If there they saw no obvious change, then they would return to where they turned off and look for the next path along.

Thadora was less then pleased at the thought of returning to the higher altitudes. She had begun to feel a little better since they had been descending. She had voted to continue, along with Grimmaldo and Basalt. She sent a little prayer up to whatever gods were listening that they would not have to go back that way.

Fero decided that as soon as the path widened they would stop for something to eat and drink, as well as a rest. If the sun was anything to go by, it was nearing the sixth hour of the day and they all felt a bit tired and hungry. They were thirsty too, because as they descended, the temperature began to creep upwards again.

They travelled for half a league on until they found wide enough place that Fero thought they could eat. All five sank down onto rocks scattered around this wider place.

'I wonder what's happenin' to the others?' said Thadora suddenly.

Fero's eyes got a bleak look in them. He had been trying not to think of Randa. They had fallen out and were not speaking to each other when Khland appeared and took the others prisoner. He could not bear the thought that she might be dead and he had not been able to make it up with her and tell her again how much he loved her.

Chapter 19
Discoveries

The meal finished, Fero stated that they should move off again. The others stood reluctantly. Thadora said that she thought she could walk, at least for some time and so she helped put their packs back on the horse's back and they set off.

They plodded on for the best part of an hour when the narrow valley they had been following ended. The path began to climb again, but not as high as previously and so Thadora did not have a return of her altitude sickness.

Then path suddenly stopped. Basalt frowned and looked around. Fero shook his head and the two young woman visibly sagged at this apparent sign they had come the wrong way. Then Grimmaldo remembered something.

'Georgic said that we should look for a rock in the shape of a dog's head. It would be looking towards a hidden cave. We need to pass through that cave.'

They all scanned the surrounding terrain until Asphodel spotted the rock.

'It seems to be looking towards the cliff face, just over there.' She pointed to a steep rise to the south. 'I can't see any cave though.'

'Grimmaldo said it's hidden,' said Thadora. 'It must be in this cliff though,' she pointed out as she trotted towards it.

The cave mouth was well hidden. It was behind a large rock and there was a bush growing over it, partly concealing it. They pushed past the bush and into the dark of the cave.

There was a bundle of torches just inside the doorway and Grimmaldo lit one with his cantrip. The mare shied at the flame, but was quickly soothed by Thadora, then they plodded wearily through the cave.

When they came out into the bright sunlight once more they found themselves in a much wider valley than the one they had just left. The cave had opened out part way up the side of a mountain to the south.

There was a small hut next to a stream that fed into a lake and three men worked outside. Some cages stood at the back of the hut. With her superior eyesight, Asphodel could make out movement in them.

The valley was wide and the lake seemed to fill much of the northern side. The valley itself ran east west. As well as the stream by the hut, others tumbled down the sides of the mountains to feed the lake, which looked as though someone had thrown diamonds onto it that sparkled as the sunlight fell on the waves.

The group was just about to descend to the valley to speak with the man in the hut when there was the sound of wings and Monilla began to whinny in fear.

Fero looked up.

'Wyverns,' he said. 'Take cover.'

All five plus dog and horse dodged into the cave they had just come out of.

Three of the creatures swooped down onto the grass near the hut. As they watched, much to their astonishment the men did not dodge back into the hut, but approached the fearsome beasts.

Wyverns were akin to dragons, but much smaller. These had greenish grey scales and long sinuous necks that they stretched out towards the man.

Wyverns have long tails equipped with deadly stings and unlike dragons, which have four legs and two wings, wyverns have only two legs and two wings.

These creatures used their wings to help them to walk, folding them upwards so that their elbows pointed down towards the ground to help propel them along.

Fero held his breath. He had come across these deadly animals before, when he crossed the Great Desert and knew how untrustworthy people thought them. Then he frowned.

These creatures did not seem quite like the wyverns he had seen before. He frowned, trying to put his mind to what differences he could see. He had not seen the wyverns in the Great Desert close to. It was not advisable to get too close.

He crept out of the cave and crouched behind a rock. Instead of running into the hut to escape from the beasts, the three men walked towards the wyverns. The creatures staggered forward on their legs and wings and reached the men. Each of the men began to scratch the animals behind their ears and the sound of loud purring came to Fero's ears.

He was astonished. Never before had he heard of anyone getting close to wyverns and living to tell the tale. One of the men patted the wyvern he had just scratched and walked off behind the hut to where the cages stood. The wyvern tried to follow, but the man appeared to tell it to stay, and to Fero's surprise, the creature did as it was told.

All the men went to the cages and each came back with something that was struggling. Fero called to Asphodel.

'Your eyes are the best of us all. Can you se what is going on down there?'

The elf peered over the rock.

'The men are bringing some sort of creatures from the cage. I can't tell what they are. They look like something I've never seen before. They are quite large, perhaps orc size, but although they look quite a bit like orcs, they seem to be different. One seems to have the head of a bear rather than an orc, and another seems to have wings, but not very strong ones.'

Just then, the men released the creatures they held and the strange beasts fled in all directions. Each wyvern took to the air and flew after one of them. As they approached the fleeing beasts, they swung their tails round and stung them. The stung things then staggered a few more steps and flopped down to the ground as the poison took hold. They still tried to crawl away as the wyverns began to tear them apart.

Asphodel turned her head away from the gruesome sight.

'That was horrible,' she said. 'I don't know what those things were the men brought out, but to die like that—well, I wouldn't like anything to die in such a way.'

The sounds of crunching bones came up to them from the valley as Thadora came out of the cave.

'What happened?' she asked.

'You don't want to know,' replied Asphodel. 'It was truly horrible.'

The young thief looked down at the wyverns eating. There was little left now.

'It's just some creatures eating their meal. It happens. They have to eat too, you know.'

'Not like that,' responded the cleric.

Thadora looked puzzled.

'Look, Thadda,' Fero said. 'Those wyverns are somehow tame. I don't know how it's happened, but those three men brought some strange creatures that looked like half orc and half something else, and deliberately fed them to the wyverns. They also seemed to enjoy the scene.'

The girl looked surprised. 'Tame wyverns? How cool is that?'

Just then, Grimmaldo approached.

'We may have a problem. Georgic's instructions said we must that valley. Now, I think we could probably manage to sneak past the hut without being seen, but with wyverns flying around…'

The five slipped into the cave and sat on the ground to think.

'Do you think there may be a way around that valley,' wondered Asphodel.

Grimmaldo shook his head.

'No, I doubt it. The smugglers always use this pass, so Georgic said. If there were another, then they'd use that in cases when this one's blocked by snow. Georgic said they used this one all the time and when it's blocked, they don't cross. Smuggling is a seasonal pursuit it seems.'

The night came quickly in the mountains. The sun sank below the mountains quite early and deep shadows stretched across the valley.

'We could use those,' Thadora pointed out. She turned to Fero. 'Are those damned wyverns of yours likely to be flying at night?'

'Hang on, they're not *my* wyverns. They seem to belong—if that's the right word—to those men in t he hut. And no, Wyverns don't fly at night. They usually hole up in a cave somewhere.'

'Then this is our chance to get across the valley,' said Thadora triumphantly. 'Those deep shadows'll hide us good and proper.'

They let the sun sink a bit more before venturing out. Thadora suggested they rub some mud in their faces and all over Monilla's light coat.

'It doesn't matter if a few bits of light show,' pointed out the thief. 'That will look a bit like a patch of moonlight, but we must coat most of her. Good job Bramble's black.'

'Wolf Moon tonight,' said Grimmaldo. 'That's when both moons are full together and Lyndor passes exactly in front of Ullin. It's supposed to be a good night for wolves hunting. They are also supposed to howl to the moons too. The wolves are supposed to be guarded by some sort of wolf god on this night. Not many people go out during a Wolf Moon. They say that if you do, the wolves will get you.'

'Complete nonsense, of course,' replied Fero, busy rubbing mud into Monilla's forelegs. 'Wolves don't get suddenly more aggressive because of one full moon passing in front of another.'

'P'raps the mysterious Wolf god'll 'elp us too. After all, we're Wolves too, aren't we? Let's 'ope those three buggers in that 'ut are superstitious and stay inside.'

Just as darkness began to creep over the valley, the five people, one dog and a very muddy horse crept down the mountainside from the cave and entered the valley.

It seemed as if the celestial wolf, whatever it was, was on their side. They passed from shadow to shadow with very little light to negotiate.

Thadora went first as she was the most accomplished in using the shadows and the others followed where she led. The shadows did not allow them to take the most direct route across the valley and so it was almost an hour before they arrived at the small hut.

It was a crude building made of wood and looking a bit worse for wear. There was a light coming from the shuttered windows and they could hear the voices of the men inside. Thadora heard the sound of ale being poured from a barrel and concluded the men decided to drink the night away.

Suddenly, she heard raucous laughter as something happened. This helped to prevent the men from hearing a curse as Thadora slipped on a piece of slippery rock. She then cursed again, but silently this time, for being so stupid. She was slipping. This being the 'Duke's Daughter' was making her forget how to be a good thief. How her old comrades would have berated her for that slip. Both the physical and the metaphorical one.

Then she smiled to herself. Perhaps this Wolf Spirit, if it existed, was looking after them, Perhaps it had caused whatever made the men laugh and drown out her own curse.

She beckoned the others to a large patch of darkness under a large tree and next to the wall of the cages where the things (she could not call them anything else) that the men fed to the wyverns had been kept.

As the others approached, a low growl emanated from Bramble's throat. Fero put his hand on the dog's nape and whispered to him to be quiet. Bramble reluctantly cut off his growl and lay down at the ranger's feet.

Thadora searched around for some new patch of shadow, but the moons shone brightly and she could not see any close by. They would have to make a run for it to the next dark patch.

'We'll need to go one by one to that shadow over there,' she whispered. 'I'll go first and hope no one comes out or that none of those bleedin' things in the cages see us and raise the alarm. The rest of you follow one by one once I'm there. Let the person before you get there before you start out.'

She was just about to go when she turned to Basalt.

'Oh, and Bas,' she said. 'Try to be quiet when you run.'

The dwarf spluttered. 'Have I not been quiet as a snowflake on the mountains? Have you heard a rattle from my weapons or a thud from my boots?'

The moons had gone behind a cloud and so Thadora had determined that this was the best time for them to run across the brighter area. She giggled and sped off towards the patch of shadow she had indicated.

Grimmaldo followed and then Basalt, still muttering under his breath about cheeky young girls. Then it was Asphodel's turn.

Unfortunately, the clouds sped away from the face of the moon just as she was passing the cages. A sound emerged from inside one of them.

'Elf,' growled a voice. 'Stop. If you have any compassion, help us.'

Asphodel paused. The voice sounded harsh and as if it found difficulty forming words. the creature slurred the words and Asphodel had trouble making them out. It shuffled over to the cage bars.

The elf started as she saw, in the moonlight, what stood before her. It looked as though it had been a hobgoblin at one time, but not any more. Its feet had become talons and one arm looked as if it had been partially transformed into a wing. Where its mouth should have been she saw a hooked beak, like an eagle's, hence the difficulty the creature had in talking.

'Come on, Asphodel,' called Thadora in a loud whisper.

'Elf,' went on the voice. 'You are a cleric I see. You must have sympathy. If you leave us here, we will be fed to those wyverns. Three more of our companions got eaten yesterday. That will last the creatures for several days, but they will need more, then more of us will die. Please help us.'

Asphodel was torn. Her natural compassion made her want to help this creature, but she owed it to her companions and to her adopted country to get away without being seen.

Fero came up beside her.

'What is it, Asphodel?' he asked.

'Look, Fero. What are these things? How have they been made and who by?'

' "When impossible beasts occur," ' murmured the dark ranger. 'The prophecy, remember? These are impossible beasts. Creatures such as these have never been seen in nature.'

'What's he saying?' demanded the creature.

'He was just wondering how you came to be. Nothing like you has been seen before.'

'Hah! That's because we were experiments. Experiments by that man who calls himself the Master of Erian.'

'But that's dreadful. Experimenting on living, sentient beings!'

'Oh, we were all volunteers. We've all been condemned to death for one crime or another. I won't pretend we're innocents. We've done some dreadful things in our time. The Master told us that if we volunteered for his experiments we'd be forgiven our crimes and allowed to work for him. Naturally, we all agreed.'

Asphodel translated this for Fero, who had been calming Bramble, who did not like these creatures at all.

While this was going on, Grimmaldo, Thadora and Basalt had crept up to se what was keeping the other two. They had left Monilla tied to the tree that was casting the shadow that they had run to.

'Are you two bleedin' mad?' demanded Thadora. 'You are standin' here in the bright moonlight for all to see. It only needs one of them blokes to glance out the blithirin' window and it'll be all up. Zol's balls, we'll be in there with 'em and fed to them bloody wyverns.'

'Thadda, these creatures are victims. This one here has been telling me that the master of Erian has been experimenting and they are the result. I think they are the failures though. I think we saw some of the successes trying to steal the dragons' eggs. Remember that we thought the orcs seemed braver than normal and they called themselves 'special orcs?''

The young thief nodded.

'These creatures want us to free them so they won't be fed to the wyverns.'

Thadora put her hand to her mouth.

'Fed to the wyverns?'

'Yes, stung to make them paralysed and then torn apart.'

Grimmaldo looked at the creatures in disgust.

'They are most unnatural. They shouldn't exist at all.'

'What are you all saying?'

'We are trying to decide what to do. You are, in your own words, Criminals that have been condemned to death. How do we know that you won't go and continue a life of crime if we release you?'

'Well, kill us then.' This was another voice. Its owner approached the bars. This creature was trying to walk as the man that he once had been, but he had the limbs of a cat and had problems standing on them. He dropped down to all fours and trotted towards them. He had a man's head, but furred like a cat's along with the cat's limbs.

'The Master is trying to make creatures with the best characteristics of many creatures. He has altered orcs to make them braver and somehow put something of the loyalty of a dog into those wyverns.'

'How do you know this?'

'I heard the men talking.' He pulled himself up on the wires of the cage so he stood upright. 'The Master chose them to be present when the eggs hatched and the baby wyverns thought they were their mothers. Then the Master took the baby wyverns and did something magical with dogs and hey presto, loyal and faithful wyverns.'

After Asphodel had translated this, Basalt said that he thought that it was a risk to free such creatures, but that he also thought that to leave them to be torn apart by wyverns was appalling. He was for granting them their wish and killing them quickly.

A quick discussion decided them that the kindest thing would be to grant the creatures their wishes and to kill them quickly and as painlessly as possible.

Fero raised his bow.

'Wait.' Grimmaldo put his hand on Fero's arm. 'Arrows don't always kill cleanly. If I can just find that scroll it may be just the thing to use here.' He rummaged in his pack for a few moments. 'I can't cast it myself yet, but the scroll will allow me to do it. Ah, here it is.'

He pulled out a crumpled piece of parchment and smoothed it out on his knee.

Asphodel withdrew. She could not take part in killing—even mercy killing—of sentient creatures. She did not argue against the others doing so if they wished. She ran to the shade cast by the tree where Monilla was calmly eating the grass and buried here head in the horse's mane as she cried.

She soon felt a presence by her side and looked up. It was Thadora.

'I couldn't do it, in the end, Asphodel,' the girl told her. 'Fighting is one thing, and killing to save your own life too, but killing in cold blood? I couldn't do it.'

Grimmaldo began to chant the words on the scroll. As he did so, the parchment began to smoulder. As it burst into flames a lightning bolt shot from Grimmaldo's hand. It struck the creature that had called to Asphodel, then bounced off it onto the cat-like creature. From there it bounced round all the creatures in the cage. Soon there was nothing left alive. Just crumpled bodies.

The three men then returned to Asphodel and Thadora.

'It's done,' said Fero.

Chapter 20
Grosmer Again

With the misshapen creatures dead, there was no need to hide. The cat creature had told them that the three men would not look out of their window nor venture outside as long as the Wolf Moon was in the sky and so Thadora took Monilla's reins and they passed across the valley in peace.

The next morning, one of the three men came out of the hut and crossed to the cage where they kept the captives.

He stopped in his tracks.

'What the...?' he exclaimed. There in the cage lay ten bodies. On closer examination, he saw that they all seemed to have died by being struck by lightning.

He returned to the hut to get his companions who both agreed that this was lighting, but how? It had been a clear night. The Wolf Moon had been clear to see. There had been no thunder.

They decided that it must be some strange phenomenon associated with being out during a Wolf

Moon and praised their decision not to even look out of the window.

The man who had found the bodies then sent a bird to Frelli to say that they needed some more food for the wyverns. The creatures did not like carrion. They seemed to need to chase their food down.

After the friends had reached the opposite side of the valley and passed round the end of the lake, the path took a westward turn, much to the companions' relief. They felt as if they had been going too far north.

Soon the mountains turned into high hills that rolled westwards towards Grosmer, and after a day's walking they found themselves in rolling countryside.

'I think we're back in Grosmer,' said Asphodel.

'Yes,' said Basalt, 'I do believe you're right.' He glanced back along the road they had travelled. 'The mountains are far behind us now. We just need to find a town or village with an inn.'

'Yes,' replied Asphodel. 'A bath and a decent bed would be good.'

'I wasn't thinking so much of a bath,' replied the dwarf, 'but a good ale would hit the spot alright.'

'I agree about the ale,' replied Fero, 'but a bath would be good too. We must all smell like a troll camp.'

'Don't remind me of troll camps,' protested Thadora. 'That one where we found Tadra stank. We can't possibly smell as badly as that...can we?'

The mention of the Troll camp and the rescue of Tadra, the yeti cub, reminded them all that half of their companions were still missing and so they relapsed into silence as they all thought their own thoughts.

Asphodel thought of Carthinal and how, in spite of his indifference to her and his marriage to Randa, she loved him. She had at last admitted to herself that this was the case and could not bear the thought that he may be dead.

Fero thought of Randa and how they had parted on bad terms. He had regretted not swallowing his pride and apologising to her for his anger when she had nearly been raped and taken prisoner by the Erian soldiers.

It had not been her fault, well, not entirely anyway. If she had not moved when the soldier had urinated on her while she was hiding in the bushes, they would not have known she was there. They were both too proud for their own good.

Thadora, too, was thinking of Randa. She was her half sister. They had only found out when their father recognised her from her likeness to his grandmother. He had publicly recognised her and adopted her, as well as providing her mother with a house of her own. She had just found a family and the sister that she had always longed for was missing.

Grimmaldo thought of Carthinal whom he had met while they did their tests in the Tower at Hambara. The pair had hit it off immediately and he hoped that the other mage was still alive.

Basalt thought of all those missing friends. He had been one of the first in the group that now called itself Wolf. He met Carthinal and Asphodel after the flood that had swept away most of the caravan all three of them travelled with. He was there when Fero turned up, and when they went to see Duke Rollo with the prophecy.

He had seen the growing feelings between Asphodel and Carthinal and could not understand why they both denied it. Now, though, it was too late. Carthinal had got the elf, Yssa, pregnant and had married her out of a sense of duty. They now had a little daughter.

He was there when they met and hired Kimi and Davrael. He had grown fond of the little Horselord girl with her common sense and had a great respect for her fierce husband. He sent up a silent prayer to Roth, god of mining and metalworking, and the god the dwarves revered.

As they rounded a bend in the path, a town appeared. It was walled, but small. They speeded their steps towards the gate.

When they got there, the guard looked them up and down. This dirty bunch also had a tatty-looking horse that could do with a good brushing. What is more, they came from the direction of Erian. Strange things seemed happen in that direction these days. Although he had not seen anything himself, one of his mates told him that a cousin of his mother's aunt, or somesuch, had seen strange beasts as he hunted in the mountains. He saw wyvern chasing it down, he said, and what was more, the wyvern carried a man on its back. Of course, the guard did not believe such stories. He was a reasonable man, after all, and such a story with so many people passing it on, well, it was probably not true at all.

He watched the five companions, their horse, and dog approaching the gate. They looked weary and as they neared him, he wrinkled up his nose. They hadn't seen a bath in months, he would say. They smelt worse than their horse! He held up his hand to halt them.

The tall dark man seemed to be the leader. At least, he stepped forward to answer any questions.

'Where are you coming from, and what is your business in Jonnerby?' asked the guard.

The tall man replied, 'We're coming from Erian. We had a bit of trouble and took the mountain road.'

'The Smugglers' Road, you mean. Do you have any goods to declare? You don't look like smugglers. You don't look like anything but a rag-tag group of dirty Travellers.'

A young girl with red curly hair answered angrily. 'Don't insult Travellers. They aren't dirty at all and they don't bloody smell like we must.'

A black-haired elf, that the guard just noticed, put her hand on the girl's arm and said, 'Thadda, enough. Don't antagonise the guard. He's only doing his job, and that is to keep undesirables out of the town.'

The girl scowled, but said nothing else. The guard noticed that the young elf was wearing the white robes of a cleric of Sylissa, albeit rather dirty ones.

'Sorry, Sister,' he said to her. 'I didn't notice you are a cleric. You must have had some difficult times in your journey.'

'Yes we did.' The speaker was a dwarf. 'Now can we come in t o town and find an inn so we can get clean?'

The guard stepped to one side to let them pass, and as he did so he heard the dwarf mutter to the elf, 'I knew that your robes were useful for something!' and he wondered if perhaps they were bandits after all. Still, they had now entered the town so it was too late to worry about it.

'Lets find an inn quickly. Now we're in the town I don't want to wait a moment longer than I need to get into a bath,' said Asphodel.

'Shouldn't we tell someone what we've found out?' asked Thadora.

Fero looked fierce. 'We tell no one until we can tell a Duke or the King. We don't want to panic the people unnecessarily. The proposed war may come to nothing, especially if the right people are told and they can get diplomats to broker a peace.'

Thadora looked chastened. 'OK, I suppose you're right, but these people are living on the border and would be the first to experience any attacks.'

'Fero's right,' said Grimmaldo. 'If we talk about preparations for was by Erian, then the very fact that this town is on the border would create panic.'

By this time, they had reached the door of an inn. It was called The Golden Goose. After tying Monilla up to a hitching post by the door, they entered the bar room. The bar was at one end of the room, opposite the door that they came through. The five passed through the room, which was empty, to speak with the innkeeper who was polishing the tankards.

'Do you have rooms for tonight,' asked Fero.

'And a bath, please,' put in Asphodel.

The innkeeper looked them up and down, especially Bramble.

'A bath for you all before you go near my rooms,' he said. 'And that includes the dog. I can find rooms for you all. Two. One for the two young ladies and one for you three gentlemen.'

He led them to the back of the inn and pointed them through to the bathhouse. There they found three cubicles and a large cauldron full of hot water. They decided that the girls would bathe first and then the three men after.

After Fero had finished his bath, he lifted Bramble up and dumped him unceremoniously into the bath he had just left. The dog objected and tried to climb out, but Fero, with a brief word, made him stay in the water until he had soaped him thoroughly and then rinsed him clean.

On being released from the bath, Bramble immediately shook himself vigorously, covering all three men with water droplets. Fortunately they had not dressed, although, Basalt was beginning to get his clothes ready to put on. Fero laughed as the dwarf spluttered.

'You see why I didn't put anything on until Bramble was bathed?' he told the dwarf.

Basalt responded with a glare as he shook water droplets off his underclothes.

All five bathed and got clean and, feeling much better, they met back in the bar. The innkeeper took them to their rooms, which he kept scrupulously clean. They felt so tired that they forgot all about Monilla tied up outside. They lay on the beds and soon fell asleep.

Grimmaldo woke to a rapping on the door. He stood and opened it. It was a boy with their panniers from Monilla's back.

'I've brought these up for you,' he said. 'I thought you might need them. Would you like me to take your horse to the stables and groom her?'

'Oh, no,' he exclaimed. 'We felt so tired that we completely forgot her. Davrael would have had our guts for garters if he were here. Yes, please do, and give her a good feed too. She's been a stalwart and faithful friend to us. I feel so bad about forgetting her, and Thadora will be devastated.'

After the boy had left, Grimmaldo woke the others and they all went down to have a meal in the bar room. Basalt declared the ale to be the best in the world and swigged down three tankards straight off. The others behaved a little more politely and drank slower, but they all enjoyed the meal and drinks.

The innkeeper came over to ask if everything was all right. After they replied in the affirmative, and Thadora had told him it was the best meal she'd had in ages—quite truthfully, of course—the innkeeper began to speak of happenings in Grosmer.

'We are on the border, of course,' he told them, 'and news doesn't reach us until a long time after the event, so I don't know when the terrible things actually happened.'

Asphodel looked up at him. 'What terrible things?'

'You haven't heard then? No, you probably haven't being as you've just come from Erian. Well, there is a new ambassador from Erian, it seems. There was a big reception for him and all the Dukes and other important people were there.' He paused before continuing, 'There was a big swan served to the High Table, where all the nobility sat.'

He went on to tell the five friends what had happened at the banquet and the aftermath. They stared at the innkeeper and it was a few minutes before Thadora spoke.

'What about the Duke of Hambara? What's happened to him? Is he dead too?'

'I'm not sure. I think he was sick, but on the way to recovering. The Duke of Frind wasn't there as he had been held up on his journey, but Bluehaven, Sendolina and Eribor are all dead.'

'What about the rest of the Royal Family?' asked Asphodel.

'It seems that Prince Almoro hadn't been at the banquet. Sulking about something. Crown Princess Helloria chose that time to go into labour and so she and Prince Perdillon left the table. The Queen and Princess Dana must not have eaten very much. It was the swan, you see. Gone off in the heat, they said. Anyway, the king and most of the others at the table were taken very ill, and many of them died. Some of the servants too. They must have pinched some of the swan, although it's forbidden for the ordinary folk to eat it.

'So we have some new Dukes and a new king. It's worrying that there is so much inexperience in charge of the country though.'

He cleared the plates and went into the kitchen.

Thadora looked ready to cry.

'I spent all my bleedin' life wanting a proper family, and just as I found one, it's all going damned well wrong. My sister is missing and my father may be bleedin' well dead. He was so good to me, the bastard daughter of a whore. Now there may be only mother and me again.'

Grimmaldo put an arm round her shoulders and said, 'The innkeeper said that your father is on the way to recovering, and as to Randa, well, we have no idea, so let's not assume the worst.'

Thadora shook him off.

'It's easy for you to say,' she glared at him. 'It's not your family that's lost and sick.'

The young mage frowned and Basalt said. 'I think we should go to our rooms. Perhaps tomorrow it won't seem so bad.'

The next morning they all set off again. Monilla seemed quite lively. She looked a different horse. Her coat had been brushed and shone in the morning sun. She had had a good feed and plenty of water and so she was ready to go again. The rest of them felt anxious to find out the truth of what lay behind the rumours that the innkeeper had told them.

Had King Gerim really died of food poisoning? And the Dukes of Sendolina and Bluehaven too. They did not know Duke Thorric of Sendolina, father to Larrin, Brand and Sandron, but Thadora had met Duke Danu of Bluehaven and had liked him. He had been a close friend of her father.

The young thief worried as they rode westwards towards Hambara, knowing that her anxiety would not be eased until she knew exactly what had happened to her father, and if her sister had arrived home.

The others felt no less anxious.

'If the King is new and very young, and the dukes are all inexperienced youngsters now,' mused Basalt one morning, 'then that will play into the hands of the Master of Erian. A young king wouldn't be too bad if he had older heads to advise him, but if they are all wet behind the ears...'

His voice trailed off.

'Exactly what I was thinking, my friend,' replied Fero. 'Now would be a good time for Erian to attack Grosmer.'

Epilogue

Hammevaro rode out of Bluehaven satisfied with the results of his poisoning of the wine for the banquet. Admittedly, all of the dukes had not died, but enough had, and the king was no more. Ideally all the royal family would have died. It was just unfortunate that the Crown Prince's wife had chosen that time to go into labour. Still, with a young, inexperienced man on the throne, and a number of inexperienced dukes and duchesses, the country was in enough chaos for an invasion to be successful. He thought that the Master would be pleased.

He trotted his horse along the road towards Eribore, whistling to himself. His horse seemed to pick up his mood as they rode through wooded countryside and danced a little until Hammevaro brought it under control. The birds sang in the trees and he could hear a distant drumming of a woodpecker. The summer sun was shining in the sky, but the trees at the roadside prevented both Hammevaro and his horse from becoming too hot.

The young mage-turned-ambassador was going around the land of Grosmer. He had asked permission from the new King Perdillon I to travel around to see if he could help to stem whatever problems had arisen from the sudden deaths or incapacity of the dukes.

In reality, he was going to try to stir up as much trouble as he could. His pleasure was broken, though, by his horse catching his foot in a hole and beginning to limp. Cursing, he dismounted and wondered how far he would have to walk, and if he would have to sleep rough that night. Hammevaro was not keen on sleeping in the open. Not at all!

The sun was going down as he came to a small cottage. It was in a clearing in the woods. Alongside the cottage was a small stream and a few hens pecked at the dirt in front of the door. There was the sound of a cow being milked in a shed at the side. Hammevaro pulled his horse to a stop and dismounted just as a man came out from the house. The man greeted him.

'Ho, traveller,' he called. 'We don't get many people past here. I see your horse is a bit lame. It'll be dark soon, so I will offer you a bed for the night. I cannot promise you great food, such as I am sure you are used to,' he glanced at Hammevaro's rich clothes, 'but you will be comfortable and warm.'

'Thank you,' replied the mage. 'I would be very grateful. I was not looking forward to a night on the forest floor.'

The older man chuckled. *'I'm sure you weren't,'* he thought to himself.

Just then, a very pretty girl rounded the corner of the cottage carrying a pail of milk. She jumped as she saw Hammevaro. He bowed to her, taking in her fair skin and jet-black hair. She was about five feet five, and when she saw him, her cheeks turned pink. Her eyes looked as blue as the sky above and long lashes surrounded them. She lowered them quickly as she caught his appraising look. Her nose was slightly turned up and she had a wide mouth that looked ripe for kissing. She was about sixteen years old.

'This is my daughter, Inla,' the man told him. 'I am Blendor. We live here, scratching a living from the forest. It's not much, but it's ours and we like living in the forest, don't we, Inla?'

Inla smiled up at her father. She reached up and pecked his cheek. 'Of course. I wouldn't want to live anywhere else.'

Hammevaro introduced himself and took his bags from behind the saddle.

'Take our friend inside,' Blendor told his daughter 'while I take his horse around the back and have a look at his foot. He can stay in the shed with the cow tonight. I don't expect she'll mind the company.'

Hammevaro entered the little cottage in the company of Inla. He looked around. It was not a very large cottage, but it was well cared for and clean. Two rooms had been built on the ground floor and a ladder went up into the roof space, where there was probably another room. In the centre was a well-scrubbed table with three chairs around it. Two more chairs, with cushions on them, stood in front of a fireplace where a fire burned in spite of the heat of the day. The room had two windows, one next to the door through which they had come and another in the back wall overlooking a small lake dotted with a few islands.

The fireplace was built of brick with an oven to one side for cooking, and judging by the smell, there was some bread in there. Hanging over the fire was a pot bubbling away from which came the aroma of a stew.

Inla took Hammevaro towards a door in the left-hand wall.

'This is usually Father's room,' she told him, opening the door, 'but when guests come they sleep in here. I sleep upstairs in the loft,'

'Where will your father sleep then?' queried the young mage.

'Oh, he has a spare pallet and he will pull it out and sleep in here.'

'I can sleep on that. I don't want to turn your father out of his bed.'

'Don't worry about that. He doesn't mind. He can get up early and see to the livestock easier if he doesn't have to worry about disturbing you.'

The room into which Inla took him was quite small and contained a bed, a small table and a cupboard. There was a window opposite the door, looking out onto a couple of fields and the forest beyond. Hammevaro put his saddlebags down on the bed.

'I'll bring you some hot water so you can freshen up. We'll be eating shortly. I'll call you when the meal is ready,' Inla told him as she departed, closing the door behind her.

Hammevaro sat down next to the saddlebags and began to rummage through them trying to find some soap to wash with. He pulled out a comb and began to comb his thick blonde hair. He was very proud of his hair, which curled onto his shoulders.

After he had combed it, there was a knock at his door. He opened it to find Inla with a jug of hot water. She handed it to him and turned to pick up a bowl from the table, which she also handed to him.

The young man put the bowl on the table and filled it with the hot water. He stripped off his jacket and shirt and gave himself a wash. After that he felt a little better, changed his shirt and went out into the main room of the cottage.

'Do you and your father live here all alone?' he queried.

'Yes. Mother died when I was only five. I can hardly remember her. We've lived here since. Father has been the best parent a girl could have.'

'Aren't you lonely? Wouldn't you like to have some company of your own age?'

'I don't really miss other girls and boys. There's always plenty to do here, although sometimes I dream of a handsome prince coming riding by and falling in love with me. Silly, I know. I do get to meet with others when we go to market though.'

Hammevaro smiled at the girl's naive dreams.

'Surely there must be a boy in the town who would like a pretty girl like you as his sweetheart.'

Inla blushed. 'Well,' she hesitated before continuing, 'There is one boy that I quite like, but I don't think that he's really the one for me. Father doesn't like him very much either. I think he doesn't realise that I am growing up. To him I'm still his little girl. He wants to keep all the boys away from me, even though I am sixteen. Jellor, that's the boy's name, once kissed me behind the town hall. Father would go mad if he knew.'

At that moment, Blendor came in.

'I'm afraid your horse has sprained his leg when he tripped in that hole. I can help him, but it will take a few weeks for him to recover enough for you to ride him. You are welcome to stay here until he is better though.'

Hammevaro thought. He should really be getting on with his travels, but without a horse it would be almost impossible. The thought of staying in this rural spot for several weeks did not appeal to him either. He was a man of the city not the country. He glanced round the room and his eyes fell on Inla. Well, here was a pretty girl. An innocent, pretty girl. Perhaps he could amuse himself by trying to seduce her.

'I suppose there is no alternative,' he answered. 'I need a horse to travel the distances I must travel. I will accept your kind offer on one condition. I must pay you for my keep.'

They agreed that Hammevaro would stay until his horse was fully recovered.

Over the next few days, Hammevaro began to work on his seduction of Inla. She was truly innocent. He brought her wild flowers from the forest and walked with her on the woodland tracks. He listened to her sweet voice as she sang while milking the cows and held her hand as they walked. Soon he decided it was time to kiss her. They had gone for a walk in the forest and she stopped to pick some flowers. (Hammevaro had no idea what kind.) As she stood up, he pulled her towards him. She resisted at first, but he whispered that he would never make her do anything she did not fully agree to. He meant it as well. He had never forced a girl or woman against their will. He may not have very high moral standards, but that was one of them.

After that first kiss there many more followed and gradually Inla began to melt until one day she gave in and they made love in a forest clearing. It was her first time and Hammevaro was gentle with her so she felt that it was a beautiful experience. After that first time, they made love many more times, always careful to be far away from her father when it happened.

When five weeks had passed, Blendor declared Hammevaro's horse to be fit to travel and be ridden and so the mage decided that he would leave the next day. Inla was distraught. That evening as she and Hammevaro looked out across the lake in the light of the Golden Moon, Lyndor, she wept on his shoulder.

He patted her back. 'I will come back for you, Inla, my little one,' he promised. 'I must go though. I have a job to do. You wouldn't want me not to complete my promised work would you?'

'N-no,' she replied, 'but can I be sure you will return for me? I love you so much. Let us go into the forest, to the glade where we first made love and make love again there.'

The next day, Hammevaro repeated his promises to Inla and rode away down the road towards Eribor. He soon forgot the little girl on the farm in the woods.

The end of Part 3
of
The Wolves of Vimar

A bit about V.M.Sang

She was born in the north west of England in a town called Northwich, which is between Manchester and Chester.

She was educated at Northwich Grammar School for Girls, which was a selective school. It has now become a comprehensive school and takes in all ability levels and both sexes. From there she went to Elizabeth Gaskell College in Manchester to do teacher training where she studied Science as a main subject and Maths and English as subsidiary.

After finishing her training she taught in several places, beginning in Salford, near Manchester, then she taught in Lancashire, Hampshire (south of England) and Croydon (a London borough)

She is married with 2 children, a girl and a boy, and 3 grandchildren, 2 boys and a girl. She likes to spend time with them as they are great fun. Her other interests are a variety of crafts (cross-stitch, card making, tatting, crochet, knitting etc) and painting as well as writing. She also enjoys gardening and walk-ing, cycling and kayaking.

She is now retired from teaching and lives in East Sussex with her husband.

Lightning Source UK Ltd.
Milton Keynes UK
UKHW012007301120
374378UK00001B/237